CW00661565

The Messenger

Happy Reading 💙
Nancy Gore

The Messenger

Nancy Gore

The Messenger
Copyright © 2023 Nancy Gore

All rights reserved. No part of this book may be reproduced, stored in a retrieval system, or transmitted by any means without the written permission of the author.

This book is a work of fiction. Any similarity to actual persons, living or dead, is coincidental. Names, characters, businesses, places, events, and incidents either are the product of the author's imagination or are used fictitiously. Scripture taken from the HOLY BIBLE, NEW INTERNATIONAL VERSION ®. Copyright © 1973, 1978, 1984 by International Bible Society. Used by permission of Zondervan Publishing House. All rights reserved.

Cover design by Nancy Gore

ISBN-13: 979-8-218-15360-1
Library of Congress Control Number: 2023903973

Published by Welrish Creations LLC
First printing, 2023
welrishcreations@gmail.com

For my husband…
And to those who wait for one last message.

Acknowledgements

Grace, thank you for the countless hours spent helping me to finish my dream. Although we met by chance, I feel our friendship was destined. Here's to many more years as friends.

ONE

Climbing into my car and inserting the key, I glance across at the ambulance bay as I flip down the visor. Fumbling with my sunglasses, I feel numb and emotionally drained. As I take a deep breath and let it out, I turn the key, only to be blasted with hot air from the vents. Jabbing at the buttons, I shut the air conditioner off. Rolling down the windows, the warm August breeze quickly invades the car.

Hearing sirens nearby, I watch for approaching traffic across the street while the car cools down. It doesn't take long before my thoughts revert to the previous hours. She looked so young, maybe only in her early twenties. Life goes on -- just not hers.

Across the street, a fire truck arrives with the ambulance indicating that their patient needed additional manpower or immediate life-saving care. I say a quick prayer for those involved before pulling out of the parking lot. While waiting at a light, I decide to make a stop on the way home.

***

Grasping the doorknob, I study the gold-painted lettering on the door: Foster's Antique Shop. As I enter, the bell over the door jingles. I love coming to this shop. An elderly woman standing at the counter looks up.

"Hello, I'm Mrs. Foster. We have quite a few things to look at and a big furniture section upstairs. Have a look around and let me know if I can help with anything."

"Thank you," I reply, tucking a loose strand of hair behind my ear.

As I begin to meander around, I tell myself: you need this. Pausing, I close my eyes and draw in a deep breath. The faint musty smell that lingers in the air has always had a calming effect on me. Rummaging through an antique store is a favorite past time of mine and brings back such fond memories.

While looking at various kitchenware and gadgets, I spot an old bowl with a blue pattern, that resembles mine. While studying it, I look up to see a picture hanging on the wall of a young girl, and immediately my mood changes. I have been involved in many different aspects of death. I have comforted families as their loved ones take their last breath and have prayed with those dying alone. My prayer is always the same; for a safe and easy transition of their souls and peace and strength for those left behind.

***

The driver from today's accident was brought in and checked for injuries as well as for driving under the influence. He was so inebriated, it made him loud and belligerent with the nursing staff and police.

"Big deal," he sputtered. "So, I hit a dawg! It shoulda been tied up anyway. You should arrest the dawg! What about *my* rights? I didn't even get my phone call!"

His lack of remorse intensified everyone's emotions; you could see it on everyone's faces.

I feel that when someone dies, even if you did not know them personally, the details can be quite upsetting. Especially if you can relate to their loss and share that loved ones' emotions. *That poor girl from today, was someone's daughter, sister, granddaughter, and friend*. You can try and disassociate yourself as a defense mechanism, but the memories often linger.

After it was all over and she was pronounced dead, Dr. Austin thanked everyone for their hard work and efforts before leaving the room. As the x-ray and lab techs gathered their equipment, the rest of us restocked and cleaned up the room. Very little talking or direct eye contact was made. This helped to shield the tear-filled eyes. While Quinn and Paige reviewed their charting, I grabbed several warm blankets and draped them over her body. As I tucked them in along her side, I realized this was just a meager attempt to make myself feel better.

It was Lexi who first broke the quietness in the room. She asked to step out after gathering instruments together on a cold metal tray. She looked over at the girl lying on the gurney and said, "She reminds me of my daughter Remi."

Paige stood up and stretched: "I think it would be a good idea if we all got some air."

Chaplain Paul walked in and tucked his cell phone into his jacket.

"Have they identified who this young girl was?" Paige eagerly asked.

"Sadly no, but I will be sure to update you the minute I hear anything," replies Chaplain Paul.

While the detainee continued his outbursts, I stood watch at the printer, anxiously waiting for his lab results. The sooner we had his results, the sooner he could be discharged and taken to jail. And the sooner the ER would be quieter and less stressful. Yes, this was a selfish thought and yes, it would be better with him gone. He was lucky to have suffered only minor bumps and bruises. He showed no signs of pain, as he lay on his back with one leg crossed over the other, blowing invisible smoke rings. Silently, I prayed that when the alcohol wore off, he would be remorseful for his actions and severely punished for his crime.

The ambulance crew had relayed to the hospital staff that the girl had been jogging in the bike lane when the driver, after weaving through traffic, hit her. He was finally stopped after hitting several mailboxes and getting a trash can wedged under his car. Bystanders covered her with blankets and were careful not to move her. An officer told the ER staff that when he arrived at the accident, he found a crowd gathered around her, quietly reciting the Lord's prayer, as a young man knelt beside her, holding her hand.

The medics secured her airway and placed a cervical collar around her neck. Intravenous lines were placed, and fluids were started. Firefighters assisted the medics in assessing and treating her injuries. She was then loaded into the ambulance as they raced against time.

Prior to approaching the hospital, one of the medics in the back yelled up to the firefighter driving: "We have lost pulses. Take the corners safely but get us there fast!"

While one medic performed chest compressions, his partner at the head of the cot squeezed the Ambu bag, trying to breathe life back into her lifeless body.

The poor girl was dead on arrival. Looking around the trauma room, you could see it on everyone's face. Nevertheless, we feverishly tried to save her life, a life that had already been taken away.

***

Willing myself back to the present, I walk over to a table in the antique store and begin leafing through an old photo album. Gingerly turning the frail, faded pages, *lucky for her it happened so fast.* Stopping in my tracks, I recount my thought. *Lucky it happened so, fast? How can you be lucky if you are dead? Sure, it is meant that there is little to no agonizing pain, but it still sounds awful.* Looking down at the faces of the people in the album, I wonder: *why there are so few smiling?* Most likely it is related to the hard times, I surmise, and close the album.

Staring at a display case, I continue to counsel myself: It is tragic that such a young life has been taken but you did your job and so did everyone else. You love being a nurse and wouldn't want to do anything else. From an early age, I knew I wanted to be a nurse. I can remember countless hours spent playing in my nurse's uniform complete with a cap and blue cape that my Nana had made. I used to love listening to her recount stories of her helping people and birthing babies. I knew I wanted to be just like her.

Up to this point, nothing has caught my eye. I never really come with the intent to buy anything, but occasionally I will find something that speaks to me. As I look around at what was once people's treasures, hopes, and dreams, I wonder what it must have been like to live back then. I guess this is why I like to read old diaries.

As I make my way upstairs to the furniture section, the voices of the two elderly shop owners filter up the stairwell. With each step, the creaking of the floorboards becomes more pronounced, like a moan. Entering the large room filled with furniture, it is so quiet, you could have heard a pin drop. The owners had done a wonderful job of staging and displaying the pieces, resembling the rooms of a home. Running my finger over the top of a dresser, a layer of dust resembles a fine dusting of snow. Maybe it was deliberate, to add to the ambiance and age of the antiques.

Glancing around the room, I spot a dresser and decide to take a closer look. The dresser has glass knobs and a wishbone-style mirror. The tag shows it's from the early 1900s with the original key. The price is reasonable too. I glance down at my watch to check the time. Well, I have spent enough time trying to clear my mind and need to start home. Gracie, our dachshund mixed fur baby will be standing with her legs crossed if I don't hurry.

As I turn to walk away, a shadow in the dresser's mirror catches my eye. I must have been so engrossed in my thoughts that I didn't notice someone else come upstairs. Turning, I look for someone standing behind me. Seeing no one, I stare back at my reflection in the mirror. Setting my purse on the dresser, I fish for a tissue. Carefully wiping off the mirror, the tissue is blackened along with my fingers from the dusty film. Retrieving another tissue, I wipe the dirt from my fingers. *My eyes are playing tricks on me. I'm still upset from earlier today. Don't be silly, you're the only one upstairs. You're not one to get easily spooked, so stop it!*

This is crazy, I say to myself stuffing the tissues in my purse. Staring at the mirror, a gray haze appears as the air grows still. Blinking, a blurred image slowly forms as I begin to notice the scent of lilacs. Sniffing at the air, I wonder why I didn't smell it earlier. The blurred image becomes clearer and appears to be that of a girl. Straining to make out her face: "Come closer," I say aloud.

As her face comes into focus, I notice she is motioning me to follow her. Scrunching up my face, I say again to myself, *this can't be happening. Someone is playing a joke. They must have rigged the* mirror and have a camera hidden. The girl then puts her hand against the mirror, as if trying to touch me.

After several seconds of watching her, I place my hand opposite hers. The mirror's coldness sends a chill down my spine, causing me to jerk my hand away. Taking a deep breath, I place my hand back on the mirror. As I study her features, I realize she looks familiar, a little too familiar. She looks like the girl from the accident. This can't be, shaking my head as I back away from the dresser.

Because she had no identification on her and no family was available to identify her, the emergency room assigned her a "Doe" name.

Watching her, I'm mesmerized, until she mouths the words, *help me*, and a tear escapes down her cheek. I rub my arms for warmth. The butterflies in my stomach now feel like bats. She turns and looks back over her shoulder and walks away until she fades out of view.

My heart rate quickly changes from a trot to a full gallop. *I wonder if anyone has ever performed CPR on themselves*. Leaning in, I examine the mirror more closely. I can see my handprint left on the glass but, where she had placed hers, there is nothing. One by one, I slide open the drawers and feel around for false bottoms or any signs of wires or cords. Then carefully, I slide it away from the wall to look for anything that could resemble a tape recorder or projector.

It's on now, I tell myself, playing detective. The idea pops into my head to use a mirror to look underneath. Removing my compact from my purse I open it up and crouch down beside the dresser. The search comes up empty except for some cobwebs.

Hearing a clock chime, I stand up and check the time against my watch. After brushing off my pants, I grab my purse and head for the staircase. I avoid the urge to look back. *This is spooky*. I make a beeline for the door leaving Mrs. Foster curious about my hasty exit. I am visibly shaken as I head for my car.

TWO

Gracie happily greets me at the door wagging her tail. "Were you a good girl?" I ask. With Gracie content in the backyard, I run upstairs to change. It feels good to be out of my scrubs. Simple chores take precedence and I push everything else to the back of my mind. I look in the fridge and I'm relieved we still have leftovers to eat. This will be a quick and easy dinner. I laugh when Gracie walks over to her dog dish and begins pushing it around with her nose to get my attention.

"Okay, I can take a hint," I tell her, filling her dog dish with kibbles.

My husband, Chris, walks in just as I am setting the table. While eating, I recount the day's events with him.

"How awful. Did they ever find out who she was?" he asks.

"When I left, they were still working on it. I couldn't get the whole thing out of my mind. On my way home, I stopped at an antique shop to try and clear my head."

"Which one? Fisher's?"

"Foster's, off Clark Street," I correct him.

"I was close," he laughs.

"Anyway, I was looking around and…"

"You want me to wipe off the table?" he asks.

Wringing out the dish rag, I toss it to him. When I start to speak, he interrupts again, "Where in the fridge do you want the leftovers?"

Pivoting, I shoot him a look. He looks up and cringes, quietly sliding the leftovers in and shutting the door. With his arms folded, he stands listening.

"I am trying so hard to tell you something, and I can't even get to the good part."

"I'm sorry, go ahead. You have my full attention," says Chris.

Clearing my throat, "So, I am looking around upstairs at some furniture, and I go over to this dresser. While I am standing there looking at it, suddenly, I see a girl looking back at me from inside the mirror! It looked like the girl from the accident."

11

He stands there, with a blank look on his face. His reaction is not what I expected. I don't know whether I envisioned him running through the house with his hands in his hair or what. "Hmm," he says, making a face.

Disappointed at his odd response, I avoid eye contact while wiping off the counters.

"Don't get mad. I don't know what you want me to say. My whole take on this, if you really want to know is, you were so upset about the whole thing with the girl in the accident and the drunk, that when you went to the antique shop your mind just wandered and played a trick on you."

"I'm tired," I announce, shutting off the kitchen light and heading upstairs. "I suppose you're right. I'm going to take a bath."

"Did you want any popcorn or would you care to watch any TV after your bath?"

"Not tonight, but you go ahead."

"I'll watch something for a little bit and come up later."

"Fine," I respond as I climb each stair feeling totally defeated and misunderstood.

Chris knows me! Living in a small town, we went to the same schools and hung out with the same friends. Plus, we have been married for the last three years. He should know, I wouldn't make this up.

As I adjust the water temperature and let the tub fill, I sprinkle bath crystals over the top of the water. "Calgon, take me away," I murmur. Gathering my hair and pulling it up, I secure it with a clip.

Rummaging through magazines from a basket beside the bed, I pick out a couple and place them beside the tub. Easing into the warm sudsy water, all the day's events speed through my mind. Trying to focus on the article in the magazine I find myself rereading the same paragraph, still unable to understand what it's about.

After staring at the same page for several minutes, I give up reading. Reclining further under the water, the magazine slips from my fingers, and falls to the floor. Closing my eyes, I am conscious only of my breathing and the faint popping sound of the bubbles. With my arms floating weightlessly beside me, I admire the honey and vanilla scent that has filled the room.

Minutes later, I startle, when something touches my arm. As I open my eyes, there is a face inches from mine. It's her face. The girl in the mirror and the one from the accident. Bolting upright, the water swishes up and over the side of the tub. And she is gone.

Getting a grip of my senses, I look around stunned. No one else is here. Realizing the bath water has turned cold, I begin to shiver. Looking at my fingers they are shriveled-up. I must have dozed off and was dreaming.

Standing at the bathroom sink, Chris comes up behind me and wraps his arms around me.

"How do you feel?"

"Better," I replied, trying to sound believable. *There's no point in telling Chris what happened in the bath,* I tell myself. *He didn't understand earlier. I doubt he would now.* As I get into bed and pull the covers around me, I feel spooked. *I know it was her that touched my arm.* As I try to force the negative thoughts to the back of my mind, I begin saying my prayers. Tossing and turning throughout the night, I will myself to fall asleep.

***

I walk downstairs to find Chris in the kitchen.

"Good morning," I say while hugging him around his waist.

"Good morning sunshine," he replies giving me a kiss.

"I see you almost have your lunch packed. Need any help?"

"Nope, 'bout got-er done'," he says in a long, drawn-out voice, placing both hands on his belt and smirking.

"Who are you?" I laugh, causing him to break out of character.

"Got your coffee poured and sitting on the counter. Did you sleep okay? You were tossing and turning quite a bit. You were even talking in your sleep at one point. I was going to wake you up but, then you stopped."

Taking a sip, I lean back against the counter.

"I wasn't going to say anything, but I saw a face last night."

"What do you mean you saw a face? Where?"

"When I was taking a bath."

"You saw a face in the bathroom window? The bathroom is on the second story."

"The face wasn't in the window."

"I'm not following you, Beth."

"I drifted off to sleep and was startled awake when something touched my arm and then I saw a face a few inches from mine."

"You were probably dreaming in that RENO state of sleep."

"It's called REM and stands for rapid eye movement, and no-- it was her face, Chris, the girl from the accident. I know it really happened because my magazines beside the tub were damp from the water and I hadn't gotten out. It was her. I know it."

"You had a small nightmare. You said so yourself that you drifted off to sleep and when you woke up it scared you. That could explain the magazines getting wet."

"Whatever it was, it really spooked me."

"That explains your mood last night."

He pulls me close, and with my head against his chest, I can feel his heartbeat.

"Why don't you try to get your mind off the whole thing and read a book or go for a walk, or call up one of your friends?"

"I'm not sure I will have time, today."

"Why is that?"

"I have a full day of running errands planned."

＊＊＊

With Chris' slacks from the dry cleaners safely hanging from the hook, I shut the hatch and get in. Staring at my list, I can finally cross off the last item. I wait to pull out of my parking space when a shiny clean car pulls in beside me. Well, I tell myself, maybe just one more stop.

I pull into the car wash and wait for my turn. Once given the signal, I placed the car in neutral and turned up the radio to jam for the next couple of minutes. High-pressure jets spew water and soap at the car as I turn the radio up even louder to help drown out the noise. Closing my eyes, one of my favorite songs is playing. As I try to sing along, I come to the realization that I really don't know the words. Laughing, I sing along with what I think are the words, bobbing my head to the tune.

I open my eyes to check my position and notice the scent of lilacs. It must be the soap they are using. It smells nice. Peering out the front I follow the big, long strips as they hit the windshield and drag up and over the car. Since I was a child, this has always reminded me of long octopus arms. Looking through the rearview mirror, I follow as they run across the back of the car window, darkening the inside of the vehicle. A small beam of light begins to shine through and grow brighter in the car. Suddenly, something's not right. It looks like someone is sitting in the backseat!

Grabbing the steering wheel, I quickly try to turn around. As I fight with the seatbelt, it tightens as I twist. The car continues making short jerks as it proceeds on the track. Turning around, I strain to see. Finally, I unbuckle my seatbelt. There's something floating in a mist. It's a girl. It's the girl from the accident. The one I saw in the mirror and the face I saw in the bathtub! When the blowers switch on, it startles me, and I look away. When I look back, she's gone.

Peering through the windshield, I follow small beads of water as they try to hang on. The windshield wipers flop about when the huge air compressors turn on. The green light located at the exit lights up as I continue staring. When the driver behind me grows impatient and honks, I quickly snap out of it, clicking my seatbelt and putting the car in drive. As I'm sitting at a stop light, I realize the radio is still blaring. I shut it off and drive the rest of the way home in silence, questioning my sanity.

***

With everything put away and dinner in the oven, I walk outside to water the plants. As Chris pulls into the driveway, he eyes me warily while I stand there with the hose in my hand. I playfully squirt towards his car as he gets out and cautiously walks towards me.

"Don't you dare," he warns me.

I squeeze the trigger shooting water close to his feet.

"Now, come on," he pleads. "You remember what happened the last time you tried this? Someone got really drenched and I don't recall it being just me!"

He dodges my half-hearted attempts to squirt him and locks me in a bear hug while he craftily "disarms" me.

"You certainly are in a playful mood," he laughs. "You must have had a good day. You usually dread a day of nothing but errands and running around."

Shutting off the hose and winding it back on the reel, I reply, "It wasn't bad at all. I had a friendly cashier that didn't mind my coupons and a grocery cart that had working wheels."

"The car looks great by the way!"

"You noticed? You can notice I got the car washed, but you don't notice when I get my hair done!"

"I was going to tell you your hair looks very nice but, you didn't give me a chance to get it out!"

I hold up my hand, laughing: "I didn't get my hair done today. I was merely stating a fact."

"Phew! I'm starving! What's for dinner?"

"Yeah, go ahead, change the subject."

Looking over his shoulder, he retreats inside. "I know when I'm beat!" he laughs.

As we set the table and prepare to eat dinner, Chris turns around and gives me an odd look.

"What's the matter?" I ask him.

Cocking his head to one side, he sniffs at the air. "Do you have a new perfume on?"

"Nope, the same one I have had for the last several years. Why? Do you want me to look for one that smells like cheese pizza?" I joke.

Continuing to sniff at the air, Chris asks, "Do you smell anything odd?"

"You can cook the rest of the week or go hungry if that's what you want to start!"

"I'm not playing. I smell the pasta and it smells delicious. When I opened the cabinet, I got a scent of something."

"Is it a good smell or a bad one?"

He peers back into the cabinet, sliding glasses and dishes all around. "Did you put any potpourri in here or any of your scented stuff?"

"Why would I put potpourri in with the dishes?"

"It's gone now, I don't smell it anymore."

"Good! Come and grab a plate."

Spooning a generous helping of pasta onto each plate with a piece of French bread, I set the plates on the table. While we eat, I hesitantly mention what happened at the carwash. Pausing, Chris sits there in silence. After what seems like a zillion minutes with my plate now empty along with his, he begins to speak.

"Look," he says calmly, "I'm just going to say this. Your mind is playing with you. This isn't normal, Beth. I think it would help you if you talked to someone, like a professional. You could talk to Pastor Dave at the church or maybe even someone at work."

"I'm not going nuts! I really saw her."

"Okay, I understand you think you saw something, but why?"

"I'm just as confused as you are Chris. Seeing things that cannot be explained is common in my family."

"It's the Adams' Family meets the Twilight Zone," he says and smiles.

THREE

I walk downstairs making a beeline for the coffee pot. Propped up by the coffee maker is a note. *Aw, he left me a note*. "Beth, I didn't want to wake you. You were snoring! Have a wonderful day. Left early to grab donuts for work. XOXO Chris."

Pouring a cup, I stir in the creamer and prepare for the first sip of heaven. "Mmmm." I have the perfect ratio of coffee and creamer this morning. As I push the lever on the toaster down, the phone rings.

"What did you forget?" I ask.

"Can I speak to Beth please? This is Ruby from the hospital."

"Oh my gosh," I laugh. "I thought you were my husband calling."

"We have had a couple of sick calls this morning and we have you down for being on-call today. I'm really sorry but, we need your help."

"I'll get my things together and see you shortly."

I pull my bagel out of the toaster and smear a generous amount of cream cheese over the top. Grabbing my bagel and cup of coffee, I go upstairs to get ready. I quickly text Chris to let him know that I have been called in.

***

I catch myself checking the rearview mirror on the drive to work. Stop it, I scold myself. No one's there. It's your mind playing tricks on you. Remember?

I clock in then stuff my purse and phone into my locker. I tuck a few extra pens into my pocket. You can never have too many pens. Someone is always asking to borrow one and I'm always laying them down.

Walking into the department, it's busy. Several patients are unstable and requiring a nurse at the bedside.

I'm supposed to take over for my friend Caleb, who stayed over to help. Caleb is a young man in his mid-twenties with sandy blonde shoulder-length hair pulled back into a bun. He followed his mother's footsteps in choosing a nursing career. He just got married to his partner of five years in May. He is so caring and genuine with such a sweet smile.

I find Caleb talking in his patient's room. "It was nice of you to stay over this morning."

"I can always use the extra money," Caleb says. "Andrew has the day off, so I'm taking him out for breakfast."

"That's nice."

Caleb then looks over at the older gentleman lying on the gurney. "This is Mr. and Mrs. Young."

I nod and smile at the woman sitting in the corner, playing with her handkerchief. Caleb then reviews with me that Mr. Young collapsed at home.

"He awakens at times but is confused," says Caleb. "He is tolerating the oxygen mask well. His blood pressure has been elevated and he's been given these medications to try and bring it down slowly," pointing at the chart.

We continue to have a bedside report as his wife listens intently. At the end, Caleb pauses and looks over at Mrs. Young.

"Do you have any questions for either of us?"

She adjusts herself in the chair and says, "I'm worried about his blood pressure. It's never been that high."

Caleb looks down at the chart he's holding and flips through papers. "I see it has come down some, but I will let Dr. Austin know it is still elevated. Beth will take good care of you," he says and exits the room.

While straightening Mr. Young's blanket, I ask Mrs. Young, "How long have you two been married?"

"Carl and I have been married for 45 years," she answers, dabbing her eyes. "Our anniversary is next month."

"Let me help you move your chair closer so that you can hold his hand."

As she gently takes his hand, I encourage her to talk to him.

She takes a deep breath and sighs. "I think I'm still in shock. We were just sitting and having breakfast and he said he had a headache. He never has headaches. I went to get him something and came back to find him slumped over. I was so scared. I hurried and called an ambulance and then our son. I have never had to call an ambulance before."

"I'm sure it was quite scary for you."

Dr. Austin walks in and looks at the monitor on the wall displaying the patient's vital signs. "Caleb informed me his blood pressure is still elevated. I have ordered another medication to try and bring it down." He takes a seat on the stool beside the gurney and looks through the chart. "Mrs. Young, the CAT Scan has revealed your husband has had a stroke. We are keeping him comfortable and monitoring him. He will be admitted to the Intensive Care Unit and his care will be turned over to Dr. Williams, a neurologist. Do you have any questions or need anything?"

She again takes a deep breath and lets it out. "I'm just trying to digest it all."

"If you should think of anything, you can let Beth know."

"Thank you, Doctor," she says shaking his hand.

"I can assure you, Dr. Austin and Dr. Williams are both excellent doctors. I would let either one of them take care of my family."

"That is reassuring to hear. You have all been so wonderful."

My colleague, Paige, walks in and relays that Dr. Williams phoned and has been delayed with another case. "He wants Mr. Young transported to the ICU and he will see him later. He is going to room 102 and you can go ahead and call report to the unit."

***

Walking into the ICU lounge, Mrs. Young is standing at the counter fixing herself a cup of tea. She turns and smiles wearily.

"They will come out and get you once they have him tucked in. It shouldn't be long," I reassure her.

"I have my rosary to keep me company and to try and ground my thoughts," Mrs. Young replies.

"I will keep you in my prayers," I tell her touching her arm.

She hugs me, "Thank you for everything. You have been so sweet."

Returning to the nurses' station everyone is sitting around.

"Why don't you go get a snack," Lexi suggests.

"Are you sure? I only have a couple hours left until my shift is done," I reply.

"We're fine and your patient was the last one to go to the unit. It's just minor stuff now."

"Okay, I'll be back shortly."

I walk into the cafeteria and look around at the various displays of treats and snacks. "Hi Beth," Violet, a cafeteria helper, and friend of mine, says from behind the counter.

"There's too many things to pick from," I tell her making a face.

"Tell me about it. We have some donuts that have been talking to me all morning!" she laughs. "I'm still trying to get rid of my baby weight."

"How is baby Max?"

"He's getting big. He rolled over the other day, and he is smiling all the time." She takes a minute and shows me a picture of her bright-eyed, brown hair cutie.

"He has got to be the cutest baby I have ever seen, Violet! He should be in commercials. And look at those eyelashes."

"We're blessed and we know it."

"Amen!" I affirm.

After finally choosing something to tie me over, I take a seat in the breakroom. I carefully peel the paper from the muffin and take a bite. Savoring the sweetness of the chocolate, I close my eyes. Chaplain Paul happens to be standing there smiling when I open my eyes.

Laughing, he tells me: "It does look good. How is your day going?"

"Okay. They had a couple of sick calls this morning, so they called me in. I just finished with my stroke patient, so I grabbed a snack to hold me over. You may want to pay a visit to his wife. They're in room 102. Such a sweet couple."

He writes the information down in his notebook and tucks it in the breast pocket of his jacket. "Do you mind if I sit down for a minute?" he asks pulling out a chair.

"Not at all."

"I heard the ER was really busy this morning. I have been trying to make my rounds and my list just keeps growing."

"Do you have any news on the girl from the other day?"

"No, but I wanted to check in and see how you are doing."

I swallow hard as I fold the edges of my napkin. Pausing, *I just need to say it.* "Actually, I'm not I... I um... I have had some weird things happening."

"How so?" he asks.

I get up and close the door to the breakroom and then return to my seat. "I have been seeing things and smelling lilacs."

"What do you think you are seeing?"

"Not 'what', 'who'," I correct him.

He looks at me puzzled. "Who?" shaking his head.

"I am seeing the girl from the accident."

"Have you talked to anyone about it?"

"I have talked to my husband, Chris. He thinks, well I'm not really sure what he thinks."

"Are you sure it's her?"

"I have seen her multiple times. Once in a mirror at an antique store, then while I was taking a bath, and then again in the car while going through the carwash."

"Beth, you know as well as I do, what stress can do to the body and your mind. I'm glad you feel comfortable enough to talk to me."

"I know Chris will be more at ease that I have talked to someone."

"I will put you in my prayers tonight," he smiles.

"Thank you," I respond taking the final bite and folding up the wrapper.

***

Walking back into the department I am just in time to answer the radio designated for ambulance traffic.

"This is medic 19, how do you read?"

"Loud and clear, go ahead with your radio traffic," I speak into the mic. Dr. Austin walks over and stands beside me as well as Karli.

"Be advised we have a 6-year-old female who was playing on the playground when she fell off the monkey bars. She is complaining of pain to the left forearm that has been splinted. She also has abrasions to both knees. She is alert and oriented with no reported loss of consciousness. The school nurse gave her Tylenol prior to our arrival and her mother has been notified. Our ETA is 5-7 minutes. Do you have any questions?"

I glance over at Dr. Austin, who shakes his head and walks back over to his desk.

"No further questions medic 19. You can go to room 2 on your arrival."

Lexi escorts the anxious mother from the lobby to room 2 where she takes a seat. Karli brings her a cup of water as she nervously tries to take a sip. After introducing ourselves, we update her on what the medics reported. A short time later, a wide-eyed 6-year-old with blond pigtails named Harriett is wheeled into the department on a stretcher with a white fluffy stuffed dog on her lap. Mom becomes teary when she sees her daughter. As we try to calm Mom down, for Harriet's sake, we begin to talk to Harriett as well as her stuffed friend. I grab the smallest blood pressure cuff available and fasten it around her furry friend's arm.

"What's his name?" I ask.

She shrugs and smiles shyly, watching intently.

"Can I take his blood pressure and temperature?"

She watches closely then allows me to do the same on her. Her abrasions are cleansed, and Band-Aids are applied to Harriet as well as her dog. After x-rays are taken, it's confirmed she has a broken arm. While her cast is being applied, I do my best to wrap gauze around the dog's arm as well. Lastly, I apply a miniature sling which brings a smile to Harriet's face.

Dr. Austin looks over and laughs, "I didn't realize you were so crafty, Beth."

"I can be," I smile.

Upon Harriet's discharge home, she tells us she has named her new friend Buddy.

***

While clocking out, some of the girls are talking about meeting at the park for a run.

"You should come Beth. We are going to run on the trails."

Hearing Chris' voice in my head urging me to take part, I agree to join them. I give Chris a call on the way home to let him know of my plans.

"That's great! I'm glad you are doing something for yourself and with your friends. I had a meeting that ran over and still have some things I need to wrap up before leaving. Have a fun time but be careful!" he warns.

Once at the park, I check my shoelaces and grab my water bottle before tucking away my keys. As our group jogs along, we talk about guys, cooking, fashion, and who is dating whom. The time goes by fast and as we walk back to our cars, we talk about trying to make it a weekly or perhaps a monthly event.

FOUR

Opening the door, I find Chris at the kitchen table. He looks up from his bowl of cereal: "How was your run?"

"It was nice. Is that what you're having for dinner?" I ask.

"Yeah, I'm too tired to fix anything."

I walk over to the refrigerator, open it, and inspect the shelves.

"Did you want anything else? I can fix you something."

"No, I'm content with my Captain Crunch, but thanks."

I pour myself a glass of orange juice and take a big gulp.

"Thirsty?" Chris asks as he watches.

"This really hits the spot."

I get out the milk and pour a bowl of cereal for myself.

"Are you having dinner with the Captain too?" he jokes.

"It's just something to put in my stomach and like you, I don't really feel like fixing anything."

"How was work?" he asks. "It stinks you got called in."

"Not horrible. I talked to Chaplain Paul today. Still no word on the girl."

"That's too bad," he adds.

"I told him about my seeing the girl and stuff."

He looks at me beaming. "I am so proud of you. I know it must have been hard for you. What did he say?"

"Something that I already knew. That stress can do a lot to the body and mind. He is going to pray for me, which can't hurt."

Chris grabs the cereal bowls and rinses them off before putting them in the dishwasher.

"Go ahead and shower. We can watch some TV together and then go to bed."

"I would be content to just lay in bed and read."

"That sounds good too. I will let Gracie out and join you shortly."

***

The next morning, I get up and decide to go for a run. *The run yesterday felt so good.* After Chris gets off to work, I stand at the end of the driveway, prepared to lose myself in the music coming from my phone, concentrating solely on my breathing. I love it when you get in the zone and your breathing feels effortless. As I run through neighborhoods, I study the houses looking for decorating and landscaping ideas. I love going past a house and you can smell the scent of fabric softener in the air.

Walking into the kitchen, I am winded. I down the rest of the water in the bottle and pour myself a glass of orange juice before heading to shower.

Once refreshed and ready to start the day, I am on my way downstairs when the phone rings.

"Hello," I answer.

"Hi. It's me, Amber Lynn. I wondered if you were free to grab lunch today. There's a new diner downtown that I have been wanting to try."

"Is it the one next to the bank and dry cleaners?" I ask.

"That's the one. How about 11:30 a.m.?"

"That will work. I'll see you then," hanging up the phone.

I have just enough time to run an errand before heading to the restaurant. I grab my purse and toss it into the car. I then scan the backseat for any extra passengers. *I remember Grandpa Theo talking about his ghost experiences, having once lived in a haunted house as a kid. He felt they were lost souls trying to move on. Mom would tell him not to fill my head with such ideas and scare me, but frankly I was intrigued.*

***

I enter the restaurant and look around for Amber Lynn while admiring the surroundings. *It's quaint.* I let the hostess know I am meeting a friend. She goes ahead and seats several other guests, while I continue to wait. After several minutes, she offers to seat me while I wait. Showing me to a booth, she informs me that our waitress is finishing with a large group and will be over shortly. I take a seat, smoothing out my top and pushing my hair away from my face. I thank her as she hands me a menu and places water on the table. Looking over the menu, I glance at the board listing their specials. *I'm not sure what I'm in the mood for.*

Amber Lynn is her usual bubbly self when she arrives. She reaches over and hugs me before sliding into the booth. Plopping her purse down, she runs her fingers through her long blond hair. "I must look a mess. I have been going nonstop this morning," she says.

Our waitress comes over and introduces herself and apologizes for the delay. After reviewing the lunch specials with us, she takes our drink orders and gives us time to decide.

"I forgot to eat breakfast," Amber Lynn says frowning. "I got Doug and the kids off and went to Pilates class."

Looking across the table, I watch as she scans the menu. She always looks so polished with just the right touch of makeup regardless of how busy she is. "Come to think of it, I only had orange juice after my run this morning. I never even thought about fixing breakfast for myself," I add.

"I can always eat, but I never seem to make time for it," she says flipping her menu over.

"I know how you feel."

We promptly hand our menus to our waitress after both ordering the lunch special. Amber Lynn folds her hands and sets them on top of the table. "So, what gives? Something isn't right. You're not yourself. When I called you yesterday after you weren't returning my texts, I caught Chris at home. He said you were going through some stuff."

Swirling the straw around in my glass, I take a sip.

Amber Lynn continues, "I'm confused. What stuff are you going through? Are you sorting through stuff in the attic, redoing your closets, redecorating? What? He didn't even elaborate, just totally left me hanging," folding her arms.

Looking down, I begin playing with the edges of the napkin in my lap.

She leans across the table and in a low tone asks: "Is everything okay with you two? I hope you know that you can confide in me. I thought we were better friends than that. I know when Doug and I have an argument it sometimes goes on for a couple of days where we don't talk, then we decide it has gone on long enough, and we make up."

"This isn't about an argument or disagreement, like you have with Doug!" I snap. Having realized too late my tone, I watch as she tries to avoid making eye contact now.

"I just thought if you guys were going to get a divorce, maybe I could help in some way."

"Divorce? No," shaking my head. "It's nothing like that. There is no reason you should be upset at Chris for not giving you all the details. I have been trying to sort through something at work."

"Is that all." Immediately, she sounds bored as she clicks her tongue.

Her disappointment of my issue being work related and not involving my marriage catches me by surprise. I begin to sense I am going to regret telling her. "Something happened and I'm just trying to understand it. It's like doing a puzzle and a piece is missing."

Amber Lynn rolls her eyes and takes a sip from her glass as the waitress breaks the tension by serving our meals.

Once the waitress leaves, I try to explain: "This is about a girl who died in the Emergency Room."

Biting my lip, I begin to tell her about the accident and the young girl. I even tell her about seeing the girl in the mirror at the antique store and seeing her face while in the bathtub. As the words roll off my tongue and out of my mouth, I notice

Amber Lynn is sitting there with her face all scrunched up.

"That's weird!" she says. "Don't they have a pill or something that you can take for that?"

Nervously, I run my hands up and down my thighs. *This isn't going the way I had played it out in my mind. What did I really think was going to happen? She, show empathy?* The waitress tops off our glasses and brings extra napkins. "Thank you," I tell her as she walks from the table. I continue to try and explain what's been going on to Amber Lynn, ignoring the amplified sirens going off in my head, signaling danger.

Taking a bite of her sandwich, she chews slowly as she mulls over the conversation. "Can't you just take a long bath or go for a good run to forget about it?"

I look at her intently and reason, "It's not that easy. I have never had anything like this happen to me, so I really don't know how I am supposed to be acting."

"This isn't the first time you have been around someone that has died."

My eyes widen as I am shocked and hurt by her comment. Feeling my blood pressure increase, I begin to feel my face getting flushed. "Yes, I have had patients die, but they haven't come back to visit me!" *If you only knew about what happened while at the carwash or how I have had relatives come to me who have died in the past.*

Nothing is said over the next several minutes allowing us both time to cool down and concentrate on eating. Having lost my appetite, I begin playing with my soup, to avoid making eye contact. Amber Lynn sees that I am upset and tries to change the subject. The voice inside my head tells me to stop trying to have her understand and just let it go. She has no experience in the medical field and can only relate to the things she's seen on TV.

She pushes her plate away, looks at me cocking her head and smiles. "I want you to know you can call me anytime. I am here to listen," using a sincere voice.

Disappointed how the whole conversation has gone, I was hoping to gain some support or comradery. "Let's talk about something else," I urge, pushing my plate aside. "What's new with you?"

The subject quickly changes to Amber Lynn being made the new chairperson and organizing the annual craft bazaar.

"What happened to Linda? I thought she did a wonderful job with last year's."

"It's time for a change. We are going to do things quite differently this year. We only have a few spaces available," she says playing with her necklace. "I am being pickier than Linda was last year. We need to weed out the flea market junk."

"Some people like that. Vintage isn't bad." I reply.

Watching her, I notice her persona change.

"If they want flea market junk, let them go to the county fair. Anyway, I knew you would want to take part like last year, so I went ahead and signed you up."

"Great."

"I will put you in the same spot as last year. Do you know what kind of fabulous things you are going to make?"

"Hmm, not really. I haven't given it much thought. When is it again?"

"Wow, you really are out there nowadays, aren't you?" Amber Lynn jokes.

"I guess I am a little preoccupied right now you might say."

"Its fine," reaching over and patting my hand. "You have plenty of time to try and get over what you are going through. The bazaar isn't until next month."

Our waitress comes and clears Amber Lynn's plate and notices mine has barely been touched. Tearing our meal checks out of her order pad, she asks, "Didn't you like it, sweetie?"

"It was great. I just spent too much time talking," trying to expel a laugh.

"I will be back with a box so you can take it home and I'll bring you some more tea."

"Beth, you have always been one of our top money makers. Maybe this will help you to get your mind off the girl," Amber Lynn suggests.

If only you could have shown compassion to me earlier, Amber Lynn, I think to myself. My head is starting to pound. Rubbing my temple, I search through my purse for my pill box. I find two ibuprofen and wash them down with the rest of my tea.

"What is the total for the booth again?"

"It's seventy-five dollars this year. We had to increase it some but we're still cheaper than most you know."

"It doesn't matter because I will donate all my proceeds like I did last year."

"You are always such a good girl, Beth. I'm saving mine up for a getaway with Doug, without the kids. Where is someplace you would go for a getaway? I was thinking somewhere warm and tropical."

As I start to answer, Amber Lynn suddenly shrieks, as she looks at her watch.

"Is that really the time? I didn't realize it was getting so late. I am so sorry to cut this short. I have a nail appointment and I'm going to be late. I have to squeeze everything in while the kids are in school. You understand." Grabbing the money off the table for the booth rental, she slides out of the booth. "This has been so much fun. We will have to do this again," Amber Lynn says.

I let out a sigh as she hugs me goodbye.

"I'll give you a buzz in a couple of days to see how you are doing and we can try and set up another time. Oh darn," she cried, stomping her foot. "I forgot to ask for a drink to go. You won't mind if I take yours and you can ask for another one?"

"Go ahead," handing her my cup.

She stands beside the table and takes a sip, "Let's try and do coffee next time."

"Sounds great," trying to sound believable.

She hurries from the table and out the door. I take a deep breath feeling I have just survived a tornado and the all-clear has been announced. Our waitress comes over and collects the money on the table. She asks if I need any change back.

"No, keep it."

She starts to walk away, pauses, and asks: "Are you sure you're, okay? You seemed sad while your friend was here and even more now that she has left."

"I guess I'm just a little out of sorts today," shrugging.

"Can I get you something else? How about a piece of pie? We have an excellent peach pie today. Marie over there makes them herself." She gestures over at a petite brown-haired woman in her mid-forties. "Hey Marie," she hollers across the room. "Don't you make the best pies?"

Marie looks up from the table she is waiting on, cocks her head to one side and grins. "I am proud of my pies," she boasts.

Just then an elderly man sitting at the counter turns around and adds, "I come in every week just for a piece of Marie's pie."

"Oh, Kirby, you really know how to make a girl blush," Marie beams.

He chuckles and turns around.

"Wow, with that kind of an endorsement, how can I refuse? Could I get a piece to go? Whatever kind you suggest."

"Sure, thing and I will get you another iced tea to go. I see your friend took off with yours."

Returning with my drink and piece of pie nicely tucked in a paper bag, she places it on the table.

"How much for the pie?" I ask as I dig through my purse for my wallet?

"It's on the house! A present from me to you. Hopefully, it will make your day a little sweeter with something to look forward to later."

"It certainly will. Thank you very much."

"Maybe you just need some retail therapy. Go out and buy something for yourself you wouldn't normally buy. I know I always feel better after shopping that is, until I have to explain it to my husband," she grins.

"I know what you mean," I laugh.

FIVE

Getting into the car, I begin to drive and for whatever reason, I find myself back at Foster's Antiques Store. Walking into the store, I have butterflies in my stomach. Mrs. Foster is busy talking with two women at the counter with a few other people browsing. Not wanting to waste any time, I grab the handrail and head upstairs. I can hear the muffled voices of the women with Mrs. Foster. The shop seems unusually busy today. I notice a sign at the top of the stairs, "twenty percent off today" which explains the busyness.

Once upstairs, I notice a man with two women looking around. Casually they walk around pointing out various pieces to each other. Eventually, I make eye contact with the taller of the two women and smile. She nods and then turns to talk to her friend. I presume she must be the leader as I watch the man and other woman follow her around. The man with them must be one of their husbands, I conclude, when I watch him cringe after checking the price tags and say, "Do we really need a new one? What's wrong with what we have?"

Cautiously, I walk over to the dresser. *It's in the same spot*, I tell myself. Carefully I slide one end of the dresser away from the wall and study the back. The number 2191 is written on the back. I look around to see if anyone is watching. Swallowing hard, I extend my hand touching the mirror. Nervously, I peer into the mirror and wait. Several seconds go by and nothing. *You were nervous for nothing*. But wait, there is a reflection. Only it's not the reflection I had anticipated. I now realize the talking from the people I had seen earlier has stopped. The reflection in the mirror is that of the two women watching me with perplexed looks.

Taking my hand away from the mirror I turn around and watch as one woman furrows her brow and shakes her head, while her friend stands staring at me inquisitively. They look at each other and laugh and then walk away. Totally embarrassed, I walk toward the stairs and hear one of the women ask, "What about this chair?"

I hear the man protest that his feet hurt, and he can't take the walking back and forth "like a couple of squirrels trying to find a nut!"

I walk up to Mrs. Foster at the counter and say, "Hi."

"What dear?" she says, tilting her head to one side. "Your voice is so soft. What did you say?"

"Hi," I repeat. "I was wondering if you could tell me anything about a dresser you have upstairs. There's a number written on the back of it; number 2191. What does the number mean?"

"The number on the back helps us with our record keeping for the larger items. We do it in chalk, so it doesn't cause any damage."

"Has anyone else asked about the dresser?" *Is it possible someone else has seen the girl in the mirror?* I wonder.

"Not that I am aware of. You were in earlier this week, weren't you dear?"

"Yes," I nod.

She leans over the counter and smiles. "I knew you would be back."

"Why do you say that?" *Was she watching me on a security camera when I saw the image?*

Looking over her glasses, she sheepishly said, "Anytime someone comes back for a second look, I feel something or someone has spoken to them. Sometimes when it's quiet around here, you can hear and feel things. Sometimes maybe it's a moan or even a groan."

Just then, her husband walks around the corner, holding his back. "The moans are just me," he interjects, "because you've asked me to move something else!"

Ignoring his remark, she smirks and continues talking. "I mean like when a dress or pair of shoes say, "Buy me, buy me!"

Mr. Foster again chimes in, "That's what you call impulse buying and no self-control!"

Shaking her head at him, she ignores his remarks.

Meekly, I ask, "Like a little voice inside you, right?"

Glancing up at me, she adjusts her glasses on her nose, "You didn't think I meant that the dresser actually talked to you, do you?"

"No!" trying to laugh convincingly, while nervously playing with my purse strap.

"These things talk to me all the time. Helps to keep me company when George isn't around or doesn't feel like talking."

"I'm glad you have someone else to talk to, Alice!" Mr. Foster chimes in.

Trying not to laugh out loud, I smile as he walks away carrying a box.

Mrs. Foster shouts, "I love you, you old coot!"

Looking back over his shoulder, he kicks up his leg as Mrs. Foster and I laugh.

"I love you too, Alice."

Mrs. Foster then smacks her hand against the counter, "Now let's get back to business, shall we?"

"I can't seem to stop thinking about the dresser," I tell her.

"Then you have had that little voice speak to you."

"Something like that. Do you have any history on the dresser?"

She looks through her notebook.

"Most of our things come from estate sales or auctions."

"Do you happen to know the name of the estate it came from?"

"I don't think I have had anybody ask for that particular information before."

"I guess I'm just curious."

She looks through the notebook again, "It doesn't seem to be written down. Sometimes, George records the information and sometimes I do. Only this time it looks like neither of us did."

She turns to her husband who is busy going through boxes piled on the floor nearby: "Do you remember the name of the estate we got the dresser upstairs from?"

"Which dresser might that be? We only have about fifty or sixty to choose from."

Ignoring his sarcasm, she continues, "You know, number 2191, the one with the mirror? You said it looked like the one your mother had."

"Oh, that one. We got it the same time we got the large trunk and that suitcase with the women's clothes."

"Oh, I remember now," she says. "Let me see if we put the name under any of the other items. Do you remember the number on the trunk or suitcase, George?"

"I don't catalog every item in my mind-- that's what we have the notebook for."

"Well, let's see now…" She thumbs through the pages. "No, no, that's not it. Wait, is this it? No. Oh, here it is! Right underneath my finger," she laughs. "The trunk is number 2192 and the suitcase is 2193. I guess I should have just looked a couple of numbers away from the dresser's number. Here's the name. We bought it from the Richards' estate sale in Florence County."

"Florence County. Where is that?" I ask.

"It's not far from here, just as you leave the Indiana State line."

"Do you still have the trunk or suitcase by chance?"

"Unfortunately, no. The drama teacher at the high school bought them. I remember him talking about how he would put them to good use for costumes and props."

I don't dare share with the Fosters anything about seeing the girl in the mirror, especially after Amber Lynn's reaction. Number one; I didn't want to scare them and number two; I don't want them to think I'm crazy. The only person I can comfortably talk to right now is Chris. Impulsively, I buy the dresser and Mr. Foster is more than happy to help me load it into the car. I don't know how I'm going to explain it to Chris but, I will worry about that later.

I'm curious what was in the trunk and suitcase. Since the drama teacher got them for props, I'm assuming it was mostly clothing. I turn the radio on to help break the silence. Looking in the rearview mirror, I have a clear view of the dresser in the back. Gradually, I notice the the soft scent of lilacs. No carwash to blame it on today, I say to myself.

***

As I wait for Chris to come home, I play over in my mind what his reaction might be to my buying the dresser. Thankfully, I am pleasantly surprised at his reaction. He is more than eager to help me get it out of the car and positioned in the guestroom.

"Next time," he says panting, "We will take the drawers out to make it lighter and manageable on the stairs."

"Honestly, I didn't even think of it. What makes you think there is going to be a next time?" I ask.

"Are you kidding? I'm married to you! I know there is going to be a next time," he says shaking his head and smiling.

As he positions the dresser on the far wall next to the window, I pop down to the kitchen. Holding the container out in front of me, I say to Chris, "A piece of peach pie for a peach of a husband! Thanks for being such a good sport!"

Sitting on the bed, he opens the container and dives into the pie while I dust off the dresser. I place an antique doily and bud vase in the center.

"Did you buy those too?" he asks holding out the fork, offering me a bite.

"No, I had them sitting on the chest downstairs. I will snip a flower for the vase tomorrow." Savoring the bite, I say "Wow, that's delicious."

"It looks like the dresser is in good condition," he says, opening the drawers. "Did you buy this too, lifting out a picture frame?"

"No, I didn't. I wonder if Mrs. Foster put it in there?"

"Maybe she decided to throw it in as a bonus?" He positions the frame next to the vase. "Whose picture are you going to put in it? You just can't leave it empty."

"I will have to go through my box of pictures to see if I have one that suits the frame."

"And if not … more shopping!" he says teasingly.

"You never know," taking his hand in mine and kissing it.

"Are you happy that you have the dresser now? I'm afraid of what you might try to bring home next."

"Very funny! I really think this is a big part of the puzzle and will help me to start getting some answers."

"I hope you're right, babe. This girl's death has really gotten in your head. Unlike any I have ever seen before. This isn't like you."

"I know... Just let me have a couple more days to try to figure this out on my own. If you still feel that I am tight roping towards the deep end I will make an appointment to see Pastor Dave, or a shrink or both. I tried talking to Amber Lynn today at lunch and when I was really getting into it, telling her everything, she blew me off to go to a nail appointment. I didn't even get to tell her about the lilac smell at the carwash or seeing the girl in the backseat. She made me feel like I was crazy. She even questioned whether there was a pill I could take!"

"Well, I'm sorry Amber Lynn wasn't there for you when you needed to feel supported."

"Can I just say, how much I love you Chris and how lucky I am?" as I give him a squeeze.

***

Chris busies himself channel-surfing while I mindlessly, let it filter through one ear and out the other. He pauses on a news station and I hear the newscaster say, "Still no clues to the identification…"

"Stop!" I yell, "Don't change it!"

The newscaster continues, "…of the girl who was killed recently by a drunk driver."

"I can't believe they haven't located the family yet." Chris says shutting off the TV.

I slide open the patio door and walk out to the patio for some fresh air. Chris cranks the umbrella closed and takes a seat beside me. Without any distractions or noise from the TV, we listen to the sounds of the fountain and the windchimes.

"I love that fountain," I announce.

"That was such a fun vacation. Do you remember seeing the bears and the waterfall in the park?" he asks.

"That's the closest I ever want to get to a bear!"

"You were a good sport biking and hiking. That is until you fell off your bike and thought you put your hand in bear poop," he snorts wiping tears from his eyes.

"If I remember right that bike ride almost killed me. Yeah, that's not as funny in my mind as it is in yours."

"With all that being said, would you ever go back to the Smokey Mountains?"

"Probably," I nod.

"Do you remember the name of the place where we bought the fountain?" Chris asks.

"Yes, it was 'Two-Eight Antiques'. Don't you remember? We were talking about the name, and you said you were glad they had more than just twenty-eight things to look at."

"I didn't know what to think when the owner overheard and corrected us. It's called 'Two-Eight Antiques' because it sounds smoother. Remember him making that hand gesture gliding through the air? Twenty-eight was his college jersey number."

"I remember the two of you, high fiving each other as we left the store and you telling him to keep it smooth. He was a really cool guy."

"Isn't it funny, how people can touch your life, like they have been put there to do just that?"

Chris lets out a yawn and I copy him. "The dresser took a chunk out of the evening," he says rubbing his neck.

"I'm sorry. I know you probably wanted to relax tonight."

"No problem. Paybacks are a …"

"Christopher Davis! Don't you dare!"

"I wasn't going to say it," he laughs. "I'm leaving before I get into any more trouble. I'll see you upstairs."

"How's the book?" I ask, walking into the bedroom.

"It's alright, but I just can't seem to get into it tonight. I have read the same sentence over about five times now."

"I won't be long," shutting the bathroom door I get undressed for a shower.

"I may be asleep before you get out," he says between yawns.

With the noise of the water rushing by my ear, even my own thoughts are muffled. Faintly I hear my name. Tilting my head, I hold my breath and listen. Quickly rinsing off, I shut the water off and reach for the towel on the hook. Hesitantly, I pull the curtain back. Seeing nothing obvious and not hearing anything else out of the ordinary, I towel off and slip on my nightgown.

Walking out of the bathroom, I start to ask Chris if he was trying to ask me something and I stop midsentence. Chris is propped up in bed with the book on his chest and his lower lip fluttering as he makes popping sounds with his lips. I take the book, place it on the nightstand, and turn out his light. He mumbles something I can't understand and is out again.

***

As I stare at the blades of the ceiling fan rotating around, I'm tired but can't fall asleep. *Maybe a cup of hot chocolate will help.* While in the hallway, I hear an odd noise. *Is someone trying to break into the house? Should I wake up Chris? Should I grab the baseball bat? Wait, you can't grab the baseball bat, we don't have one.* It sounded like a good idea as I make a mental note to ask Chris if we should get one.

After several seconds of holding my breath and listening, all is quiet downstairs. *The noise came from somewhere, but where? Did I leave the window open?* I look into my craft room and flip on the light switch. The ceiling fan propels papers off the table and into the air. While I am picking them up, I hear a voice beside my ear. Bolting upright, I become dizzy from the sudden movement. After tossing the papers back on the table, I flip off the switch.

Walking into the hall, the moonlight shines through the skylight in the guest bathroom. I feel drawn to the guest room and when I switch on the light, I notice the soft scent of lilacs and see the vase lying on its side. Seeing no damage, I set it upright and do a double take. The empty picture frame isn't empty. It now holds a picture. I pick up the frame and it's cold, like it's been in the freezer. It reminds me of when I touched the mirror at the antique store.

Looking at the picture, I see the face of a young girl. It looks like the same girl I have been seeing. I sit down on the bed and open the frame to examine the photo itself. Written on the back is *Addy D. - 1912*. Now I have a name to go with the picture. *Are you Addy? If you are the girl from the accident, why me? Why did you appear in the mirror? Is the dresser linked to you?*

This is real. I can feel it, touch it, and smell it. The picture smells musty and the edges are brown and worn. *I know now why I was deliberately drawn to the room to see the picture and to see you, Addy. I wonder if Chris found the picture and if he did why didn't he say anything? Unless it wasn't Chris who put it there.*

The downstairs clock chimes midnight and I carefully replace the picture. My mind is reeling with unanswered questions, but I need to go to bed. As I turn off the light, I whisper: "Goodnight, Addy." From behind me, I hear a voice softly reply: "Goodnight."

SIX

Hearing a buzzing sound, I open one eye to realize it's not a dream. Sadly, the clock reads 5:45 a.m. As I sit up and dangle my feet, Chris pokes his head from the bathroom wearing streaks of shaving cream on his face.

"Good morning. I hit the snooze and gave you an extra fifteen," Chris says.

Stretching, I thank him for the extra winks between yawns.

"I heard you get up. What time did you come back to bed?"

"Late," I say trying to muffle a yawn. "I'm sorry I woke you."

"You couldn't sleep, huh?"

"My mind just wouldn't shut off. I got up to make hot chocolate. Today, I am seriously going to need a jumpstart."

"The coffee is brewing as we speak. That should help you."

***

At work, several people have come in with food poisoning after eating at the Lucky Duck Chinese restaurant. Chris will be disappointed. He loves their sweet and sour pork. Hopefully, the future of the Lucky Duck will turnaround.

Living in a small town and being the only hospital, people get to know you and vice versa. The doctor offices in town go out of their way to manage what they can in the office. We usually have a mix of complaints and ailments that make the shifts go by fast. And we have a good team. Everyone at the hospital realizes they are just as important as the next guy.

Chaplain Paul walks into the nurses' station smiling. The two of us go way back. He was one of the very first people to welcome me to the hospital, not to mention warn me about the coffee in the cafeteria. One thing you can be sure of, you will always find him wearing a colorful shirt and tie. He is great with the patients and their families. Many people have said his voice has had a calming effect on them.

Autumn walks into the nurses' station and says, "On the news last night, they said they still haven't identified the girl from the other day."

"I saw it too," Chaplain Paul said. "Sadly, I haven't received any updates from the police."

"That poor family," Madison says, shaking her head.

Lexi stands up and says, "We need to keep them all in our prayers."

"Amen." Chaplain Paul adds.

The group disperses to get back to work. Chaplain Paul puts his hand on my arm and leads me a few steps out of earshot. Looking into my eyes, in a low tone, he asks: "Are you okay? You don't seem yourself today."

"I'm okay, just didn't sleep much," I reply.

"I know this has really bothered you. I'm glad you shared what's been going on the other day."

"It's just so sad. Some mom and dad aren't aware that their daughter won't be having any more birthdays or holidays because she died. How can we not know who she is? Why hasn't anyone reported her missing?"

"Beth, why don't you come to the chapel after work, or we could meet in the cafeteria and talk over a cup of coffee."

"I'm okay, really. I appreciate the offer." I take a deep breath and turn around to greet an ambulance crew who has brought in a gentleman who fell from a ladder. As I direct them to a room, Lexi hands me a chart. As I focus my attention on the ambulance crew and patient, I push everything else away. Listening to the medics' report, I find out the patient was cleaning out his gutters when he missed some steps on the ladder.

Several hours later, my "ladder jumper" is discharged home in a cast with crutches and pain medication. I added to his discharge instructions to have someone else finish cleaning the gutters while he delegates from a chair with his leg propped up.

Close to the end of my shift, a young college student comes in with a high fever, headache, and stiff neck. Right away we are concerned about meningitis. With it being highly contagious, she is put in an isolation room to protect the other patients and staff. Madison is assigned as her primary nurse with me and Autumn helping her. Madison was able to get the girl's fever down with Tylenol and intravenous fluids after several hours. When we left for the day, they were still waiting for her lumbar puncture results.

***

Shortly after getting home, I let Gracie out and strip down to my birthday suit to wash my uniform. Heading for the shower, I turn on the radio in the bedroom for noise. Pinning up my hair, I pull a razor out of the drawer to shave my legs. Listening to the music, I hum along. Bent over with my foot resting on the edge of the tub, I take each stroke carefully. I've never been great at shaving my legs, evident by the small pieces of toilet paper I end up wearing on them.

While listening to the music, I hear someone say something. *Did someone just say my name?* Peeking my head out around the shower curtain, I listen to the noise of the music and water. *Could Chris be home already?* After several seconds, I presume it's my overactive imagination. As I continue with the other leg, *You need to get a grip girl! Your imagination is running wild. The other night you thought you heard something and there wasn't even music playing.*

I towel off and slip on my robe. While brushing my hair, I hear my name again. I walk over to the radio and shut it off. As I turn around, I cry out, "Jesus!" She is standing right in front of me. Then in a flash, she's gone.

Shaking, I sit down on the bed. I'm nauseous from the rush of adrenaline. As I look around the room, I find myself directing my voice towards the ceiling. "Addy, you can't keep scaring me. You are going to give me a heart attack and then I'm not going to be able to help you." Waiting for a response, I shake my head. *What am I thinking? She isn't going to just start carrying on a conversation. She's a ghost, a spirit or something.*

***

During dinner, Chris and I discuss the highlights of each other's day. "Work was okay," I tell him, "but I need to tell you about what happened last night. I couldn't sleep so I walked into Addy's room."

"I thought you got up to make hot chocolate?" asks Chris.

"I started to but never made it to the kitchen."

"Whose room did you say? 'Addy'? Who is that?"

"Addy is the girl from the accident."

"Did they tell you her name at work?"

"No, we didn't hear anything. But listen... I don't have to look for a picture anymore for the frame. There's a picture in it now!"

"You had one?"

"Not exactly. One just appeared, like the picture frame. I thought maybe you put it there?"

"I didn't put any picture in a frame." He rubs the back of his neck. "I'm confused. So, you're telling me a picture miraculously appeared on its own in the frame? The frame that we found in the drawer of the dresser."

"Yes," I nod.

"I guess I don't understand why you are calling this girl Addy. You said they haven't identified her."

"Her name is Addy. She is the girl from the accident. She is the same girl I saw in the mirror and the face I saw in the bathtub. I know what and who I saw. She is the same girl who was in the backseat at the carwash. Chris, she has even spoken to me! I have heard her call my name and this afternoon I saw her standing in our bedroom. And her picture is now in the picture frame!" Taking a much-needed breath after rattling it all off, I sit waiting for him to respond.

"Wow, you have had quite a day. I am curious to see the picture."

"Awesome!" I eagerly respond, clearing the dishes.

"Slow down, we have all evening."

"I know, I'm just excited you want to see it."

As we head upstairs, I recount finding the picture in the frame. "I now know her name," I tell Chris. Chris closely watches my mood and expressions. "I have even smelled lilacs. Last night, I thought we had a burglar, and I was going to grab the baseball bat, but then realized we don't have one. Do you think we should get one?"

"Wait a minute, a burglar? When? Why didn't you mention any of this earlier?"

"I heard a noise after I got up to go downstairs. It turns out the vase on the dresser was knocked over somehow. Probably so I would notice the picture. When I took it out of the frame, that's when I saw the name on the back. When I was looking at the picture, I smelled lilacs like I did at the car wash."

Listening, he is giving me a look like I am someone he no longer knows. "I came to bed when I heard the clock chime midnight. I said, 'Good night, Addy,' and I heard her say goodnight back."

"You don't say," rubbing his face.

"Why are you making that face, Chris?"

He sits down on the bed and lets out a deep breath. "Did the flower that's in the vase appear on its own too?"

"No, I put it there."

"Listen, I have never seen you act like this before and its beginning to scare me."

Biting my lower lip, "I haven't even told you about today."

He pauses for me to continue.

"When I got home, I took a shower right away because I had a patient with possible meningitis. While I was in the shower, I heard something. At first, I thought it was you coming home early, then I assumed it was the radio I had been playing. When I shut the radio off and turned around, there she was, standing in our bedroom."

Sitting quietly, he looks up at me as I stand with my hands on my hips waiting for him to say something.

"Well, aren't you going to say something?"

"Like what?" he asks.

"How about 'Holy moly, I can't believe all this is going on and yes, you are sane Beth!' You think I am making all of this up, don't you? If you are thinking I have gone off the deep end, you're wrong. This all happened, I swear it." I take the picture out of the frame and hand it to him. "How can I make this up?"

Chris looks at the picture, then flips it over to see written on the back is "Addy D. 1912." "This picture was taken in 1912. How can it be that 98 years later, this same girl is in an accident, and dies again, and is now contacting you?"

"There is the afterlife," I remind him.

"I know how strongly you feel about that, but I'm still on the fence." He stands up and hugs me. "I'm tired and with all that you have gone through, you have got to feel drained. Let's go to bed."

SEVEN

Taped to the steering wheel I find a note from Chris: Make this a good day, I love you. Smiling, I fold it and tuck it neatly in my pocket. Once at work, there is little time to think about Addy or Chris. My shift begins with Mr. Edwards who has suffered a heart attack. Thankfully, we get him stabilized and transported to the Coronary Care Unit.

Swinging the gurney around, we guide it back into the room. Locking the brake, Rachel and I then begin putting the room back together. "Mr. Edwards was so nice. I hope he does well." Rachel says as she wipes down the gurney.

"Be sure and remember them in your prayers tonight," I remind her. As I straighten up the back counter and throw away trash, I'm surprised to look up and see Chris standing in the doorway.

"Is everything okay?" I ask, looking him over for injuries. "Is it the folks?"

"Everyone is fine," Chris says reassuringly.

"Beth, I can finish here. Go ahead," Rachel urges.

"I was in the neighborhood and thought I would come by and see how you're doing this morning."

Looking around, I notice we are being watched. I grab his arm and we move out into the ambulance corridor. If Chris is here to stage an intervention, I don't want everyone to see me being taken away.

He leans against a gurney and begins with, "You fell asleep so fast, I didn't get to tell you goodnight or that I love you."

Looking up into his eyes, I fumble with the items in my scrub pockets. "So, when does everyone come out?" I ask.

"Come out?"

"Is this where you are going to do it?"

"Do what? I'm not following you."

"Do I have to say it. The intervention!"

"What? No sweetie," he laughs. "I knew you might be hungry at lunch time, so I brought you your lunch you left on the counter. I went back home this morning to get some papers I had forgotten. And because I am such a nice guy, I might add, I brought you a chai tea latte and a blueberry muffin for a morning snack."

"Aw, you are a nice guy," kissing his cheek.

"You really thought I was going to stage an intervention? Who would take care of me or Gracie?"

Looking over my shoulder, an ambulance arrives with a new patient. "I better get back to work." I take a quick sip from the cup, "Hmm, thanks for the goodies!" Walking back into the nurses' station and seeing Chris has put my mind at ease.

"I wish my husband would bring me coffee and a muffin. Better yet, I wish your husband would bring me coffee and a muffin," Karli snickered. The nurses' station erupts with cackles.

***

I pull into the driveway and notice a flyer stuck in the screen door. It turns out to be for a new pizza place in town. Just what the doctor ordered, I tell myself. Looking over the flyer, I narrow down our choices. The phone rings and it's Chris' Mom.

"Hi Peggy, how are you?" I say.

"We're good Beth. The reason I'm calling is that Chris' Dad and I, have been invited to our friends' condo in Florida. Our flight leaves Saturday morning. We were hoping that you and Christopher could check on the house for us. I have tried to divide what needs to be done among the boys. Andy is going to keep Winston. He gets along well with their dog and they're going to run us to the airport and pick us up. The only thing left is just keeping an eye on the house."

"That shouldn't be a problem," I tell her.

"I have just a few things that I would like done while were gone. I will text Christopher the list."

"Sure Peggy, have a wonderful time."

"You should still have a spare set of house keys."

Looking over at the key rack, I see a large dolphin keychain hanging from their keys. "I'm looking at them now," I answer.

"We will give you a call when we're back and set up a time for dinner."

"Sounds good, have fun."

With the pizza ordered, I set out paper plates and napkins. "I think it will be fun to eat in the dining room. What do you think Gracie? I will even get out some candles."

Chris arrives just in time to meet the pizza delivery person and pay for it. Walking in, he is balancing the pizza box with one hand. "Your pizza madam," he announces, setting it on the counter.

"Did you change jobs and not tell me?" I joke.

"Very funny," he smirks.

"I thought it would be fun to eat in the dining room tonight. We need to start using it more and not just for holidays."

"Okay by me," he says lifting up the lid and allowing the steam to escape. "Does this ever look good."

***

Chris suggests a walk after dinner and stands up to blow out the candles. I quickly clear off the table and put the pizza away while Chris gets Gracie's leash. Walking hand in hand, as Gracie walks in front of us scouting the way, Chris turns to me and blows out his cheeks.

"What's up?" I ask.

"I ran into Amber Lynn," he tells me.

"You did. When?"

"This morning. When I was picking up your muffin. She was there having coffee with someone."

"A guy or a girl?"

Hesitating, "I think it was a guy or an ugly girl."

Smacking his arm, "That's not nice. Funny, but not nice!"

"Anyway, she told me you need to call her with your bazaar items, so she can list you in the program."

"There's a program, this year? I forgot all about the bazaar after having that awful lunch with her."

"Are you sure you still even want to do it? When is it anyway?"

"She told me, but I don't remember exactly, sometime next month."

"Do you have anything already made up or maybe something from last year's bazaar that you can use?"

"Nope. I donated it to the hospital for their silent auction to raise money for toys for the pediatric wing."

"Well, I guess that takes you back to square one and empty-handed."

"I didn't want to tell her 'no'. I have a problem with that."

"I know you do. Tell me about it."

"Oh, come on now, I'm not that bad!"

"No, but when you volunteer both of us and not tell me until the last minute, that's when I have a problem with it."

"You've already told me how much that upsets you and I've tried to consciously not commit to something where it will eventually include you. Amber Lynn told me at lunch how I have been one of the top sellers and how I can help make the bazaar an even bigger success."

"She went through the whole thing with me too while I was waiting in line. She seems to think with her being chairperson this year, that everyone is looking at her."

"All I can say is that our lunch didn't go well and I'm not in hurry to get with her any time soon."

"I can tell my bringing her up is upsetting you. Let's change the subject," Chris suggests.

"Did you talk to your mom today?"

"Yeah, she told me there was a list of things that we need to do while she and Dad are in Florida. It's probably taking out the trash and watering the plants.

I'll look when we get back to see if she's sent the text."

"It will be nice for them to get away. They need to since they are retired."

"Pop's so worried about saving money. They need to enjoy life."

"I don't think I want anyone to count on me for anything right now, Amber Lynn or your mom. I'm not sure if I can give anyone one hundred percent."

We stop and he looks into my eyes. "You sound so sad. You aren't a person who gets depressed. We are going to figure this out. I want you to remember that."

"I hope so."

When we get home, Chris looks at his mom's list while I grab a pencil and paper.

"It looks more like a ransom list," Chris jokes.

1. Take out trash Sunday night.

2. Water plants.

3. Bring in the mail.

4. Bring in newspaper.

5. Check the house every day to make sure everything is okay.

6. Mow the lawn diagonally and trim. If need to mow a second time, mow the opposite way please.

"I don't know how were going to do all this and work. This is crazy," he says dialing the phone.

"Who are you calling?"

"My brother. I want to see if he wants to trade.

'Hey Andy, it's Chris. So, the folks are leaving, and I understand you are taking them to the airport and picking them up and watching Winston'."

"Are you calling to see if I want to trade?" Andy interjects.

"Well, I just didn't know if maybe the chores Beth and I have would work better with your schedule or not."

"Well let me read you my list of demands, I mean requests," he jokes. "Number 1. Take Winston to groomers. He has an appointment set up for Monday at eight o'clock. Number 2. Pick up Winston from groomers promptly. He gets depressed if he has to stay in cage and will sulk for hours later. Number 3. Take Winston outside as soon as he wakes up and especially before he goes to bed. Number 4. Make sure he has his dog bed positioned in your bedroom so he can see you and not feel he is alone. I am worried he is going to miss us terribly. Number 5. Feed Winston dinner at 5 p.m. Number 6. Give him treats but no more than 2-3 a day. He needs to watch his weight. Number 7. Brush his teeth at least every other day. He is self-conscious of his underbite and won't smile if you don't. Number 8. Brush him daily. The round brush is his favorite. Number 9. If he starts scooting, don't give him any treats and take him to the vet. They will know what to do. Number 10. If he acts like he isn't sleeping or wanting to play, try watching TV with him. He gets very homesick for us and likes to sit on your lap and watch programs about dogs. P.S. We do not let him watch shows with violence.

"Has Mom always been a little goofy?"

"Yup, but it's gotten worse since they both have retired. Pop has even mentioned it," Chris answers.

"So, do you still feel like you want to trade?" Andy asks.

"I can see your list is just as bad if not worse."

"I'm dropping Winston off at the groomers before work and Faith will have to try and pick him up and not disrupt Charlie's nap."

"How is my little nephew?"

"He's starting to smile a lot more now. You need to come over and get your cuddle time in. We're taking applications for babysitters if you two want to practice. When are you two going to get around to starting a family, anyway? We've tested the water for you. Go ahead and jump in!"

"Yeah, we would love to start a family. We're just making sure the time is right, I guess," Chris says looking over at me.

"Lack of sleep is probably the major downfall but when he looks at you and coos, you know it's all worth it."

"Well, give our best to Faith and baby Charlie and we will try and get together soon." He hangs up, shaking his head. "There is no way we want their list, it's worse than ours."

"Did he ask when we are going to have a baby again?"

"Yeah, but don't be upset at them."

"I'm not. I was relieved when your mom didn't bring it up. Thankfully, she was too busy talking about her trip. Chris, you know I would love to start a family with you. But honestly, it's up to the man upstairs whether or not we're blessed with a baby. It's not like going to the store and getting one off the shelf. We haven't been trying that long anyway and at this point, I don't know if I want to go through all the probing and treatments. Besides, I have always thought, if we couldn't have one of our own, we would adopt."

"Let's put it in God's hands and see what happens," he says rubbing my arm. "Besides, it's fun practicing," he grins raising his eyebrows up and down.

EIGHT

Standing in the parking lot, several of us talk about the day.

"I couldn't believe we had two heart attack patients back-to-back," Lexi says.

"Everything went so smoothly," Paige added.

"Our teamwork is amazing! So, what does everyone have planned for the weekend?" I ask.

Paige sighs and says, "My weekend is going to be filled taking my kids around to their sports activities. Grant has National Guard this weekend, so he's not going to be available. Normally, we divide and conquer to get everyone where they need to be."

"What about you, Madison?"

"We're taking the kids to the zoo this weekend for a picnic," replies Madison.

"How old are they now?"

"Carson is 5 and James is 2, and this one," patting her tummy, "is 6 weeks."

"Oh my gosh, congratulations!" we all squeal.

"Lexi, how about you?" I ask.

"I'm taking Remi and Lizzy shopping and then out to lunch. Remi is coming home for the weekend," replies Lexi.

"How old is Lizzy now?" Madison asks.

"She's fourteen going on thirty," she laughs. "She thinks we need to get another dog to make up for Remi being gone."

"What about you Beth, any plans?" Paige asks.

"I have a craft bazaar coming up, so probably getting ready for that," answers Beth.

"Is it the same one you did last year?" Lexi asks.

"That's the one."

"You'll have to let us know when it is. I'll come and start my Christmas shopping early."

"My heart just isn't in it this year."

"You have seemed quiet and not yourself since we had the girl from the accident," Madison says then looks at the others. "We're worried about you."

"Her death affected many people," Paige says.

Waving goodbye, I get into my car and watch as they pull out of the parking lot one by one. I didn't *think Addy's death affected anyone but me.* Feeling numb, I start the car and immediately shut off the radio. I don't want to hear anything right now. The calm in the car is interrupted when Chris calls.

"What about meeting me for a quiet dinner tonight?" Chris asks.

"Okay, I guess."

"Are you okay? What's wrong?"

"A bunch of us were talking about what we were going to do for the weekend and Madison pointed out how I have seemed quiet and not myself since we had the girl from the accident."

"I've got to tell you Beth, I'm concerned that your coworkers are noticing it now. You can't let this girl start affecting your work performance."

"I don't feel that it has."

"They're picking up that something is wrong and that it started after the accident." After several seconds of silence, an idea pops into his head. He convincingly suggests we go away for the weekend and have a change of scenery. He proposes going to the Gate House Inn. "We could even take our bikes. You have always really liked it there."

"It sounds nice," I reply, remembering how the Inn is nestled in the middle of a small Amish community with shops. Chris and I have been there a couple of times and have really enjoyed it. One year, I took Mom and Peggy up there for lunch and shopping as part of their Mother's Day gift.

"We can grab a quick bite on our way out of town," Chris says. "I'll call your folks to see if they mind watching Gracie."

"Wait Chris. What about watching your parents' house and your mom's list?"

"We can stop by on the way home and take out the trash and check everything then."

"Okay," I say perking up. The rest of the way home, I am eager to start the weekend. *This is just what I need.*

***

As I head upstairs to pack, I tell Gracie she is going to Grandma and Grandpa's for the weekend and can play with Sadie. Sadie is a stray mutt that Dad found a couple of years ago and has been the best dog for them.

After changing my clothes, I pull the suitcase off the closet shelf and begin looking at what to pack. Filling the case, I remind myself it's just for a weekend. Pausing at Addy's door, I glance at the dresser and her picture. "This is going to be a break from everything, including you Addy. I not only have Chris worried but my coworkers too."

After dropping off Gracie with her dog bed and toys, we head out of town and grab a sandwich to eat along the way. With Chris driving, I close my eyes and take a deep breath. It feels so good with the warmth of the sun coming into the car and the windows partially down. The leaves sparkle as the sun shines through the trees. I pull down the visor and look into the mirror, to freshen my lipstick. Hesitantly, I look behind me. Relieved to see no extra passengers in the backseat, I let out a sigh.

"You okay?" Chris asks.

"Perfect! I need this," I reply.

"I know you do," he says as he takes my hand and kisses it. "It's going to be fun."

***

After checking in at the Inn and scoping out our room, we decide to take a stroll and look around.

"We can get an early start in the morning after we have breakfast," Chris says.

"Fine by me," I reply.

"We can probably catch the bike trail there," he points.

We continue making small talk, as we both dance around the topic of Addy. "I don't want you to get mad," he starts out saying as he holds my hand.

"When you start out like that, it's not reassuring," I remind him.

"I just need to say this. I want this weekend to be about us. Not about the girl from the accident, not about the dresser, not about what you have smelled or seen. Just us! I don't think I am asking too much. You must admit you've been disconnected. I know I am no doctor, but I do know that it's not healthy."

"I promise to not think or talk about Addy," I say while holding up my hand.

***

The breakfast area is cheery and bright. A large stone fireplace is the focal point of the room with oak tables and high back chairs. Overstuffed chairs with a couch and loveseat invite a person to sit and relax with a cup of coffee or tea. There are pictures of beautiful country scenes all around the Inn. Looking at Chris' face, he's in heaven as he makes his selection.

"I forgot the breakfast bar was included with the room," he beams.

With breakfast done, we head back to the room to finish getting ready for our bike ride. While Chris gets our bikes ready, I take a minute to call Mom. "Mom and Dad said 'hi'," I tell Chris as I put on my helmet.

"I even packed snacks for us!" Chris says proudly.

"What a beautiful day for a ride." The scenery is gorgeous which makes the ride more enjoyable. After stopping for snacks along the creek, we finish the ride and arrive back to the Inn with a chunk of the afternoon left. Deciding to do our part and conserve water, we shower together. After all, this weekend is about us. The closeness reminds me just how disconnected I have been. Feeling sleepy we decide to reward ourselves with a nap. Chris is still dozing when I decide to go for a walk.

***

After walking past the lobby, I follow the signs for the indoor courtyard. I am in awe enjoying how they have taken a large area and made it appear to be several rooms by positioning antiques and furniture. In the far corner, there's an old-fashioned schoolhouse that doubles as a small meeting room. Peeking in the window, I notice the chalkboard with the day's assignment. *"I'm glad those days are over for me."*

Directly opposite the schoolhouse is an old stove with big pots on it. It gives you the impression that if you wait long enough, you might see someone stirring something. Next to the stove stands a hutch with a variety of dishes.

An older couple walk in and the woman takes a seat on the red velvet sofa and is talking on her phone. Her husband heads for the cantina and returns with coffee and cookies. I watch as he carefully balances the cookies on top of each cup and even has one sticking out of his mouth. *He's good. He kinda reminds me of my Uncle Ted.*

Uncle Ted had the biggest heart and a laugh to match. Boy, I miss him. I still remember the day Mom told me he had a heart attack and died. We cried while reminiscing with one another. I remember Mom telling me that God needed a special angel that day and called him home.

The woman closes her phone and says to her husband: "There was no answer, so I had to leave a message. I hope they weren't in an accident."

"I'm sure they're okay, probably just stuck in traffic," the man says trying to comfort her. After enjoying their snack, they get up and look around to pass the time. Trying not to eavesdrop on their entire conversation, I intently study the various pieces displayed.

In the corner, a bedroom is set up. Beside the bed is a nightstand with an old lamp and alarm clock. There is also a desk with an old-fashioned typewriter and telephone sitting on it. On the dresser there is a perfume bottle with a picture in a frame. In the corner stands a coat rack with a dress, slip, and hat hanging from it. Shoes sit beside the chair. A pair of nylons are draped over the radiator. *I feel like a kid playing house.* I glance around for any signs requesting guests not to sit on the bed. With no signs visible, I sit down on the bed to take it all in.

As I sink down on the mattress, the springs on the bed squeak. *I would have loved to have lived during this era. I know it would be hard but, I would love the challenge. I wish there were such a place where you could go and spend a day living in the era you choose -- Disneyland meets Fantasy Island.*

Uncrossing my legs, I clumsily flip my sandal off. While reaching for it, it slides further under the bed. Kneeling, I reach under the bed to retrieve it. Grasping my sandal, I feel something else. Dragging it out, I discover a large photo album. Placing the book on the bed, I slowly open it. *This has to be pretty old.* Many of the pictures are badly faded. Intrigued by the book, I carefully turn the pages.

I check my watch and realize I've been gone close to 30 minutes. Chris will be wondering where I am. Turning to the last page of the book, I see a picture of a girl standing beside a dresser. *Hmm. The dresser looks similar to mine.* Studying the face of the girl, she has sweet features with her dark hair pulled off to one side. *Who are you and why do I keep finding pictures with girls in them?*

Hearing something, I look up to see Chris standing there.

"Hi, look at this picture. The dresser looks like mine," I tell him pointing at the picture. "This might be another picture of Addy."

Shaking his head, he turns around, "I'm done Beth! I can't do this anymore. You need help!"

"What? Chris wait!" I plead while trying to stand up and not drop the book. "Don't go!" Leaving the album sitting on the bed, I chase after him. "Let me explain. Chris stop! Chris please! I'm begging you!"

"Beth honey? Beth, wake up. You're dreaming," he says jostling me.

"Huh?" I open my eyes and look around.

"You were yelling out my name. Are you okay?"

"Yeah," rubbing my eyes. "What a horrible dream. We had an argument, and I was trying to talk to you, but you were walking away."

"What was the argument about?" Chris asks.

I don't respond right away as I think to myself: *He's not going to understand that I can't just shut off my brain and not dream about her, it's not that easy.* "I don't want to go into the whole thing right now. It was just something dumb."

As we enter the Inn's restaurant, I look over at Chris and smile. "Every time we come here, I feel at home." Each table has an oak turntable in the center of it with a glass oil lamp that is lit. Jelly jars hold arrangements of mini carnations, daisies, and baby's breath, which are my favorite flowers. The dinner is nothing less than outstanding with Chris having fried chicken and me having chicken and noodles. Too full for any dessert of our own, we share a dish of cinnamon ice cream.

***

After dinner we stroll around the courtyard and look at the various rooms with antiques. When we reach the bedroom, I start to feel anxious. This feels too much like my dream. Am I pulling out the bits and pieces from earlier visits here or am I reliving the dream I just had?

"They have changed it quite a bit since we were here a couple of years ago," Chris says. "I don't remember there being different rooms or a bedroom set up."

"It's cool isn't it, with the old phone and typewriter?" Alarmed that my dream might be coming true, I look under the bed. Not finding anything, I start to open drawers.

"What are you looking for?" Chris asks.

"Nothing just being nosey."

"You're not normally like that," he says as he walks on.

Walking out to the lobby, I step up to the registration desk and ask if they know anything about a photo album among the antiques in the courtyard. The young man at the desk doesn't have any idea of what I am talking about, even though I am trying my best to explain it to him. He goes into the back office and asks the evening manager. An older woman with gray hair, walks out folding up her glasses.

"I'm afraid I don't know anything about an album. Did you lose one?" the woman asks.

"No, it's not mine. I saw one this afternoon and wanted to show my husband," I reply.

The woman goes on to explain, "To my knowledge, there are only pictures in frames, some books and sparse knickknacks scattered around to make it look lived in."

Thanking them for their time, I catch up with Chris.

"Where did you take off to?" he asks.

"I went to the front desk and asked about some of their furnishings," I reply.

Totally confused by the dream and what is real, we quietly walk back to the room.

"That argument we had in your dream must have been something. I can tell you have a lot on your mind you're struggling with. Do you want to talk about it?"

"Nope, not tonight. I just want to go to sleep," faking a yawn. *Seriously, you are now lying to your husband.*

NINE

After fixing a slice of toast and grabbing a yogurt parfait, I grab a cup of coffee and choose a seat. Peeling back the lid on the creamer, I carefully pour it in my cup and stir. I take a sip and look around at the other couples and families in the room.

"How did you sleep?" Chris asks before taking a bite of his toast.

Pausing to muffle a yawn with my hand, "I don't remember any specifics of what I dreamt, but I know

I could have slept a little longer. Maybe it's just the fresh air," taking a sip. "The coffee is good."

"Drink that one and I will get you a refill you can take back to the room. You will need it for shopping." Chris jokes.

***

Walking towards Chris who is sitting on a bench, I hold up my shopping bag victoriously. "You should see the Christmas presents I bought. I got a really pretty scarf for my mom and a purse for your mom. Plus, some miscellaneous items for stocking stuffers for your pop and my dad. I even got this for Gracie to wear," giggling as I pull it out of the bag.

"What is it?" Chris asks making a face.

"It's a hat. See the candy cane on the top? Wouldn't it be cute for our Christmas photo."

"What's wrong with how we do our pictures? I like just wearing casual attire. I have never been a fan of the ugly sweater theme. This way people can set them out all year long."

"Or they can display them on the refrigerator in the laundry room, like we do. Your mom just cuts off the Xmas greeting and leaves the picture, but then you don't know what year it is from. I can tell you're not a fan. I actually got this for your mom for Winston. It was on clearance. I only paid a couple of bucks for it. You know how she likes to dress him up."

"Mom is going to love it and Pop is going to hate it along with Winston. What's the thing you say, when you're having a good shopping day?"

" 'The shopping gods are upon us', " I reply. "I'm finding quite a few things to get my shopping started early!"

"I could use a pretzel and something cold to drink, how about you?" he grins.

"Are you buying?"

"If I'm buying, I'm getting my own!"

"Whatever you say, boss."

The pretzels are huge, warm, and delicious. Chris is a happy boy dipping his pretzel into the warm gooey cheese. Sitting on a bench, we watch as people walk by. Chris could sit there all day and be content. He has always enjoyed people watching. Take him to the mall and he is happy sitting there just watching people go about their day. An Amish buggy passes by and the man driving looks at us and tips his hat. Leaning over, I give Chris a kiss.

"Thank you, I really needed this."

Tearing off another piece of pretzel, he plops it into his mouth and smiles as he chews.

***

On our way to the room, we walk by several game tables with board games set up in the courtyard. Chris challenges me to a game of checkers. After several games, I gather my loot and we head back to the room.

"You were just lucky. I was getting a cramp in my hand and having trouble moving the pieces," he says flexing his hand.

"Apparently, the cramp was keeping you from moving them in the right direction," I laugh.

Back in our room, Chris stretches out on the bed and turns on the TV while I look through an area tour book filled with various things to do. It's not long before he is asleep with the remote in his hand. Just like at home. Well, this time, I'm staying in the room. I'm not taking any more chances. Who knows what I might find or see after finding the picture album! Lying down beside him, I cover up under the quilt and it's not long before I fall asleep myself.

***

Waking up, the curtains are pulled making the room dark. I get up and splash cool water on my face, trying to wake up. While brushing my hair, the doorknob to our room begins to jiggle. I look through the peep hole to see Chris standing with his hands full and a bag dangling from between his teeth. I open the door and take the bag out of his mouth as he walks in.

"Hello sleepy head."

"What's this?" I ask.

"Dinner!"

"Why didn't you wake me? I could have gone with you."

"Are you kidding? This is the best sleep you have had in days."

Looking through the bags there is enough food to feed an army. We clear off the table and I pull over the chairs. He carefully opens the containers and sets them down. "For your dining pleasure this evening, we have chicken and biscuits with mashed potatoes. There is meatloaf with mashed potatoes, and gravy. We have green beans and homemade applesauce. There are white and wheat dinner rolls with peanut butter spread and also apple butter. And for dessert we have apple pie and chocolate cake. To wash it all down you have your choice of hot or iced tea."

"Wow, it all looks and smells amazing."

After sampling a little bit of everything, we're stuffed and only take a bite to taste the cake and pie.

"That apple pie is amazing. It reminds me of my Aunt Millie's. She was a wonderful cook," I say.

"She was certainly quite the hostess," Chris adds. "Her fried chicken was some of the best I've ever had."

"That's so sweet of you to say. Even better than your mom's?"

"Yes, and that is to be kept between me and you."

After tidying up from dinner, Chris gets comfortable and lays on the bed flipping through the channels. Quite full and content, I let out a yawn. "I'm going to take a relaxing bubble bath while you watch TV."

Slipping into the tub under the bubbles, I'm totally relaxed and close my eyes. I see myself standing in my Aunt Millie's kitchen, and I watch as she opens the oven door to show me the pie. After pouring us each a cup of coffee, I take a seat at her dinette table while she stands at the counter cutting slices of banana bread. Nibbling on the bread, we talk while enjoying the aroma from the oven. "Someday, I won't be here Beth, but I want you to know you can always still talk to me."

Patting her hand, "I don't even want to think about you not being here! But I feel the same way. I think when people die, they're gone in the physical sense along with their pain. But the memories we hold in our mind and hearts will live forever."

"That's beautiful Beth. You should write a book," she laughs. The timer goes off and she gets up to check the pie.

There is a knock at the door, and I wake up to see my bubbles are gone. Chris peeks his head around the door. "I thought I better check on you."

"I actually drifted off," I tell him wrapping a towel around me. "I'm the most relaxed I've felt in days. I actually dreamt I was in Aunt Millie's kitchen."

"That's nicer than the dreams you've been having. I know how close the two of you were. I hope you can go back home rested," he says helping me pull back the covers.

***

As Chris waits for his waffle to get done, I stand guard at the toaster watching my bagel. "You were out as soon as your head hit the pillow. How did you sleep?" Chris asks.

"Not bad, considering the bed is a little firmer than ours at home," I tell him.

"That's why you need to go away once in a while, to appreciate the things you have at home."

After breakfast, we return to the room to start packing. Chris opens up the suitcase and sets it on the bed. He picks up his clothes from the floor and chair and tosses them into the case. He then gathers his things from the bathroom and stuffs them into his shaving kit. Satisfied, his packing is done, he flips on the TV and situates himself among the pillows on the bed. Looking through the different stations, he settles on a movie already in progress.

While gathering things from the desk, I notice a piece of paper sticking out of the Bible. I open it to the page and examine the paper. "Did you put this here?" I ask Chris.

"Nope -- haven't touched it," Chris answers.

"It's blank on one side and has numbers on the other."

"It probably means something to whoever put it in there."

For whatever reason, I feel compelled to take a picture of the paper with my phone. I replace it and flip through the other pages. With nothing else found, I tidy up the desk and return to packing. Chris and I share the leftover desserts before checking out.

***

Walking into the house, it feels good to be back home, even though it was just the weekend. I love our house. I tell this to Chris pretty much every day. I hope someday to be able to fill it with children. Gracie seems excited to be home too. As I sort through the clothes and make piles, she is having fun running through them. I begin tossing clothes on top of her until she's nearly covered. Chris returns just in time to see Gracie wearing one of my bras on her head.

"Nice look, Gracie," he laughs.

"That didn't take long at your folks," I say.

"Nope. I found a note from Pop that he stopped the mail and newspaper. Their neighbor is going to mow and water the plants outside. As far as the plants inside, I checked them, and they didn't need it. I only had to set the trash can out. Their neighbor stopped me and told me he would take care of the trash can after it's picked up to save me a trip. It was a quick in and out."

"You got off easier than Andy it sounds like."

"You're probably right. I will try and give him a call and see how they are doing."

Gracie suddenly takes off running down the hallway dragging my bra behind her. "Do you mind picking that up and setting it back on the pile? I would hate for someone to come to the door and see that." Chris grabs the laundry pile on the floor and carries it into the laundry room. While double checking to make sure I have removed everything from the suitcase, I notice a white piece of paper sticking out of a pocket. I pull it out and turn it over. Swallowing hard, I can't believe my eyes. It looks just like the paper from the Bible. I search through the rest of the pockets, and I'm relieved they're empty.

Chris is talking to Gracie in the laundry room. I decide to show him the paper later and tuck it in my pocket. I take a handful of things upstairs along with my jewelry case. With our toiletries put away, I open up my jewelry case causing my heart to race. There sitting on top of my earrings and bracelets is an old photograph. It looks a lot like the one in my dream. How did it get in there? I take the piece of paper from my pocket and sit down on the bed. It was a dream, right? I take a deep breath and go downstairs.

"Chris, I need to talk to you."

"You look serious. What's up?" replies Chris. We take a seat in the kitchen.

"The bad dream I had that I didn't want to talk about was about Addy. I knew if I told you, you would be upset that we were talking about her. You have to understand that I can't just shut off my mind. It's not that easy."

I take a deep breath and continue, "In the dream, I looked around while you were napping. You know, in the courtyard where they have it set up like different rooms. I went over to the bedroom area and was looking around. I found an album that was tucked under the bed. Looking through it, I found a picture of a girl. You walked in and I said something like this picture has a dresser like ours and I didn't know if this could be another picture of Addy. You got really mad and were yelling. You were saying you'd had enough, and that I needed to get help. I started running after you and yelling for you to stop, so we could talk."

He sits in silence, letting me finish. Biting my lip, I pull the paper out of my pocket and place it in front of him.

"What's this?" he asks.

"Look at it."

He unfolds it. "Is this the paper from the Bible you told me about?"

"I think so."

"Why did you bring it home? We agreed to leave it in case the person came back for it."

"I didn't bring it home. I was wondering if you stuck it in the suitcase."

"Me? Why would I do that? I didn't really care what happened to it."

"I know. I have something else to show you." I then hold out the picture in my hand. "This is the picture from my dream."

"Is this the picture you were talking about and why you went to the front desk?"

Looking down, I nod.

"This isn't like you, to take stuff. First, you are seeing things, then talking to people who only you can see, and now you're stealing stuff. Really, what's next? Tell me!"

"I didn't take it!" I shout, fighting back tears.

Chris gets up abruptly and walks out the front door.

Left alone in the kitchen, I flip over the picture, and read what's written on the back: To my best friend Adeline, Love Milda. I set the picture and the slip of paper aside on the table. I make a cup of tea and go back to straightening the house. Opening the box of muffins that Mom gave us, I arrange them on the cake stand. I continue working on the laundry and putting things away while waiting for Chris to return.

***

Sitting in the family room on the couch, I try not to stare at the clock. Hearing the back door open, I run to the kitchen. Chris walks in and fixes himself a glass of water.

"Where have you been? I was getting worried. You were pretty heated when you left." I wait for him to take several long drinks before he pauses to answer.

"I didn't mean to worry you. I'm sorry. I had to get some fresh air. I walked over to the park and sat on a bench for a while, thinking," Chris replied.

"You have to understand, Chris. Something is going on. I'm really starting to get spooked too. This is a message from someone. Maybe from Addy. All these strange occurrences somehow fit together. She is trying to tell me something. You have to help me! But more importantly, you have to believe me!"

Hearing the desperation in my voice as well as seeing it on my face, he pulls me into his arms. "This is just so weird," he mutters. "You couldn't make this up if you wanted to. It sounds like something from one of those ghost shows. I'm just wondering why you, Beth? What are you supposed to be doing for her?"

"I don't have the answer, but I hope to." I show him the picture I took on my phone earlier. "It's the same paper. The numbers are identical."

We walk upstairs to Addy's room, and he sits down on the bed and looks at the dresser. I prop the picture up beside the one in the frame.

"So, the picture in the frame is the one that appeared on its own and the picture beside it is the one you acquired."

"I didn't acquire it, Chris. It appeared on its own. I found it in my jewelry case. Look at the picture in the frame and then the other one."

He studies one and then the other. "They're not the same picture. Is it the same girl with a different pose."

"I wonder if they are twins."

"They look to be around the same age."

"Read the message on the back."

"These pictures may not even be linked, Beth."

"They must be linked. They were placed there so I would find them."

Chris leaves and returns with a magnifying glass, "Let's take a closer look."

"Okay, Watson."

Chris rolls his eyes. "I agree the girls look to be about the same age. But I don't know if they are twins. They may not even be related. The picture of Addy is a close up. In the other picture, the girl is standing by a dresser holding a hat. One thing they have in common, is that neither one looks excited about having their picture taken."

"Times were hard back then. We have it easy compared to what they had."

"I agree. Since the dresser seems to be a major factor, let's take a closer look. Let's start with the obvious. There is a swivel mirror in the middle," Chris says.

"Yup."

"Each drawer has a keyhole and glass drawer knobs."

"So does ours," I confirm.

"The feet are the claw type in the picture, I don't think ours are."

I bend down to look at the feet, "Guess again. What do you think it means?"

"There were probably a lot of dressers like yours made and it's a coincidence that it looks like the one in the picture," Chris says.

"You are probably right. I remember when I bought it, Mrs. Foster said it looked like one her husband's mother owned."

"Where did you get the vase again?"

"It was my Aunt Millie's. Why?"

"There's a vase in the picture, and it looks similar to yours."

"I didn't even notice there was a vase in the picture."

"Beth, I think I've had enough for one day. I don't know what any of this means and I'm just as confused as before."

Lying in bed, I review the day's events, trying to make sense of it all as I wait to fall asleep.

***

Smelling the sweet aroma of coffee, I sleepily walk downstairs and put my arms around Chris' waist. He turns around, "Did you forget you have to work today, sleepyhead?"

"No, I just don't feel like rushing around this morning," I answer.

"How did you sleep?"

"Okay, I still feel kinda groggy. Did you already eat breakfast?"

"I had a piece of toast and a banana."

"I can see that," brushing the crumbs into my hand and tossing the banana peel into the trash.

Pouring a cup of coffee, the phone rings and as Chris reaches over to pick up the receiver, he reads the caller ID screen. "It's the hospital. You're in trouble now!" he smirks.

"Hello," I say into the phone.

"Good morning, Beth, it's Lexi," she says.

"Hi Lexi, what's up?"

"Well for one thing – ME! I thought I was supposed to come in early and it turns out, I am not even scheduled to work today. Would you mind if we traded shifts? I don't want to go all the way back home only to come back tomorrow."

"Sure, that would be fine!"

"Then I will let them know you will be here tomorrow in my place."

Hanging up the phone, I explain to Chris, "I now have the day off. Lexi came in on the wrong day, so I am going to work for her tomorrow."

"That's good because you would have been cutting it close," he scolds. "Someone upstairs is watching out for you," he says pointing up.

Chris leaves for work and I grab a muffin and my coffee and go back upstairs. Leaning against the door frame, I look around Addy's room. "I don't know what you are trying to tell me, Addy. I need a sign." As if planned, the phone rings.

"Wow, you work fast," I murmur while walking over to the phone. I glance at the call screen before answering.

"Hi Mom!" I say into the phone.

"Hi Honey, how are you this morning?" Mom answers.

"Great, I'm just getting the morning started. Chris left for work, and I'm enjoying coffee and a muffin."

"As I was calling, your father told me he thought you were working today. You're not sick, are you?"

"No, a girl at work came in on the wrong day so we traded. I'm working for her tomorrow."

"Since you're off today, would you like to meet for lunch?"

***

Just before noon, I pull into the parking lot of Murphy's Café. I lower the visor and check my makeup in the mirror after taking off my sunglasses. Before opening the door, I check to make sure I have my phone. I have more than once misplaced it or set it somewhere. Once I even left it sitting in the refrigerated area of the Save More Club. Luckily, someone turned it in. Chris hates it when he can't get a hold of me for several hours.

As I am searching through my purse, my phone begins to play, "Start Saying Goodbye," by one of my favorite artists. Shaking my purse, I dig deeper into the crevices. How ironic I picked that ring tone. Yeah, I am saying goodbye because I can't find my phone to say hello. One of these days, I am going to buy a purse in which I can easily locate my phone.

I finally find my phone after first trying to answer a package of tissues and a pack of gum, but the caller is gone. The call is from a number with a 113 area code. Weird. It's probably a telemarketer from a foreign country. Now that I have found my phone, I hurry so Mom doesn't wait any longer. I toss my phone back into my purse, only to be lost at the bottom once again.

TEN

Mom looks up from her menu and waves. Her face lights up as I walk towards the table and sit down.

"Hi sweetheart. How's my girl today?"

"I'm fine, just frustrated with my purse," I reply.

"You couldn't find your phone again?" she laughs.

"How did you ever guess?"

"I have that problem too sometimes."

"I think I should just get something to wear around my neck like tourists have for their passports."

"It certainly would be an interesting look. How are things with you?"

"Great. I got my laundry caught up this morning and just have a couple of errands to run on the way home. It's a shame Daddy couldn't join us."

"He's busy tinkering in the garage today and wanted to give us some girl time."

"Aw, that's sweet."

After our waitress takes our orders and collects the menus, I proceed to tell Mom about the dresser.

"Your dad was talking to Chris the other night and he mentioned you bought a dresser. Where did you end up putting it?" Mom asks.

"It's pretty neat. We put it in the guest room."

"I think every piece of furniture has a story to tell, don't you?"

"I am beginning to think that more and more. I set Aunt Millie's vase on it, and it looks really pretty. I have been thinking about her so much lately."

"She sure thought an awful lot of you."

"Why didn't they have any kids? She and Uncle Dell would have made great parents."

"They wanted them but never had any. Sadly, she had several miscarriages. Do you remember your Aunt Mae?"

"Barely."

"Well, I know you wouldn't remember Aunt Margie."

"What about them?"

"Margie and Mae were twins. Millie was around five when they were born. Did you know twins run in our family?" Smiling as she raises her eyebrows. "Margie and Mae got married to two brothers," Mom continues. "Mae adopted a little girl Daisy, after having suffered several miscarriages herself."

"How sad they both had miscarriages," I add.

The waitress brings our food and tops off our drinks as we continue talking. "Were you close to them?" I ask.

"I thought an awful lot of them. They didn't have an easy life. After the accident, no one was really the same," Mom shares.

"Accident? What accident?"

"Margie was walking home from the store when she was hit by a car."

"Did she die?"

"Not right away. She was able to say goodbye to Robert."

"Who's Robert?"

"Her husband," Mom says before taking another bite.

"How awful!"

"Remember, back then it took a while for an ambulance to come. They went and got Robert who had come home for lunch and took him to her. Margie had been at home preparing his lunch when she went to the store for something. She died in his arms."

"Did they find out who hit her?"

"It was an elderly man who had suffered a heart attack and lost control of his car. His poor family went through a lot of guilt. They ended up moving away to start fresh. What's even sadder is Margie was expecting. She had made Robert a card telling him the news. He was reading it when they came to tell him about the accident."

"I don't think I can eat anymore," I say pushing my plate away with tears in my eyes. "I can't believe I didn't know any of this?"

"Honey, this happened a long time ago. Let's talk about something else," Mom urges. "I didn't mean to make you feel down."

"Life can sure be sad sometimes, can't it?" I sigh.

"Don't forget, it can also be filled with many beautiful and precious moments, sweetheart."

***

After kissing her goodbye, I stick my food in the car and walk over to the park next door. They have painted the gazebo since last year and have the fountain working again. This is such a nice little place for someone to walk and sit a spell on the benches.

I take a seat and look around at the various businesses. The pizza parlor is still in business, no doubt with the help from the fire station next door. The furniture store is still there too.

Looking up at the City County building, I read the engraving: *A.D. 1912. I wonder why I have never noticed it before. 1912. Hmm. That's the same year that's on the back of Addy's picture. It's also Addy's initials. I need to remember to tell Chris.*

As I walk back to the car, Chris calls. "I wanted to give you a call and see how your day is going."

"Good. I just got done having lunch with Mom."

"How is she?"

"She's good."

"Did your dad come?"

"No, just Mom. Dad stayed home tinkering in the garage to give us some girl time."

"Your dad probably stayed home so he wouldn't have to go shopping after lunch. Whose kidding who?" Chris laughs.

"You're probably right."

"So, did the two of you catch up?"

"She asked me about the dresser. I told her some stuff, but not everything. I don't want her to think I'm losing it."

"Some of it is pretty out there. I think it's smart to filter what you tell her for the time being."

"I found out today one of my aunts was hit by a car and died when she was pregnant."

"Recently? Which one?"

"My Aunt Margie and it happened a long time ago when I was a baby."

"That's awful. I hope you guys had a nice lunch despite the sad conversation."

"We made it nice."

Beth continues, "I want to ask you about a missed call I got on my phone. Have you ever heard of the area code 113?"

"What's the rest of the number?" asks Chris.

"Hold on while I pull it up. The number reads 113-122-418."

"I don't think it's a legitimate number. It's probably from a telemarketer."

"You're probably right. Okay then, do you know what it means when a building has A.D. on it and 1912?"

"If I remember right, A.D. means 'in the year of the Lord' and then 1912 would be the year the building was erected. Why do you ask?"

"I walked over to the park after lunch and noticed it on the City County building. It matches what is on the back of Addy's picture. I took a picture with my phone to show you."

"Don't forget to add it to your timeline."

"Well, I'll let you get back to work. I'm headed home to look through old pictures. I want to see if I can find any of Aunt Margie."

"Aunt Margie?"

"The one that died."

"Well, good luck."

"Thanks."

***

I lug the step stool upstairs and position it in the closet. Yanking on the string of the light fixture, I move the menagerie of items and boxes around on the shelves while dodging the light bulb by my head. Feeling a cool breeze on the back of my neck, I stand motionless as I hear a soft whisper of my name. Goosebumps run down my arms. As I hang onto the door frame for support, I crouch down and scan the room. Seeing nothing unusual, I go back to looking. With just one box left, I find it. *It's always the last box.*

Stepping down off the stepstool, I toss the box onto the bed and begin rummaging through the pictures. This is going to take forever. I need to have some sort of system. I will try and sort them into piles, familiar and unfamiliar faces. Photo after photo reveals special moments and occasions together that leave me smiling but disappointed. I have looked through this entire box and not one picture has been of Margie. I need a break!

When I stand up to stretch and glance back at the photos on the bed, I notice a photo wedged in the corner of the box. As I take a closer look, it's a picture of a young couple standing arm in arm. Turning it over it reads, Forever in Love, Margie and Robert. I found you! What a cute looking couple!

Moving the box, I discover an old dry-cleaning slip with numbers written across the top of it. Looking at the numbers, I ask myself, what's so special about these numbers. Why do I keep coming across slips of paper with numbers? Opening the dresser, I retrieve the paper from the Bible. Then suddenly a thought crosses my mind. What about the weird phone number?

Running downstairs, I get my purse and spill out the contents onto the kitchen table. Sorting through tissues, makeup, gum, mints, barrettes, and a couple of old receipts, I finally find my phone and come to the realization that I seriously need to clean out my purse. Looking closer at my phone, I realize I've missed another call. Ignore it for now. You're on a mission. I quickly jot down the previous number from the call log and toss the items back into my purse. This is why you can never find anything, I tell myself.

Running back upstairs, I sit down on the bed with the paper from the Bible and the number taken from my phone. One by one, I compare the numbers 113-122-418. My mouth drops as I realize the numbers match exactly. I glance down at my lap and realize things are about to turn even weirder. The numbers written on the dry-cleaning slip also match the other numbers.

Remembering the missed call I ignored earlier, I listen to my messages. There are only two -- one from Chris' folks checking in and one about an upcoming dentist appointment. Whomever the number belongs to isn't leaving a message. They called at 1:12 p.m. today and 2:24 p.m. yesterday. Both are from the same number: 113-122-418. How can it be that the phone number matches the other numbers?

Returning from a pit stop, when I approach the doorway, I feel a cool breeze and smell the light scent of lilacs. Looking at the bed, pictures are strewn all over. What happened to my neat piles? I didn't know when I got up, that I had upset them all. All of the images in the photos are starting to blend into one big blur. Giving myself a few minutes to gather my thoughts, I decide to streamline the process by quickly looking at the picture and sticking it back in the box. I haven't found any of Aunt Millie and only the one of Margie and Robert.

Finally, the bed is clear of pictures except for one. Picking it up, it's a picture of a girl with a hat in her hand. Who is this pretty little girl? Flipping over the picture, I look at what's written on the back. Milda, to my best friend, Love Adeline. I don't remember having someone named Milda in the family. I walk into the bedroom and phone Mom.

"Hi Mom, it's me."

"How are you doing with the pictures, Honey?" asks Mom.

"Well, I am sick of looking at old pictures, I can tell you that much. I did find a picture of Margie and Robert. They were a good-looking couple. I found a picture of a young girl with the writing on the back: 'Milda to my best friend, Love Adeline'. Do either of these names sound familiar?"

"Milda was your Aunt Millie's formal name. I don't know any Adeline though."

"I was hoping to find a picture of Aunt Millie or Margie."

"I will look through the albums we have here. I'm sure we have a few. I'd like to see the photo you found of Margie and Robert the next time we get together."

"I'll lay it out so I don't forget. Give my love to Dad, Bye."

***

I wait until after dinner to tell Chris I have added extra pieces to the puzzle. "Do you want to play detective, Mr. Watson?"

He lets out an exasperated sigh, "Not especially," he replies.

"What's the matter with you tonight?"

"To be honest Beth, playing more detective games about this girl isn't really what I had in mind. I was looking forward to eating dinner and relaxing."

"What happened in the last couple of hours to make your day so bad?"

"One of our tile workers got hurt and it's going to delay the whole job. I have been fielding calls all afternoon and my head is pounding," he says rubbing his head.

I pour a glass of water and hand him a bottle of Tylenol. Disappointed by his lack of enthusiasm, I go upstairs to clean up my mess. I put the picture of the girl I found and the dry-cleaning slip along with the other papers in the top dresser drawer for safe keeping. The rest of the pictures I put back in the box and on the shelf.

I carry down the step stool and find Chris standing in the same spot. "If you're so worried about it, why don't you finish the tiling if you can't get anyone else? You've done it before." Pausing, I can see the wheels turning as he mulls over the idea.

Chris grabs his phone and makes a call. I pick up a circular ad and take a seat in the family room. He comes back in and sits next to me. "Well, I think I'm going back to my days of doing it all. I called my boss and he's okay with the idea. Your suggestion will help keep us on track."

"Good, I'm glad I could help you figure out a solution. How's your headache?"

"I think it's easing up, with the work situation figured out. Look, I know I disappointed you. It just seems like every waking minute we have, were talking about this girl."

"Do you want me to save it all up for the weekend so you can't sit in front of the TV and scan the channels? You're going to complain that I took up the entire weekend then." Not giving him a chance to protest, I blurt out, "I wanted to tell you that when I was looking through the pictures, I felt a soft breeze, smelled lilacs, and heard my name. I also found a dry-cleaning receipt that had numbers written on it. It was in the box of pictures. But most importantly, the numbers from the paper in the Bible and the dry-cleaning receipt all match. What's even weirder is they match the phone number of the missed calls I have been getting. I need your help figuring this out. I'm trying not to let this consume me or affect my work, but like it or not, it has."

While I wait for his response, I watch as he carefully chooses his words. "I will help you, number 1, because I love you and number 2, because I want things to go back to the way they were. You have to realize this and be feeling it too. You are not the same person. This is consuming you and you are trying to get it to consume me, and I can't. One of us has to stay grounded and not get sucked into this whole thing. And another thing, you're not eating. I think you have lost some weight."

Surprised at his tone, I swallow hard and take a deep breath.

"I know I'm not the same. I feel like I may never be the same again. And with the weight loss, you're exaggerating. Who can't stand to lose a couple of pounds?"

He rubs his forehead and sighs. "Go take a hot shower. It will help relax your muscles. When you're done, I will meet you in Addy's room and we can talk."

ELEVEN

While letting the water beat against his neck and shoulders, Chris thought to himself: God, give me strength. How am I supposed to tell her about all the phone calls from friends and family? I was totally caught off guard by Chaplain Paul's call today. Everyone is voicing their concern and I'm with them.

As he wrapped the towel around his waist, he says aloud; "Addy, you're not even real!"

Suddenly, there before him is the image of a girl, floating. He jumps nearly losing his balance. His mouth drops when he hears her speak.

"But I am!" Addy says.

"Jeez," he yells, gripping his towel firmly. As he stares at the image before him, he tries to regain his composure.

Hearing a noise from upstairs, I walk over to the stairs and yell, "Are you okay? You didn't fall, did you?"

He stands frozen as the image before him fades and disappears.

Several seconds pass before he's aware of my yelling.

"No, I'm okay," he says weakly. "I will be down in a few minutes."

Down? I'm coming up to meet you in Addy's room. Alarmed, I walk upstairs to see what happened. "Are you alright? What happened?"

He hesitates before answering. "I thought I saw something."

As I look at him, I notice his color is pale. "Are you sure you're okay? You look pale!"

Quietly, he says, "I saw her."

"Saw who?"

"I don't know what she looks like to really know."

"Who are you thinking you saw?"

"The girl? Addy?"

"I was running over some things in my head, and I said out loud, 'Addy you're not even real'. Then I saw her floating in front of me and she said, 'but I am'. Then she disappeared. I almost lost my bodily functions!"

Looking down at the floor, "Well, I'm glad you have good sphincter control," I laugh. "If I'm going crazy, I guess I'm taking you with me," patting his hand.

"This isn't funny!" he says raising his voice.

"I never said it was. Now you know how I feel."

"I haven't even told you about all the phone calls."

"What phone calls? She's calling you too?"

"Beth, stopping making jokes. This is serious!"

"Okay, I'll let you finish."

"I'm talking about the phone calls I have been getting from friends and family who are worried about you."

"What are they telling you?" I ask defensively. "That maybe I need a psychiatric evaluation and maybe I'm going off the deep end? Are you forgetting that I have already spoken to Chaplain Paul. I'm not stupid! I know what people are saying. I'm guessing my mom has called you along with Amber Lynn who is just worried about the bazaar!"

"That's not fair, Beth! You can't blame your mom for being worried about her daughter. You would be doing the same if the tables were turned. As far as Amber Lynn goes, she's a friend and is worried about you as well. One person who I didn't expect to hear from was Chaplain Paul."

"When did he call you?"

"This afternoon. He's worried about you. Everyone that called pretty much said the same thing, that you're not yourself and you're unusually quiet and distant."

"What did you say to everyone that called?"

"I just listened. You don't have to worry. I didn't offer information about what has been going on with you hearing and seeing things. Several of our friends figured out something wasn't quite right after bumping into you at the store. As far as your coworkers go, I don't think you realize how well-liked and what a good nurse you are. You have been at the hospital awhile and are looked up to. If this sends you off the deep end, then what about the others that may follow?

"I have to wonder if there is anyone else having trouble dealing with the girl's death. I'm not saying that others are seeing things, but at this point, we don't know. I'm wondering if you should ask your manager about a group counseling session with Chaplain Paul. There may be others that could use a neutral place to vent their feelings."

"You're right. I guess the thought never entered my mind that this could possibly be happening to someone else or that someone else may be having trouble dealing with her death. I will try and talk to my manager and Chaplain Paul tomorrow. Can I still show you some things in Addy's room?"

"I will make you a deal. We will go over some stuff and when I have had enough, we will put it away for another time."

"Deal. That's more than fair."

***

"Now entering 'Addy's room,' " I announce as we walk into the room.

"Why do you call it Addy's room? I'm not trying to pick a fight. I just want to know," asks Chris.

"This is where I feel her."

"Even though you have seen her in other places?"

"Yes. This is where I feel her the most. I know it sounds strange, but maybe it has something to do with the dresser." I open the top drawer and stop when my attention is drawn to the pictures. "Addy is gone! Chris, look at this! It's like she has been erased from the picture. Are my eyes playing tricks on me?"

"That wouldn't explain how I can be seeing the same thing."

"You didn't switch pictures, did you Chris?"

"Now why would I do that, and more importantly, how could I possibly find another picture?" He gives me a look of disbelief as he shakes his head. Picking up the frame, he examines it closer. Taking the picture from the frame, he reads the back out loud, "Addy D. 1912".

"I wonder if it has anything to do with you seeing her. Remember you said she wasn't real?"

"Yeah, I remember," he says rubbing his head.

"You still have your headache?"

"Yeah, I think I just need to go to bed."

At least he tried, I sigh, as I flip off the lights and walk out of the room.

Staring at the ceiling, trying to force sleep, there's a noise at the foot of the bed. Rising up off the pillow, I presume it to be one of Gracie's toys that has fallen. Instead, it's Addy! She softly whispers, "I had to show him I'm real," and disappears. Plopping my head back on the pillow, I'm mad at myself. I should have asked her if that's why she was gone from the picture.

***

As were getting ready for work, Chris reminds me about the group counseling session. Relieved that his headache is gone, I decide it's best not to start out the day talking about Addy. I will update him at some point. "I'm going to have a muffin and leave shortly. Maybe I can talk to some of the staff before my shift starts."

"I'll see you tonight then. I'm going to stop by the job site to assess the tiling job before going to the office."

Later, as I sit in the nurses' station, charting, I am pleased that both my boss and Chaplain Paul are onboard with the counseling session.

"How does it feel being Lexi today?" Quinn asks.

"Nice. It's fun getting to work with some of the people you don't normally get to," I reply.

"If you like working a different shift so much, any chance you would pick up a couple of hours for me?" Quinn asks. "I need to take my mom to a doctor's appointment. My dad has been taking her but he is getting overwhelmed with my mom, and we are having to adjust some of her medications."

"What day do you need covered?"

"Actually, it's tomorrow. I have been asking around and not having any luck."

"Do you need the entire day off?"

"No, just the first part of my shift. So, I can get my parents settled back at home and get them lunch. I will even throw in a batch of cookies."

"Chris will enjoy the cookies. It's more important that you are at the appointment with your parents."

We both quickly jot a note in our calendars and then go check on our patients.

On my way home, I call Chris.

"How's my favorite nurse?" he asks.

"Good. I'm just heading home," I reply. "I picked up a partial shift for Quinn tomorrow who is taking her mom to the doctor. She couldn't find anyone to pick up her hours and I felt bad for her. It's just the morning part and I will still have the afternoon to get stuff done."

"Were you able to speak to your manager or Chaplain Paul regarding the group counseling?"

"I did. It's set up for nine on Monday morning. They both thought it was a great idea and are going to put up notices. How bad is the tiling job going to be for you?"

"Actually, not bad. One of the guys has a cousin that does tiling who can start tomorrow."

"Sounds like we both have had good days. I'll see you at home in a little bit."

***

Walking upstairs, I pause in the doorway of Addy's room. As I look at the picture frame, I'm surprised to see that Addy is back in the picture. Picking up the frame, I run my finger over the glass, and notice the soft scent of lilacs. *Welcome back Addy.* Gracie sits at my feet and whimpers. "Okay girl let's go!" I say to her.

Opening the patio door, Gracie runs out as I start to walk out. "Whoa there, turbo," I warn, taking a seat in the glider. Putting my head back, I close my eyes. *Addy, what does all of this mean. It's not just Chris anymore who wants things back to normal.* Thinking about what Chris said about Addy consuming me, I decide to take time and call a friend.

After several rings, it goes to voicemail. "Hi, it's Beth," I say. "It's been a while since we've talked, and I thought we could catch up. Miss ya. Call me." Hanging up the phone, I realize that sounded desperate and pathetic! Chris jokes that I can never leave a short message. I go on and on. He's right. I admit it.

Next, I decide to call my friend Heather. Luckily, she's home and we are able to catch up with each other. Hanging up the phone, I pick up a magazine and read the latest diets, recipes, makeup tips, and hair styles.

Chris comes home and lies down on the couch with his head resting in my lap. Gingerly, I stroke his head and play with his hair.

"What's for dinner?" he asks.

"Leftovers. I just need to heat things up," I reply.

Letting out a deep breath, he takes my hand in his and kisses it.

"I'll wait right here then," he smiles.

"You will be shocked to learn I called not one but two girlfriends today."

"That's great."

"I called two because the first one didn't answer," I laugh. "Heather and I got to chat a while which was nice."

"It was good you got to catch up," he says letting out a yawn.

"Let me get up and warm up dinner so you don't fall asleep in your plate."

After dinner I gingerly approach the subject of Addy. "Do you think we can go over Addy and the numbers now?"

"Numbers?" he repeats.

"The numbers on the piece of paper from the Bible at the Inn? You remember they all have the same sequence of numbers as the dry-cleaning slip and the weird phone number. And I almost forgot to tell you, she's back."

"Whose back?"

"Addy. She's in the picture again. I noticed it when I came home." I run upstairs and grab the papers from the top drawer. I set them down beside Chris and take a seat across from him at the kitchen table.

"Could I see your phone?"

I hand him my phone and watch as he looks through my recent calls. He then begins to make a list of the date, time, and number of the missed calls. "Did you know you missed a call from the hospital today?" Chris asks.

"No. When?" I wonder.

"They probably want you to work another shift," he says handing me my phone. I listen to the voice mail that turns out to be from Chaplain Paul. He was calling to check in on me. I will try and touch base with him tomorrow.

"Maybe he is calling with an update on the girl."

"I would love any information at this point and her name is Addy."

"Getting back to your missed calls, whoever has been calling you, is really trying to get your attention. This was when you got the first call, right?"

"That would have been the day I had lunch with Mom."

"Which was on Monday the 20th," he adds, "but looking through your missed calls, you got the first one the day before, Sunday the 19th. See here. That would have been the day we came back from the Inn."

Retrieving the calendar from inside the cabinet door, I verify the date. "It's also the day I found the slip of paper in the Bible."

"You also got a call today."

"Really?"

"Are you sure you didn't know about the missed calls?"

"I'm positive."

"Did you have your phone turned off or on vibrate?"

"Not that I am aware of. Are all the missed calls even from the same number?"

"Yes, but I don't think it's an actual phone number. The numbers remind me of a lock combination or page numbers."

"What about Bible verses? We could use some divine help about now and the paper was in the Bible," I remind Chris.

Thumbing through the pages of my Bible, we start with the first sequence of numbers and begin scanning page numbers and Bible verses looking for anything that could relate to Addy. After an hour, Chris shuts the Bible, arches back in his chair, and stretches. "Were not getting anywhere."

"I think the numbers all go in sequence somehow."

"What happened when you dialed the number?"

"I never tried it. I was afraid I would get charged some astronomical fee for it being somewhere outside the country."

"Just for peace of mind, let's try it," Chris suggests.

While I read off the numbers, he carefully punches the numbers into the phone. There is a long pause and then a recording. "The number you have dialed cannot be connected. Please recheck the number and try again, AD 1912," Chris recites, ending the call.

"What did you say?"

Chris begins to repeat the entire message and I stop him.

"Just say the last part."

"AD something?"

"Dial the number again," I ask.

"Why when we're just going to get the same recording."

"Please, I need to verify the very last part."

As Chris redials the number, he places it on speaker so we can both listen. Sitting there, I don't even think Chris notices that I am holding my breath. The message is no different than the first one.

"What is the significance of 'AD 1912'?" Chris asks.

"I have had several things now that reference it. It's on the back of her picture and they're Addy's initials. Plus it was on the building I told you about."

"I remember," Chris nods.

"I want to show you something upstairs."

When we walk into Addy's room, there is the faint smell of lilacs. Chris quickly snaps his fingers. "That's the scent I smelled in the kitchen cabinet."

"I smell it a lot when I come in here. I relate it to Addy."

He sits down on the bed as I walk over to the dresser. Grabbing the picture, I hand it to him. "See... She's back in the picture."

"Yup, you told me earlier."

"What I didn't tell you was she appeared to me last night, after you had fallen asleep. I heard a noise and woke up to see her floating at the end of the bed. She told me she had to show you that she was real."

"That she did!"

"Take the picture out of the frame," I urge him.

"I've seen this before, remember?" As he turns it over, he reads, "Addy D. 1912".

I then hand him the picture I found in the suitcase. He looks at it then reads the back, "To my best friend Adeline, Love Milda."

"Now, look at the picture I found while going through my box of old photos."

He flips it over after glancing at the picture and reads, "Milda, To my best friend. Love, Adeline."

"Mom told me that my Aunt Millie's formal name was Milda."

"So, Addy could actually be short for Adeline."

"I guess so. I never really made the connection until you just said it."

"Do you think the names are just a coincidence or do you think your Aunt Millie gave that picture to Addy in a past life?"

"I love the thought, that life goes on after death with the connection of friends and loved ones. It helps me deal with the challenges and sadness life brings."

"So, looking at this picture of the girl named Milda, I think it's your Aunt Millie."

"You do? Why?"

"You did say you found this picture in your aunt's belongings. Plus, there is the vase. These two things tie Addy and your aunt together."

Standing there, I silently pray that Chris is jumping on board and not secretly picking out the colors for my padded room.

"So, tell me about the other bizarre things that have been happening. Start at the beginning so that I can try and meet you halfway."

I glance over at the clock. "You don't know how badly I want to, but it's getting late and we both have to get up early. I think it's best if we save it for tomorrow."

"What if I pick up dinner on the way home and we go over everything then? If you have some time tomorrow, start making a timeline. Between the two of us, we should be able to make sense of this."

Crawling into bed and snuggling into Chris' arms I let out a sigh. "Such a heavy sigh," says Chris, smoothing my hair from his face.

"I feel like I can take a deep breath again," I say to him.

"Well, we don't have it all figured out yet, but we'll get there."

"I know," I say closing my eyes.

TWELVE

Quinn walks into the nurses' station and sets down her bag. "How did the appointment go?" I ask.

"It went well. We will only have to adjust a couple of Mom's medications. We even had time to grab lunch before I dropped them off back home. I really can't thank you enough. I owe you big time. If you ever need any hours covered, don't hesitate to ask," replies Quinn.

After checking my charting and giving Quinn report on her patients, I grab my stuff and head to the breakroom. Before leaving for the day, I decide to give Chaplain Paul a call and tell him about learning Addy's name and stop myself. How are the police going to find her identity with just having a possible first name and first letter of her last name. Are they even going to take me seriously, after hearing that I'm trying to help a ghost? I'm only calling her Addy after finding the picture that read "Addy D. 1912". I need to think about this some more.

Chris calls as I am walking out to my car. "I could really go for these short shifts," I tease. "It's nice getting off early. It makes me feel like I am playing hooky."

"I have never done that, so I wouldn't know what that feels like," Chris says in a mature voice.

"I'm sure you don't!" I laugh.

"What's on your agenda now?"

"I'm going home to start on the timeline so we can go over it together."

"Good girl. What about burgers from the Burger Barn for dinner tonight?"

"Sounds great. We can start going over things while we eat. We can call it 'operation Addy'."

"Operation Addy?" he repeats before hanging up.

On the way home, I begin trying to organize the timeline in my head. After changing my clothes, I grab a pad of paper and head outside to the patio with Gracie. Just as I shut the screen door, the phone rings.

I'm surprised to hear my boss' voice. "Hi Beth. I wasn't able to catch you before you left. I have been in meetings. I wanted to make sure you knew about the change with the counseling session. I hung a notice in the breakroom and have been trying to make sure everyone is updated."

"Change?" I ask.

"In speaking with the other managers, we have decided it would be best to include all the departments involved, such as the lab and x-ray departments, as well as the house supervisor and social work departments. Not everyone is going to fit into our small breakroom and in order to accommodate everyone, we are moving the meeting to a larger room."

"Even better," I add.

"With that said, we had to change the time, unfortunately. I am personally calling everyone at home so that no one is inadvertently left out."

"Thanks for the heads up. When is it?"

"We've moved it to 3 p.m. this afternoon in the large conference room. I hope you can make it, since it was originally your idea."

"I had something to get done this afternoon, but I will definitely be there."

I jot down a couple of notes that stick out in my mind and then for the next hour or so stare at the pad of paper. *I know there has to be more than this.* I'm trying to force my thoughts and I can't think because of the anticipation of the counseling session. Feeling the need to look presentable, I change out of my comfy clothes. As I look at my reflection in the mirror, I tell myself, *This will have to do*, painting my lips with lipstick.

In the car, I play over in my mind how the meeting will go. One thing I can bet on -- there won't be a lot of people voicing they have been seeing an apparition that looks like the girl from the accident.

***

In the elevator, I keep busy by fumbling with my purse strap on the slow ride to the second floor. I take a deep breath and say a quick prayer before walking into the large conference room. Scanning the room, I search for a familiar face. Chaplain Paul sees me walk in and smiles. He's wearing my favorite tie with a lavender shirt. The colors in the tie against the shirt resemble a stained-glass window.

"Hi Beth," Chaplain Paul greets me.

"I see you have my favorite shirt and tie on," I tell him as he casually smooths out his tie and nods. Once I have signed in, I take a seat next to Madison and Lexi. Paige walks in with Rachel

and sits behind us.

A couple hours later, its finally over. Walking out to my car, I'm relieved. I was quite surprised at the number of people who attended. I hadn't even thought about the police officers or the fire and rescue personnel attending. It was so sweet of Chaplain Paul to go the extra mile and obtain permission to extend the invitation to the outside agencies and crews that were involved, realizing not everybody has the resources. He did an awesome job encouraging everyone to talk and share their feelings and to ask questions. I feel like a huge weight has been lifted. I was more nervous than I thought thinking about what could possibly be said or happen during the meeting. Addy's death certainly impacted more than just, me.

***

I pray for no more interruptions, so I can get the timeline done before Chris comes home. Taking the list I started earlier, I go up to Addy's room and take a seat on the bed. *Maybe it will be easier to remember things in here.* Reviewing what I already have jotted down, I start with the day of the accident and then seeing her in the bathtub. Next, is the carwash where I smelled lilacs and saw her in the backseat. Chris said he smelled something when opening a cabinet and later said it smelled like lilacs. This was the same day I had lunch with Amber Lynn and bought the dresser. Mrs. Foster told me it was from an estate sale in Florence County. We found the picture frame tucked in the top drawer.

Continuing the timeline, late at night, I heard a noise and found the vase lying on its side. That's when I noticed the picture with "Addy D. 1912" in the frame. I started calling her Addy after that. I said goodnight to Addy, and I heard goodnight back. There was the time that I took a shower and thought I heard my name and then saw her in front of me. I got a flower from the garden and put it in the vase. Looking at what I have jotted down, I know some of these are out of order.

I look around to see if anything can jog my memory. I forgot to list the trip to the inn and finding the picture of the girl that read: "To my best friend Adeline, Love Milda," which was a major event. That's also when I found the paper with the numbers "113-122-418" written on it sticking out of the Bible and then later mysteriously tucked in our suitcase. I had lunch with Mom and went to the park and noticed the City County building with "A.D. 1912" on it. I started having missed calls then with the area code 113. I looked through the box of old building pictures and heard my name called as well as felt a cool breeze. I found the dry-cleaning receipt with the same numbers on it. There were pictures strewn all over the bed and I found the picture that had, "Milda, To my best friend. Love, Adeline."

Chris also had his own sighting after he announced she wasn't real. We noticed she was gone from the picture and when I went to bed that night, I heard a noise and saw her floating at the foot of the bed. She told me she had to appear to him. Then the next day Addy was back in the picture.

I feel like I am getting writer's cramp and this is as much as I can remember right now. I am relieved to have the timeline and the counseling session both done. I just wish they would make a formal identification of Addy.

***

Chris sets the bags down on the table and the aroma fills the air, making my stomach rumble. I go to the fridge to get out the ketchup while he unloads the bags. "It smells amazing!" I say.

"I know," he says grabbing a fry and tossing it in his mouth. "They're just perfect."

"I have a question for you. How many orders of fries did you get and how many came home?"

"Very funny. You know the saying: you can't eat just one."

I grab a fry from the bag and pop it into my mouth, savoring the salty goodness. "If you can't beat them join them."

At the table, Chris pauses between bites. "Did you get your timeline done?"

"One better! I got both the timeline and the counseling session done."

"I thought the meeting wasn't until Monday."

"My boss called me after I got home. The meeting was moved to accommodate more people who expressed interest in attending. The police along with the fire and rescue crews were there."

"How do you think the meeting was perceived?"

"This is just my opinion, but I feel that everyone that wanted to, had the opportunity to share. Chaplain Paul did a wonderful job overseeing it. He opened and closed with a prayer for the girl and her family to find closure as well as for all of those affected."

"Chris, I want to thank you for suggesting it. There were a lot of people there and I am sure it helped."

"How about you? Do you feel better now?"

"Yes, I do."

"Did you share anything with the group?"

"Yes, but not about seeing Addy or anything that has been going on. That would be too weird for anyone else to handle. I am still trying to come to grips with it myself. I just said that I have had a tough time and it's so sad her family doesn't know that she is dead."

Chris gets up from the table and throws his trash away. Looking at my food, "Aren't you going to finish? You've hardly eaten anything."

"I am just going to get some plastic wrap to put around it and I will reheat it later or tomorrow. I am not hungry anymore. I must have snitched too many fries from the bag." Watching me wrap my plate and put it in the fridge, he looks annoyed.

"Do you want to go over the timeline here at the table or somewhere else?" I ask.

"How about we sit outside and get some fresh air, maybe it will help kick start your appetite," Chris suggests.

Bothered by his mention of my not eating, I plop the dishcloth in the sink. He walks over and puts his arms around my waist. Backing me up against the sink, he pulls me close. "I am worried about you. I'm trying to help you through this and that includes making sure you are keeping up your strength. I am no medical professional, but I do know you need glucose and sleep to help your brain function."

"Okay. I get it. I will try to be more mindful of my eating and sleeping. I am going to run upstairs and grab the timeline. Can you take our cups of glucose out to the porch?"

Chris shoots me a look, clearly not amused.

I sit down next to Chris and proudly hand him the timeline. "I think I pretty much have everything," I boast.

"There's a lot here," he says skimming over the list.

"I might have a couple of things out of order," looking over his shoulder.

"I think it would make it easier to follow, if you added the dates of when it happened."

I sigh and turn away rolling my eyes.

"I can tell you're upset. This is a good start," he reassures me.

I go and get a calendar and hand it to him. "If you want to see it in big print, here you go."

"This is going to take longer than just tonight."

Feeling totally deflated and nauseous, I can't tell if it is from the lack of food or lack of support. I take the list and calendar and walk inside with Chris following.

"Don't you agree?" he asks.

"Right now, I don't want to agree about anything. I am getting a headache." I open the cabinet and get out a pill bottle as he hands me a glass of water.

"It might be because you haven't eaten much today," he says bluntly.

Glaring at him, as I swallow the pills. I set down the glass. "Not now, Chris."

"You have quite a bit of stuff here," he says, trying to back pedal.

"I don't want to talk about it anymore," I announce.

"I really don't see how you could be fabricating any of this."

I immediately see red. "What did you just say?" I asked knocking over the glass. Reaching for a dishtowel, I begin mopping up the water. "Why would I feel the need to make any of this up! What possible motive would I have? Please tell me because I would really like to know. This is just mind-boggling, because up to now, I thought you were trying to help and understand what I have been going through. But now, I can see you have just been going through the motions. I get really hyped about trying to tell you about everything that has happened and then I see you sitting there looking at your phone or staring at the TV. I'm not blind, you know."

His face reddens as he avoids making eye contact.

"I know when to throw in the towel," I yell tossing the wet towel onto the counter.

"Let's just call it a night. You are probably just as tired as I am," he says. He tries to pat my back but I turn around and retreat upstairs. "I will be up shortly," he says.

Trying to walk up the stairs I feel like a lead weight is holding me down. My spirit's broken. It's not about having to redo the timeline. I am exhausted and need to be free from this emotional baggage.

As I step into the shower, "I just don't know anymore." Playing over and over in my head is Chris saying, "I don't know how you could be fabricating this." As the water roars loudly in my ears, I faintly hear the words, "try harder, try harder."

Grabbing the shower curtain and pulling it to one side, I jump when I see Chris standing there, holding out a towel.

"Sweet Momma!" I holler, bracing my arm against the wall of the shower.

"I'm sorry, I'm sorry," he laughs. "I thought it would be nice if I got a towel for you. I wasn't trying to scare you. I have been standing outside trying to talk to you. You must not have heard me."

"Thank you," accepting the towel and wrapping it around me. "And no, I didn't hear you."

With my nightgown and robe on, I glance back in the mirror, surprised to see Addy looking back at me. With the bathroom mirror much larger, I'm able to get a better look at her, despite the mirror being slightly fogged. I take a towel and wipe the mirror. Speaking into the mirror, I say, "Addy, I'm trying. You must believe me. I don't know what I'm supposed to be doing. You've got to help me. I can't do it by myself." Looking straight into my eyes, she nods and then begins to write on the mirror.

Chris asks, "Who are you talking to?"

I bring my finger up to my mouth and motion him to be quiet and come closer, pointing at the mirror.

He stares into the mirror, shaking his head in disbelief. "I don't believe what I am seeing," Chris whispers.

"Chris this is Addy," making a formal introduction. She looks over at him and then goes back to writing on the mirror. She looks very disheartened.

"I need my phone," says Chris.

"Who are you going to call, Ghostbusters?"

"Very funny, but I have to tell you if they were available, I would seriously consider it." Several seconds later, he walks in carrying his phone. "I want to take a picture of her."

"I don't know how the image of her will look, and I don't want to do anything to upset her."

"I don't either, but we won't know until we try." He takes the picture and quickly looks at the image. The only thing visible is a partially written sentence and the image of me standing beside Chris. Addy is not in the picture but oddly, there is a bluish-white circle above the writing.

"There she is." I point out to Chris.

"Where? I don't see her," he responds.

"She's there in the form of an orb. Don't you ever watch any ghost shows?"

"No, I can honestly say I don't because I am not sure that I believe in all that stuff, like you do."

"I only do because I saw it firsthand at my Grandparent's house that was haunted."

"What do you think she was trying to say?

" 'Please try', was all she had written before you took the picture."

As we both stand staring into the mirror, the letters in front of us become dimmer and dimmer until they disappear.

"Well has any of this changed your mind, Chris?"

"Yes, it has," putting his arms around me. "I'm sorry that you felt I wasn't there for you. I don't ever want to hurt you. I was coming to apologize when I brought the towel. We will have to add this to your timeline. We can look at everything tomorrow and maybe it will make more sense after a good night's sleep," he says pulling the covers up around him.

I lean over and kiss him goodnight.

"I am still worried about you, Beth. What if we don't ever get this figured out? Then what?"

"Everything will look clearer in the morning with fresh eyes," I announce, switching off the light.

Turning on my side, I try hard to think about nothing, as Chris yawns and says, "Goodnight."

"Goodnight," I reply.

Then with the quietness of the night, I hear Chris say, "Goodnight, Addy." With that, I smile and close my eyes.

***

I lay and watch the hands turn on the clock until I can't anymore. Maybe a cup of tea will help, as I head to the kitchen. I switch on the undercounter light and turn the burner on for the kettle. The clock on the stove reads 12:30 a.m. After selecting a tea bag, I pour the water into a cup. Dunking the tea, I try and reason with myself. You must have dozed off at some point, as the vague memory of a dream begins to flood my mind. I take a sip as I look out the kitchen window.

"What is that?" squinting to make out what it is. "Did I leave something on the clothesline?" The tea kettle whistles loudly, startling me as I hurry to the stove. I thought I shut you off. I quickly turn off the stove and remove it from the burner. I carry my cup over to the table and pull out a chair.

As if on cue, I'm joined by my four-legged friend, Gracie. "Can't you sleep either girl?" rubbing the scruff of her neck. With that, she stretches and yawns. I will take that as a "yes."

I grab the laundry basket and walk outside with Gracie. The dim lights from the porch subtly illuminate the backyard. Looking out around the yard and then back at the clothesline, my attention is frozen. "There isn't anything on the line. What was it that I saw?" Cautiously, I walk over to the clothesline. There is a mist-like figure floating above the ground. Straining to see due to the lack of light, I call out, "Addy is that you?"

Her image slowly comes into focus, and I can see her faint outline. In a soft whisper she says, "You need to know, I haven't much time left."

"I need your help as well, Addy."

"I must deliver my message, Beth, and you are who I have chosen."

"Honestly, we have been trying to figure it out. This isn't easy for us either. I don't know why you picked me. You haven't given me much help with clues. I'm a nurse, not a detective."

"But you're wrong," she answers back. "You may be a nurse but in your everyday life, you are always looking for clues to help you diagnose and help others."

Listening intently, I conclude she is right. "I will try harder, I promise, but wouldn't it be easier for you to just tell me what the message is, instead of me having to piece everything together?"

"You wouldn't understand the message then."

Looking down at my feet, Gracie is standing beside me cocking her head from side-to-side listening.

"Hello sweet friend," Addy says.

"This is Gracie. I'm surprised she's not barking at you."

"We have already met, and she knows why I'm here. Maybe you should ask her for help?"

"That would be like asking a pencil to write down the answer for you."

"Exactly, now you are on the right track," Addy nods.

"I was joking!"

"I must go now. Please hurry. I need you." With that, she disappears and Gracie and I are left looking at each other.

"Let's go girl, you've got some talking to do!" I laugh.

Racing in the back door she stops beside her treat jar. "Addy seems to think you know the message." Giving her a treat, I sit down at the table with a pencil and see if what Addy said is true. I hold the tip of the pencil against the paper and after several minutes, nothing happens. Feeling silly for even trying, I tell Gracie, "I'm glad you were the only one to see that."

I take a sip from my cup and the tea is now cold. The clock on the wall shows it's 1:15 a.m. I have been up longer than I thought. I peek into Addy's room as the light from the streetlight casts a glow within the room. Not wanting to risk waking up Chris, I stand in the dark, praying for answers and guidance to help Addy complete her message and continue her journey. Back in bed, I hear a soft moan from Chris. Tomorrow is going to be rough, I yawn.

THIRTEEN

The aroma of coffee has me scurrying to get downstairs. Chris is busy emptying the dishwasher. "Who are you and what have you done with my husband?" I ask.

"Funny. I thought I would just be the nice guy that I am," Chris replies.

"I appreciate it," leaning over to mimic his movements and give him a kiss. Pouring myself a cup of coffee, I eagerly take a sip. "This hits the spot."

"You still look tired," Chris says, handing me a piece of toast. "Did you sleep okay?"

"I'm a little tired this morning. I got another visit from Addy this morning only this time Gracie saw her too. Addy told me that she and Gracie have already met. She also told me that she is running out of time. I asked her if it would be easier if she just told me what the message was, and she said I wouldn't understand it then. She said that I need to have Gracie help me because she holds a clue."

"Is this why you didn't get much sleep last night?" The smirk on Chris' face almost makes me choke on my coffee. "Wow, Gracie, you're better than having Lassie. Gracie, can you tell us if Timmy is in the well, too?" he laughs.

"Hold onto your hat, it gets better. She also told me to sit down with a pencil and paper and let my mind and hand relax. The pencil knows the answer."

He closes the dishwasher and takes a bite of his toast. "That's pretty bizarre wouldn't you say?"

"I would have to agree. I was even dumb enough to try it. And no, it didn't work. I can't understand why her family hasn't come forth. For her to appear to me with a personal plea, I'm worried."

"I came up with an idea this morning. Maybe her next of kin is ill and unable to let anybody know that she hasn't been around." He opens the front door and collects the newspaper.

"So, are you suggesting I try and contact all the surrounding hospitals and nursing homes? That would take weeks and maybe even months. Besides, they may not divulge any information."

Chris begins combing through the newspaper as I wait for his response. I start to repeat what I said, when he interrupts me.

"You are going to want to see this." Spreading the paper out on the counter, we stare at the bold headline "Missing 22-Year-Old Girl Linked to Traffic Accident Victim". "I think you are starting to get your answers in bold print now," he says.

I try to speed read through the article as I watch the time. "Could I take the paper to share it with the girls at work?"

He folds the paper and hands it to me. "Here you go."

"I will bring the article back home, so you can read it. I promise."

"Make sure you eat lunch today."

"You are starting to sound like my mother, Chris. Have a good day. Love you," I holler, closing the door behind me. Opening the door again, "Hey, let's get a bite out tonight and then go to the grocery, okay?"

Closing the door, I hear him say, "Yippee," to Gracie.

"I heard that," I yell opening the car door. Scanning through radio stations, I try to hear any updated information on Addy. At least I have the article to share. Some news is better than none.

***

The busyness of the department soon takes precedence. Hours later, the department settles down after having several patients from a motor vehicle accident involving a couple of cars, a mail truck, and a garbage truck. Finally, we have a minute and I pull out the newspaper.

Karli picks up the article and begins to read it aloud, " 'Recent accident victim identity believed to be that of Adeline Dyer, 22-year-old of Cook County who was reported missing by her employer after she failed to report to work for several days'."

"It was her employer who reported her missing. Why not her family?" Madison asks.

"It doesn't make any sense," I sigh. Claiming the next patient, I grab a clipboard and chart and meet them in the room.

"Let's tag team it," Autumn says handing me a blanket.

Hours later, the patient is discharged and I'm helping them into their car. Putting the wheelchair back in the designated alcove, I walk over to the triage desk. Lexi looks up from the computer and smiles as I walk towards her.

"So how is it going out here?" I ask.

Rachel returns from making a pot of coffee and sits down. "We have gone through a lot of coffee this morning."

"I just discharged the last one from the accident. It should taper off now," I tell them.

Everyone had minor injuries except for the one who was admitted and went to surgery for a nasty ankle fracture.

"There are a lot of people who need to be thanking the one upstairs or somebody," Rachel sighs. "How lucky can you be?"

"It could have been so much worse," I offer.

"I wonder if my mail will be delayed today," Lexi asks.

"I guess it would depend on if you had the same route," Rachel answered.

"Why was the kid playing in the car?" Lexi asks.

"The officer said the mother left him strapped in his car seat with the car running, while she ran inside for her purse. The kid got out of his car seat and somehow got the car out of gear. It then rolled down the driveway in the path of the garbage and mail truck. They both tried to veer away from each other as well as the car that was passing the truck. The driver of the garbage truck said he saw the mother running after the car, yelling, and flailing her arms."

"I'm glad I didn't see it. I can't stand to watch stuff happen. I'm okay taking care of the aftermath, just don't let me see it happen," Rachel expressed.

"I couldn't agree with you more," I nod.

Lexi turns to greet the people approaching the desk while Rachel pauses to listen. As I turn to walk away, Lexi asks, "Beth, will you let us know when an ambulance arrives with a fall patient?" She then motions with her head as my eyes follow in the direction of a woman sitting with a little boy on her lap. "She's waiting for her mother to come in."

Walking over to the woman, I watch as she rubs the boy's back while gently rocking him. "Sally is that you?" I ask. Sally and I worked together on a Medical/Surgical floor where she started as a new nurse.

She quickly tries to stand, while juggling her balance with the boy. The little boy sees me and quickly puts his head on his mother's shoulder, trying to bury his face. He then looks up sheepishly as his mom continues to try and soothe him. "Oh my gosh Beth! Am I glad to see you," says Sally.

"What's wrong?"

"I got a call from the ambulance crew that Mom fell at home. I told them I would meet her here."

As I take a seat next to her, she goes on to explain. "My dad's out of town. He's going to be so upset. I haven't called him yet. I'm going to wait to hear what the doctor has to say. I can't see worrying him."

"That makes sense," I reply as I smile at Ben. Reaching into my pocket, I pull out a small container of bubbles and hand it to Sally. "Maybe this will help pass the time while you wait. Let me go check and see if she's here."

"Thanks Beth. I'm so glad you're working today. I feel better, just talking to you."

Walking through the double doors, I check with the unit clerk to see if we have gotten any radio traffic or incoming ambulances. Paul checks the clipboard and says "Just one, a fall with ankle pain. They are pulling in now. We have them going into bed 6. Madison and Quinn are getting the room ready."

I peek my head into the room. "Do you guys need anything?"

"Nope, I think we are set with a blanket, extra pillows, and ice for the swelling," Quinn says.

"Can I offer you a clipboard then?" I ask.

"That would be great," Madison says as she takes it out of my hand. As the ambulance crew arrives, Mrs. Laney sees me.

"Hi Beth," Mrs. Laney says. "I'm just so embarrassed. I could cry."

"No need for that. Sally and Ben are waiting in the lobby. I will let her know you are here."

"I was trying to get the attic organized while Keith is away. He puts everything right at the top of the stairs and you have to push your way through to even get up there."

"Hmm, that sounds familiar," I say looking over at Madison and Quinn who are both nodding. "It must be a guy thing," I chuckle.

"I was done and climbing back down the stairs when I forgot to shut off the light, so I went back up and that's when I must have missed a step."

Quinn gingerly picks up Mrs. Laney's foot while Madison places pillows underneath. She then places a bag of ice in a pillowcase and gingerly wraps it around the swollen ankle. While Quinn and Madison are with Mrs. Laney, I step out of the room to update Sally. She sees me walking through the door and stands up. "Is she here? How is she? It's not a hip, right?" she nervously asks.

It doesn't take long to learn that once a person breaks a hip, complications can happen. Too many people end up having blood clots or even strokes. Some are never the same with walking or dealing with the pain.

Sally adjusts Ben to her other hip.

"You got him okay?" I ask.

"Yeah, thanks. I'm trying to be strong, but I am just a wreck inside," says Sally.

"I know you are, but you are holding it together."

"How did she fall?" Sally asks.

"Your mom said she was working in the attic when she came down the attic steps wrong and landed on her ankle. It's pretty swollen. The doctor will be in, and they will get some x-rays and give her something for the pain."

"I hope she takes it. Mom isn't one to take pain medication."

After walking them back to her mom's room, she stands outside her mother's door. She reaches for my hand. "You are such a Godsend, Beth. You have no idea."

"We need to try and get together and not just see each other at work," I tell her, giving her hand a squeeze. "Let's try and set up lunch sometime," I suggest.

"That would be great once everything settles down a bit," brushing Ben's hair away from his face.

Snuggling up against her, he closes his eyes. As I start to walk away, Sally says: "I almost forgot, a girl in the lobby asked me to tell you something. She said something about a message. With worrying about my mom and trying to keep Ben content, I wasn't fully paying attention to her."

"Was she with anybody?" I ask nervously.

"I didn't notice anyone."

"Did she happen to tell you her name?"

"No, I didn't think to ask either. I'm sorry Beth," she says looking puzzled.

"No, it's fine. Go and see your mom," I tell her waving goodbye.

Karli peeks her head out of a room and asks, "Can someone run and get a wheelchair for me?"

"I will," I volunteer. *I want to have another look in the lobby anyway.* I walk past Lexi and Rachel who are checking in a patient. I go over to the children's area near the aquarium and look around. Picking up stray cups and wrappers, I walk over to the trash can and toss them in. I decide to use the excuse of tidying up while I continue to look around to see if I can see the person who asked for me or possibly even Addy.

I walk over to the chairs where Sally and Ben had been sitting and pick up a magazine. Flipping it over, my mouth drops as I read the cover: "Divine Inspiration Magazine: 'There Are Angels All Among Us'." The label name on the subscription reads "Addy Dyer, 113-122-418". I fold up the magazine and walk over to the triage desk as I try and maintain my composure. "Still holding down the fort, I see," I say as I set the magazine on the counter.

"Thanks for tidying up," Rachel says.

"You're a peach," Lexi agrees.

"Did you guys happen to see the girl that was talking to my friend Sally?"

"There have been a lot of people walking through. There was a girl sitting by herself earlier. Later on, when I looked, she was gone. Did she leave something here?" Lexi asks.

"I'm not sure. Sally said she told her to ask me about a message. I found this magazine near where they were sitting."

"We did away with magazines a while ago," Lexi says.

"The only thing I am aware of are the various health brochures on the wall," Rachel says.

"It has to be a magazine someone forgot," Lexi adds as she takes it off the counter and begins to look at it. "This one has someone's name on it."

I take it out of her hand and fold it back up not wanting her to read the name. I'm not sure if she's read the paper I brought in or if she would even make the connection. "I'll hang onto it since she is trying to contact me. I can ask if it belongs to her when I see her."

"I think she did leave a message for you," Rachel says.

"You do?"

She nods at the magazine, "We all know you are an angel."

"I can go the other direction at times too, I suppose," I laugh.

"Girl," Lexi says.

"Can't we all," Rachel laughs.

I grab a wheelchair and take it to Karli for her patient. I then go and check on my patients.

After clocking out, I stop by Mrs. Laney's room and peek in. "How's the patient?"

"We're going home soon, just waiting for the paperwork," Sally says.

"You watch it with those crutches, Mrs. Laney, no races now," I joke.

"Not a chance," she laughs.

"Take care," I say shutting the curtain.

Holding onto the magazine, I'm anxious to look through it and show Chris. What a strange day this has been. I decide to give him a call as I walk out to my car. "Hi. Something really weird happened at work."

"Before I forget," he interrupts. "I need to tell you I ran into Amber Lynn when I was picking up donuts this morning. You have got to call her. I can't answer all her questions that she has for the bazaar."

"I'll call her later," I grumble. "Something really weird happened I repeat and I have something to show you after dinner."

"What are we having tonight?" Chris asks.

"Are you kidding me? We are going to get something out and then run to the grocery store. I told you this morning when I was leaving."

"I remember now but my stomach didn't."

"I honestly don't know how you don't weigh 300 pounds!"

"Just for your information, I might get a salad when we go out."

"Aw, do the donuts have you feeling a little guilty, my friend?"

"Maybe," he says sheepishly, "and the fact that you think I should weigh 300 pounds."

"Do I dare ask how many you ate?"

"No, I think there is a bad connection. I can hardly hear you. Do you hear that static?" he asks as he makes screeching noises into the phone. "I will talk to you at home."

"Bye," I laugh.

***

While fixing myself a cold drink, the phone rings. Glancing at the caller ID screen, I see it's Amber Lynn. "I hear you have been anxiously waiting to talk to me," I say into the phone.

"I just figured you were avoiding me since I have asked your husband multiple times to have you call me."

"I'm not avoiding you. I'm just busy with work and everything else." Taking the phone into the family room, I set the glass down and curl up on the couch with the magazine from work.

"So, what's new?" I ask.

"Well, there have been several people in the bazaar that I have threatened to pull out if they don't up their game."

"What do you mean by that? You wouldn't really do that would you?"

"Wow, I didn't think I dialed Miss Goody Two Shoes," she barks into the phone, "but I can totally see I have."

"That's not a very nice thing to say Amber Lynn!"

"Sometimes you just have to admit, Beth Davis, you are not fun to talk to or be around."

Starting to see red, "I'm sorry you feel that way."

"So then," she asks, "what have you decided you are doing for the bazaar? I will need to know so I can list you in the program."

"Hmm, I really haven't decided yet. Let me give it some more thought and I will give you a call later this week."

"You know today is Friday, right?"

"I guess it is," laughing. "I even worked today and still forgot. I will let you know Monday, or Wednesday at the absolute latest."

"Are you sure you're okay?" she asks. "You are just so preoccupied anymore."

"I am fine, contrary to what you've probably been hearing or telling others." Amber Lynn is silent for once and I decide it's a good place to end the conversation. I tell her I need to go, say goodbye, and hang up the phone. "Well, that was pleasant," I tell Gracie rolling my eyes and shaking my head.

FOURTEEN

Chris arrives home and after feeding Gracie, I grab my grocery list off the fridge, and we head out to grab dinner.

"Where do you want to eat?" I ask. "It doesn't matter to me."

"How about Jake's? It's close to the house and on the way to the store," Chris suggests.

On the drive over, I tell Chris about seeing Sally and how she met a girl in the lobby who asked her to tell me something about a message. She wasn't sure if she had the girl's wording right, being preoccupied with her mom. When I went out to the lobby to look for myself, I found a magazine where Sally had been sitting called "Divine Inspiration" with the topic "There are angels all among us." It had Addy's name printed on it with the same sequence of numbers as the missed phone calls. We don't even have magazines in the department anymore, just wellness brochures.

"I know there are a lot of different magazines out there for everyone, but I don't think that's one I have ever heard of before," he says.

We're pleased to be seated shortly after arriving. I take a sip of water and I look over the menu. "Are you still having a salad?" I ask Chris.

"What?" looking up from his menu.

"You said something on the phone about having a salad. Are you still having one or are you going to order something else?"

The waitress comes over to take our orders. I order the Cobb salad and Chris proceeds to order a full order of BBQ nachos with sour cream on the side.

"I can take the leftover's tomorrow for lunch," he smiles.

As we wait for our dinners to be brought out, I tell him about my conversation with Amber Lynn.

"She got really upset with me when I questioned her about threatening to pull people out of the bazaar. She actually called me 'Miss Goody Two Shoes'!"

As he begins doctoring up his nachos, I sit across from him stabbing at my salad. "I don't think Amber Lynn is a good friend for you," Chris says.

"She also told me that sometimes I'm not fun to talk to or be around."

He licks his fingers before grabbing another nacho. "I don't like the way she talks to you Beth."

Taking another stab at my salad and moving it around on the plate, "I second that. I'm a fun person."

"Finish your salad so we can have a nice relaxing time grocery shopping," he jokes.

"That might be more believable, if you didn't have sour cream on your chin." I take a couple more bites of my salad and push it away. "I'm done. I'm not hungry anymore."

The waitress brings Chris his box, we pay the bill and then head to the grocery.

***

After trying out several carts, Chris finds one he is happy with. As I look at my list, I begin heading for the produce area. While choosing a container of strawberries, I look over to find Chris juggling oranges. A little kid watching tries to imitate him, sending oranges all over the floor. His mother begins yelling at him, making him cry. Chris feeling bad, helps him pick up the oranges to try and smooth things over. I can't help but laugh as I gather my items and move to the next aisle. Sorry Buddy, you're on your own for this one.

Steering toward the dairy aisle, I say over in my mind, orange juice, milk, and creamer. As I begin looking to see which dairy case holds my creamer, I spot it on the shelf and notice there is only one left. As I start to open the door, I realize the door opens the opposite way. A woman then reaches in, grabbing the last one. "We were reaching for the same thing," I tell her. "I just opened the door from the wrong side."

"Sorry, this one is mine," she says holding it up like a trophy and smirking before putting it into her cart. As she walks away, her phone rings and I hear her say, "Hello, this is Amber Lynn."

Oh, my – another Amber Lynn! Please tell me they don't all share the same personality. Bending down, I check to see if I can see another row of creamer on a different shelf. I see a man standing in the cooler on the other side stocking the shelves. I get his attention and ask if there are anymore. While he checks, I grab a few more items close to the creamer case. As I am studying the varieties of orange juice, a gentleman in a white coat walks up to me. My mouth drops when I see his face.

"Here you go, Beth, your hug in a cup, right?" the man says.

"Uncle Ted?" I respond dazed. He hands me the creamer and smiles. "Are you an angel?" I ask.

"They're all around us," Uncle Ted beams as he looks around.

I put the creamer in my cart and when I look up, he's gone. There is no one else in the aisle to even ask if they saw him. I reach down and touch the creamer. It's real. I rub my forehead and look down at my list. I need to get done and find Chris. I see Chris walking down the aisle towards me with a bag of dog food, a can of peanuts, a container of peanut butter and a box of dog treats.

"I have been walking down the isles looking for you. Good thing I am so fit, otherwise I wouldn't be able to carry all of this," says Chris.

As he puts the items into the cart, I say, "This is taking way too long so let's try to stay together. Plus, a woman grabbed the last creamer in the case and my Uncle Ted brought me out one from the back."

He stops the cart, making a face. "Uncle Ted? Uncle Ted?" raising his eyebrows, "as in dead Uncle Ted?"

"I only have one Uncle Ted and yes, that one."

"I think I need to open these peanuts so that you can have some protein."

I put my hand over the top of the can to stop him. "I don't like it when people do that. It isn't paid for yet."

"If I was a diabetic and having a fit on the floor and needing sugar, you wouldn't hesitate."

"Yes, I would. I wouldn't give someone peanuts. They could choke."

"They could choke on a piece of cheese too," he adds.

"Where is this going?" I ask, annoyed.

"Well, I am just going to take my peanuts and leave you to your shopping."

"I need you to stay with me and quit joking about the peanuts. Something weird is happening!"

"Okay, but I'm pushing the cart," he says walking ahead.

As I look over my list, I cross off the items I have already put in the cart. "I forgot to get the milk and orange juice when I was in the dairy aisle. Would you go and get them for me?"

"Can I take the cart with me?" he bargains.

"You don't have to guard your snacks. I'm not going to put anything back."

While he heads in the opposite direction, I head to get sandwich wraps for our lunches. I walk down the bread aisle and pick up a loaf of bread as well as a package of buns. While I continue to scan the shelves for the wraps, I stare at the variety of donuts, cupcakes, and snacks. Deciding to do something thoughtful for my little boy, I pick up a box of snack cakes for him to pack in his lunch.

With my hands almost full, I continue searching for the wraps. Seeing a man kneeling who is stocking and straightening the shelves, I ask, "Do you know where I can find the sandwich wraps?"

He turns around and says, "They have been moved to the deli aisle."

My heart races and I tear up as I realize I am looking into the face of my grandpa, Theo. He looks at me with the same sparkle in his eyes that I remember. "Hi Beth," says Grandpa Theo.

"Grandpa, why are you here?" I say, blinking.

"We're here to remind you that you're not alone. We're always here, just in a different form."

I turn around to see if anyone else can see him and when I turn back, he's gone.

"There you are. I keep losing you," Chris says.

Standing with an odd look on my face and my arms full, he senses something isn't right. He unloads the groceries from my arms and puts them in the cart. Feeling numb, I glance over to where I saw my grandpa.

"What's wrong? You look like you saw a ghost!" asks Chris.

"I just spoke to my grandpa," I answer.

"Was Grandma with him? Let's catch up with him so I can say 'hi'."

"No," I shake my head. "Not that one. Grandpa Theo."

"You saw your grandpa that died? We need to get you out of here. Are you sure you don't want to open something and get some sugar in you? Maybe your glucose is just low. Let me have the grocery list." He takes the list from my hand and compares it to what is in the cart. "What else do we need in this aisle?"

"Sandwich wraps for your lunch, but they are in the deli area now," I tell him. "My Grandpa Theo told me."

"Okay. Grab the cart and walk with me." Chris takes over the shopping and continues to get things on the list as well as things off the list. We grab the wraps from the deli area and then are ready to go. "Is that everything now?"

"I think so," I answer numbly.

As we place the items on the conveyor belt, I try to nonchalantly look around. Chris puts his arms around my waist and gives me a kiss. I smile as I watch other people busy checking out. Then I notice her. Several lanes over, there is a clerk bagging. "She looks just like my Aunt Imy," I mumble.

Chris leans over, "What did you say?"

She makes eye contact with me and smiles. I put my hand up and wave. Chris sees me waving and turns to look. "I don't see anybody," he says.

"She's right there," I insist. "She is bagging groceries."

He swipes his credit card and puts the rest of the groceries in the cart while waiting for the receipt. Grabbing my hand, he places it on the cart as we walk toward the exit. Turning around, I pause to take one last look before leaving the store. There standing together, are Grandpa Theo, Uncle Ted, and Aunt Imy smiling. I smile back as I blow them a kiss and wave.

Chris looks at me in disbelief, shaking his head. "We're not seeing the same thing Beth. I don't see them."

Once we get out to the car, Chris opens my door and even helps me fasten my seatbelt. Loading the groceries into the car, I wait for the shoe to drop. He returns the cart and then opens the door as I take a deep breath and wait. Starting the engine, he looks over at me. *Here it comes,* trying to prepare.

Before he actually speaks, I put my head back against the headrest and bite my lower lip.

"I have to say you are really scaring me. You are seeing DEAD people now."

It's not just now, I think to myself. *Addy is dead, remember?*

The drive home is quiet as he stares straight ahead and I stare out the window, having nothing else to say to each other.

***

Chris unloads the groceries from the car, setting the bags on the counter while I begin putting everything away. I set out Chris' peanuts on the counter and open them up. Popping a couple into my mouth, I enjoy the salty crunch. He then walks over and grabs a couple himself. Chris breaks the silence and asks, "Did they say what it is like up there?"

"I didn't think to ask," I reply. "Uncle Ted said something, like there are angels all around us. Grandpa Theo said all of them are here to help me, just in a different form."

"What about your Aunt?" putting another handful of peanuts in his mouth.

"She didn't say anything. She just smiled and waved at me. When I left the store, all three of them were standing together, waving."

"What do you think any of this means?" he asks.

"I'm more confused than I was before."

With the groceries put away, I fix us both a cup of tea. I make a point to show Chris the magazine before going upstairs.

"I can't believe that it has Addy's name on it," Chris says.

"Her name and the strange long number," I add.

Upstairs, I begin pulling out containers of silk flowers from underneath the bed. I'm surprised how much craft stuff I have accumulated. I then open the closet door and start retrieving wire cutters, pliers, wire, floral tape, and a hot glue gun with extra glue sticks. Chris walks in and his mouth drops. "What happened?"

"A flower shop blew up," I laugh.

"Are you even sure we need to go to the craft store?"

"I still want to go to get some ideas. I don't exactly know what I am making yet."

"Well, something with the flowers, I hope!"

Chris offers to set up a table for me to work on. As he comes out of the closet, something falls and hits him. As he backs out of the closet and turns around, I begin laughing as he stands there with a wire wreath frame around his neck.

"How do you like my necklace?" he asks.

"You just gave me an idea. What about making flower wreaths?" I suggest.

"Well, you certainly have the flowers for it, and you have a couple more wire frames in the closet." He pulls them down and sets them on the bed, just as the phone rings. "I'll pick it up in the bedroom," he says walking out of the room.

Straining to hear, I try to guess who Chris is talking with while looking through a drawer of assorted ribbons. The conversation becomes louder as Chris walks in. He places his hand over the phone and says, "It's Chaplain Paul," as he hands me the phone.

"Hi Chaplain Paul, how are you today?" I ask.

"Good. I was wondering if I could set up a time that I could come and talk with you, at your home and not at work, if that would be okay?" he asks.

"Sure," I nervously reply. "Does it have anything to do with the girl from the accident and the article in the newspaper?"

"Yes, it does, but I don't want to go over it on the phone. When I start explaining things to you, I think you'll understand why. Would tomorrow be okay?"

"Sure, how about ten o'clock?"

"Perfect, I'll see you then."

"Well? Chris asks.

"He's coming over tomorrow morning. He says he has some news about Addy and didn't walk to tell me at work. He said I would understand why after he tells me."

"Are you going to bring up that you have been seeing your dead family members?"

"I will wait and see how the conversation goes. I work with him, remember? I don't want him to think I'm nuts." Looking at the floor, bed, and table,

I shake my head. "Having this craft stuff spread all over is going to drive me nuts."

"At least you have it contained to just this room," Chris says.

"For now," I laugh.

"Maybe this will help push you to get it done and get a certain monkey named Amber Lynn off your back."

"A rather big monkey, don't you think? I think I will get up and go to the gym in the morning. It will help clear my head before my meeting."

"It can't hurt," Chris adds.

FIFTEEN

As I walk into the door of the gym, I'm caught off guard. The building is dark inside. I touch my face to make sure my sunglasses are off. The row of TVs on the wall are all shut off as well as the overhead music. The girl behind the counter informs me that the power is off but I can still work out, just no weightlifting. Pointing into the darkness, she informs me that the treadmill and stair climber machines aren't working. With the light from the entrance doors, I can see the shadows of those working out.

Lastly, she advises me to use the light on my cell phone when walking around and especially when entering the locker room to avoid possibly falling over one of the benches.

Armed with the light on my phone, I enter the dark, eerie-feeling locker room. I put my purse and keys in the locker and attach my lock. As I turn to walk out, I bump into someone, dropping my phone.

"I am so sorry. I thought I could do all this in the dark. It's a lot harder than I thought," she laughs.

I pick up my phone and shine the light towards the wall, so she can find a locker.

"Thanks," she says, as I hear her putting her things in the locker.

As I walk towards the exit, I hear her say: "Addy told me you would help me, Beth."

"How do you know Addy?" I ask. With no reply, I begin looking around. "Hello?" I call out.

Shining the light around, I walk over to the bathroom stalls. I bend down checking for feet. A staff member then walks in. I can tell by her voice that she is the same girl I spoke to at the front desk.

"I would strongly advise against taking a shower until the power is back on. We don't want any injuries," she advises.

"I'm not going to take a shower. I am looking for someone. Did you see anyone just walk out?" I ask.

"No, but it's kinda hard to see in the dark," she says sarcastically as she turns and leaves.

I point my phone towards the row of lockers and see my red lock hanging. I then go over to the area where I thought she put her stuff. I begin opening and shutting the lockers one by one. How could she just vanish? How does she know Addy?

Giving up the search, I climb on a bike and begin pedaling. A brief time later, there is a loud noise and rows of lights, TVs, and machines light up as the power is restored. Cheers erupt from the determined who have been exercising in the dark. I choose a treadmill and drape my towel over the side. With the lights now on, I try to look at the other females who are exercising. *This is not helping me clear my mind!* Feeling frustrated, I cut my workout short and go home after having one last look for the girl.

***

"I didn't even get a good workout in because I was trying to look for the girl."

"How do you think she knows Addy?" he asks.

"I haven't a clue," I reply walking upstairs to change.

Chaplain Paul arrives promptly and I introduce him to Chris who is going outside to mow. I pour us each a glass of water before taking a seat at the kitchen table.

He looks around and then comments, "You have a very nice home."

"Thank you, Chaplain Paul."

"You can call me Paul," he interjects.

"Really?"

"My wife does all the time," he says laughing. His humor helps to break the tension and put us both more at ease.

I take a breath and begin our conversation. "I have never had a patient's death affect me like this. I don't know if it's because I was overly tired and sensitive. There has been a lot of tension between Chris and me since the accident. Chris feels I'm not coping well. I told you about seeing Addy in the antique store while taking a bath. It has been happening more often and Chris has even seen her."

"When was the last time you saw her?" he asks.

"A couple of nights ago. Gracie our dog has even seen her!"

He takes a sip of water and looks at me with a grin. "I want you to know that I am not going to judge you on anything that you are sharing with me today or have in the past."

"I would hope that you wouldn't but hearing you say it is a comfort."

"It all sounds so strange I would agree," he says. "When you were sharing with the group at the counseling session, I wanted so badly to share with you what I was going through. I felt you were going through something, Beth, and needed to talk about it."

"When Chris and I went to the grocery store the other day, I saw several of my family members."

"That's nice. I'm always running into people from the hospital or church," he says.

"The family members I am talking about, Paul, are ones that have died. Two of them even talked to me."

"Oh my! What did they say?"

"Basically, that there are angels all around us and I'm not alone.

"Do you mind coming upstairs with me? I would like to show you Addy's room and the dresser where I saw her first in the mirror."

As we walk into the room, Paul begins looking around and sniffing.

"What a cheery room. Is that lilacs I smell?"

"Yes. The lilacs started happening after I first saw her." I begin telling him about looking at the dresser at the antique store and continue through to the incident with the girl at the gym this morning, providing him with a condensed version. "It's here in this room, where I feel her the most."

"It's a beautiful dresser."

I pick up the magazine along with the pictures and papers and we carry them downstairs.

***

Paul clears his throat and begins. "Since the accident, I haven't been sleeping well myself. With great prayer, I have been searching for an answer or message."

"What did you say?" I ask.

"I have been trying to figure out an answer or message," he slowly repeats.

"I'm sorry to interrupt you, it's just so weird you would use the word 'message'."

"I now wake up with a couple of words or an entire Bible verse in my head and get out of bed to write it down so I can further research it when I am fully awake. I will have several verses written down and not remember getting up. This has changed recently."

"How so?" I ask.

"The handwriting has changed, not always looking like mine. I attribute it to being half asleep and so the writing is messier."

"Or," I interject, "you are the medium and someone else is guiding your hand to write the message. Addy told me to sit down with a pencil and paper and let the message come through. She said that the pencil knows the answer and my hand would be guided. I tried it but didn't have any luck. Did you bring any of the stuff you have written down?"

"I did." He opens the folder and carefully removes the pages. "Here we go," fumbling through the pages. "I started writing down the date in the upper right-hand corner after the first several times." Pulling out a sheet, he looks puzzled.

"Apparently, you made a partial grocery list in your sleep too," I laugh.

"I don't remember putting this in there."

Thumbing through the pages, "I see what you are talking about with the handwriting." I skim over the last page.

"These two Bible verses are interesting." I read aloud:

"1 Corinthians 13:12 -- Now we see but a poor reflection as in a mirror; then we shall see face to face. Now I know in part; then I shall know fully, even as I am fully known.

2 Corinthians 4:18 -- So we fix our eyes not on what is seen, but on what is unseen. For what is seen is temporary, but what is unseen is eternal."

I then show him the paper I found in the Bible and the dry-cleaning slip. "Chris and I combed through the Bible looking for verses but didn't have any luck," I add.

Looking at the numbers from the Bible verses and the numbers on the papers, my eyes grow wide as I realize the correlation.

"Wow!" I exclaim. "I first saw her in a mirror and then she started appearing face to face and now it's here in the Bible."

"I also need to share with you, Beth," Paul says. I can see Paul is trying to find the right words. "My wife also asked that I seek counseling. I can honestly say that in all the years of my career as a person of faith and a follower of Christ, I have never had anything grip me so hard. I can't sleep and when I do, I wake up to dreams where a girl is asking me to help her. What is even weirder is it looks like the girl from the accident."

Placing my hand on his, I say, "You're not crazy, I can assure you. The vision or girl in the dream as you call it, is Addy. The picture in the frame is a picture of her." I remove her picture and show him what's written on the back. "Addy D. 1912". "We found the frame in the dresser and the picture appeared on its own the next day."

"What are the other pictures?" he asks.

I hand him the pictures to look at. "This one is a mystery. I had a dream while we were staying at the Gate House Inn, that I found an album with this same picture inside."

He turns it over and reads aloud: "To my best friend Adeline, Love Milda."

"Isn't the Gate House Inn a neat place," he interjects, "My wife really likes it there too."

"The third picture I found while looking through a box of old family photos says, 'Milda, to my best friend, Adeline'."

"Who is Milda?"

"Actually, I have an Aunt Milda who went by 'Millie'. Chris and I think somehow Addy and Millie are connected."

"Do you think they were friends?" he asks.

"Chris said the exact same thing. I also found a slip of paper with numbers written on it sticking out of the Bible in our room at the Inn. The numbers on the paper match the number that I have been getting missed calls from. The caller never leaves a message. We tried calling back the number and got a weird recording. It said, 'Your call cannot be completed, AD 1912'. There have been several clues to the meaning of 'AD 1912'.

"When we got home, I found the paper sticking out of a pocket of our suitcase and the picture in my jewelry case. Chris thought I stole them. I had to convince him that I wasn't a clepto! Most recently, I found a magazine at work with Addy's name on it and the strange numbers."

Paul looks at me and sighs, "Why us, Beth?"

"I was hoping you would have an answer."

"I have been involved with helping families and friends grieve their loved ones, and deal with loss and hardships in the Church as well as in the hospital, but this one is so different. I don't want you to think that I am holding out on you but…" Our conversation is halted by the phone ringing.

As I answer, the familiar voice on the other end startles me.

"Hi Beth, it's Pastor Dave. You aren't going to believe this, but I had a dream about you and thought I might need to call you. Is everything all right with you, Chris, and the family?" We met Pastor Dave when Chris and I took classes before getting married. We had an immediate connection with him and asked him to perform the ceremony when we got married. He is the lead Pastor at the Church now.

My mouth drops as I look around the room. "Well," I hesitate… "there has been a lot going on. Right now, I would like to ask that you just keep us in your prayers and we will see you at Church on Sunday."

"I will certainly do that, and you be sure to let me know if anything changes."

"Thank you." *God certainly moves in mysterious ways,* I affirm.

I take a seat back at the table and return to my conversation with Paul. "Why would I think you were holding out on me?"

"Did you see the newspaper article yesterday about the accident victim?" asks Paul.

"Yes, I shared the paper at work with the staff."

"There is more than what the paper is saying. I contacted the editor at the newspaper and was given the girl's employer's name and called them. As it turns out, 'Addy' as you call her had been working at the nursing home as a care assistant for several years."

"Which one?"

"Bryansford," he answers.

"They are supposed to be one of the best in town. Does the nursing home know anything about her family?"

"Well, that is one of the reasons why I wanted to meet with you. She has a family member in the nursing home where she worked and according to the director at the facility, it is her only next of kin. 'Addy' got a job there so she could be closer to them."

"I hope we start to get some answers."

"The director didn't want to give out too much information over the phone. I have set up a meeting with her for Tuesday at 1:00 p.m. Would you go with me, Beth?"

"I will add it to my calendar."

He looks down at his watch. "I didn't realize it was this late."

Chris walks in to get a drink of water. "How are things going?" he asks.

"Things are starting to look up I would have to say, wouldn't you Paul?" I smile and ask Paul.

"Yes, I would," he smiles.

"I'm glad to hear that. I want my Beth back," says Chris.

"You aren't alone. My wife, Susie, feels the same way," adds Paul.

Chris nods and says, "Well, I have the yard done, so I'm going to head upstairs and take a shower. Nice meeting you and I hope this all gets resolved real soon."

Paul replies, "Nice meeting you as well, Chris, and I will do everything in my power to help Beth deliver Addy's message."

Chris thinks to himself as he walks upstairs, I didn't expect to hear such a blunt statement from Paul.

Paul then gathers his papers. "I will see you at work on Monday and I will come by and pick you up at 12:45 p.m. on Tuesday."

"That sounds perfect," I respond.

"See you then," Paul says and waves, walking out to his car.

As I close the door. Chris walks in refreshed and smelling amazing. "How about grabbing some lunch?" he asks.

"Great! I know just the place and I will treat you to a slice of Marie's famous pie," I offer.

"Is that where the peach pie came from?"

"It is."

"Hot diggity dog," he says clapping his hands.

In the car, I lean over and kiss him. "The black clouds are moving, and the sun is peeking through!" I proclaim, putting on my sunglasses.

***

We choose a booth by the window. Chris comments on the quaintness of the diner, as he looks at the shelves above the lunch counter lined with antiques and collectibles. Our waitress comes over to the table with water and menus and without making eye contact, begins to rattle off the daily specials. She stops and then nudges me on the arm.

"How are you?" asks the waitress. "You know I have been thinking about you ever since you were in. You looked so sad that day."

Chris watches as our conversation goes back and forth then asks, "Do you two know each other."

"Nah," the waitress laughs. "I just helped make her a day a little sweeter with a piece of Marie's pie, that's all." She extends her hand to Chris and says, "I'm Milda, but people call me Millie."

Chris shakes her hand and watches as my mouth drops.

"I had an Aunt named 'Milda'. What a quinky dink," I laugh.

"You know my sister, Mae, used to say that."

"Your sister 'Mae'?"

She looks up and smiles. "Boy, I miss her. But I know I will see her again someday. She's gonna be at Heaven's gates waiting to take my hand. I haven't thought about her in days," she says tapping her pen against her order pad. "You really miss the ones that are gone," her voice trails off. "You two look over the menu and I will be back in a couple of minutes."

"Did you hear what she said?" I ask Chris.

"Which time," he says studying the menu. "She's not one that is at a loss for words."

"Her sister is named 'Mae' like my aunt."

"That's a coincidence," he says. "You must have made quite an impression for her to remember you."

"Lunch with Amber Lynn was disastrous and Millie made me feel better with her kindness. Let's decide so we can order. My stomach is asking what the holdup is."

"I am going to try the blue plate special. What about you?" he asks.

"I am going to have the child's portion of the blue plate special." Millie returns with our drinks and takes our order. "Don't forget to save room for some of Marie's pie."

"We could split a piece," I suggest to Chris.

"Yea, I suppose we could," Chris frowns.

"Well since you have been such a good boy, you can get your own and I will get mine. Whatever we don't eat, we can take home for later."

"Perfect," he says, straightening up in his seat, smiling.

While eating, I discuss my conversation with Paul. I notice Chris tries inconspicuously to let out his belt, as I try not to laugh. Looking over the dessert menu, I choose fresh strawberry pie with whipped cream and Chris chooses chocolate cream pie.

"Can you make them to go please?" I ask Millie. I take my fork and spear a large strawberry with whipped cream and take a bite. "Oh my gosh, this is amazing," I gush. Several minutes later, I close my box. "I will save the rest for later."

"Not me," Chris replies, licking off the fork after scraping the last bits from inside the container. Wiping his face with his napkin, he looks quite content. Millie walks over to the table and turns around and shouts over to Marie at a nearby table.

"He finished it all. I owe you five dollars, Marie," she chuckles.

"It's always the men that can eat it all," Marie grins.

Content with our full tummies. "Where to now? Chris asks.

"Do you mind going to Hobby Town and walking around? I need to get some project ideas for the craft bazaar."

"I'm all for you getting your mind on something other than Addy."

SIXTEEN

At Hobby Town, Chris grabs a shopping cart while I glance through their flyer. As I walk down the aisles, I look at the various categories while reading the overhead signage displaying the aisles. Stopping to look at the endcap displays I pray to channel my creative mojo. Time is running out, in more ways than one.

Chris stops the cart and breaks the silence when he asks, "What exactly are you looking for?"

"I'm not sure. Right now, I only know that I am going to make flower wreaths, to use up all the frames I have. I want to use a lot of the things I already have."

As I walk towards the floral department, Chris says, "Don't you have enough flowers already?"

Giving him an irritated look, he abandons the cart and goes looking around. Picking out a couple different varieties, I hold them together in one hand while studying them from different angles. Deciding I need to concentrate on filler items for the arrangement, I begin browsing through various stems of berries and leaves. Hearing a familiar voice call my name, I turn to see Carolyn standing with a shopping basket on her arm. Carolyn is one of the ladies with the craft bazaar. She is very tight with Amber Lynn. "Oh, my poor dear! How are you feeling?" She says touching my arm.

"I'm okay. Why?" I respond.

"You've missed all of the bazaar meetings."

"I was never informed of any."

"Some of us questioned where you were. Amber Lynn told us you were seeing dead people and on the verge of a breakdown."

"She did?" I can feel the color leaving my face, as I begin to feel cold. I turn away for a moment to try to gain my composure. After several seconds, "I'm fine," I tell her smiling. "Would you be a dear and let everyone else know that as well?" I can tell she is watching my facial expressions and body language like a hawk, to report back to Amber Lynn and the others. "Chris is here with me, so I need to catch up to him. It was nice to see you, Carolyn."

"You too," she says walking away smugly.

After she leaves, I stand and try to collect my thoughts. I am not going to let her or Amber Lynn get the better of me. I am stronger than that. I feel like I am back in high school and dealing with mean girls. Why is it bullies don't grow up, they just move to a different level playing field? It the same way with cliques!

As I catch up with Chris, I am surprised to find him looking at paint by number sets. "I've always wanted to finish one of these," says Chris. Looking at his face, I can tell he is serious. Going through the selection on the shelf, he moves them around, studying all the choices.

"If you really want one, get one," I reply.

"I don't want one. I just said I would like to finish one. I got one as a kid for Christmas and never finished it. I accidentally used the wrong sequence of colors for the numbers, and it didn't look right so I never finished it. Mom got mad and never bought another one. She knew the chances were slim of me finishing a second one."

"You could break the cycle and give it to her for Christmas. I think it would be kinda cute."

"Really? I like that idea, but I don't think I want to wait that long to give it to her."

"I just thought it would give you plenty of time to complete it," laughing at what I just said.

"I'm a whole lot older now," he says in a serious tone. "I should be able to knock this out in a couple of hours."

"Well then, how about shooting for her birthday which is in a couple of months?"

"Now you're talking," smiling like a little kid on Christmas morning. "Do you like the Mona Lisa, the boat, the dog, horse, or kittens?"

"Hmm," looking them over. "I am rather partial to the dog, but you get whichever one you want. I'm sure she will like any of them."

"Okay, in that case, I will get the boat. Maybe the folks will want to hang it in the living room."

I just got a glimpse of what you were like when you were 10 years old, I think to myself. I offer to take the shopping cart so he can have his hands free and look.

"I'm glad you suggested coming here," he says.

"I know you are," wondering what else was in his pie.

While looking through a bin of craft supplies, Chris walks up and tries to nonchalantly place several items into the cart. Turning to see what is up, I ask, "Okay mister, now what? A wood burning kit, a moccasin kit, and a pottery wheel with another paint by number kit. Are all of these for you or is there a toy drive I didn't know about?" I ask.

"They're for me," Chris answers quietly.

"Chris, when are you going to have time for all these crafts? Who is the moccasin kit for?"

"I thought I would make them for my dad since I was making something for Mom."

I pick up the box to look at it closer. "Are these even the right size for your dad to wear? You don't want them to be a little kid's size and then he can't wear them. Honey, I hate to break it to you, but these go up to a kid size thirteen shoe, not men's," handing him back the box. "Who's the extra paint by number kit for? Are you making them both for your mom?"

"No, I was going to do one for our house, maybe our living room. I got the dog one you liked."

"That would be nice. And the wood burning set?"

"Well, you see, there is a story behind that. My brother Andy got one for Christmas one year and he left it plugged in and walked away. I picked it up and burnt my finger. I ended up dropping it which caused a burn mark on the carpet. Mom was madder than a hornet at us. We were told not to use it without supervision, but we were kids and accidents happen. Plus, we both felt we were supervising each other."

"So now since you are older you are going to try it for yourself?"

"I bought a package of wood spoons to try it on."

"Really? Hmm, that would be cool if you did designs or pictures."

"Maybe you could sell them at the craft bazaar or add them to one of your crafts?"

"You have me thinking now. I'm going to go look at the ribbon."

"I'll go put the moccasin kit back," he says.

"Okay," steering the cart down the aisle. *I never did ask him if there was story behind the pottery wheel.*

Thirty minutes later, I have my project ideas for the bazaar with the supplies needed in the cart. Chris walks up and I am excited to share my news. He stands holding something at his side. "Which is it now?" I tease, "an edible bug maker machine, or another paint set?"

"I found a moccasin kit for adults!"

"I'm sure your dad will be glad you thought of him. I'm ready to go when you are," looking over my project list.

Standing in line, he asks, "Are you going to make apple dumplings again this year with the cinnamon bundles for the bazaar?"

"Just the cinnamon bundles because I'm adding the banana bread. I had to cut the dumplings out."

"Really?"

"Don't sound so disappointed."

"The guys at work have already been asking me when you are going to have them and if they can preorder this year."

"You're kidding, right? I can't this year, so you will have to let them know."

"Okay, but there are going to be a lot of disappointed guys."

"Don't do this, please. I have so much on me all ready and it has been such a nice day."

Looking shocked by my plea, "You know you will have help."

"As it is, I'm going to have to enlist help from my mom and dad again. You will need to be ready to roll up your sleeves too. Last year was a lot!"

While we wait in line, Chris leaves to return the pottery wheel after telling me it doesn't look all that fun.

"You know if you were interested in taking a pottery class, they have them for adults. We could take one together," I suggest.

"Maybe someday," he says.

Once at the checkout, I begin to unload the cart and watch as the price scans onto the screen. The cashier, a young teen-age girl with braces, picks up one of the paint sets and examines the picture. She offers, "My little brother got one of these and did the wrong color and it looked horrible. He never did finish it."

I watch Chris' reaction out of the corner of my eye. He clears his throat and says, "That's too bad. Maybe when he is older you can get him another one so that he can try it again."

"Maybe for his 30th birthday," the clerk says sarcastically and laughs.

"Well, any age would probably be fun," he spouts back.

As we put the bags in the car, Chris asks, "Did you happen to see her name on her badge?"

" 'Blessing', I think her tag said," I answer.

"She wasn't very nice."

"She's just a kid, so don't let what she said bother you. You're going to finish yours this time," patting his arm.

"I just hope someday her brother gets one and can complete it."

"There's more to you wanting to finish the paint set. I think it's bothered you that your parents spent the money, and that you upset your mother. You feel like you let her down and want another chance to please her. You need to finish it for yourself first and in doing so, it will make her happy. As far as the other crafts, spread your wings, try new things, make life an adventure and have a great ride."

He turns and looks at me. "When did you get your PhD in psychology?"

"Nope, no PhD but I saw it on a greeting card commercial. Am I right though?"

"Maybe," scrunching up his face.

" 'Blessing', huh? It's going to be a blessing if I get everything done," I tell Chris.

***

I dump out the bags onto the table in my craft room while Chris looks at his paint sets.

"I think I will give it to her early and not wait for her birthday," Chris says.

"It's totally up to you. When do you think you are going to start it?" I ask.

"Maybe tomorrow or the next day. I'm not sure."

"I would like to see what you can do with the wood burning kit and the wooden spoons."

"I'll put the paints on the back burner then and see what I can do with the spoons."

"I appreciate it. If they don't work out, I'll have to go to plan B. I didn't tell you that I ran into Carolyn at the craft store."

"Who is Carolyn?"

"One of Amber Lynn's puppets. She told me that Amber Lynn told her and a bunch of people at a planning meeting for the bazaar that I was seeing dead people and was on the verge of a nervous breakdown."

"Wow! Amber Lynn just doesn't know when to quit."

"That's for sure!" I say sadly. "I don't feel like starting a project tonight. Let's go downstairs and raid the refrigerator," I suggest.

SEVENTEEN

As I walk downstairs, Chris walks in from the garage blowing on a glowing charred ember that resembles a torch.

"Nice torch. Are you leading the search party for Frankenstein?" I ask.

"Very funny, this is going to take more practice than I thought, not to mention spoons," Chris says as he blows some more on the glowing wooden spoon.

"Put that in the sink and run some water over it. We don't need to catch anything on fire."

"Or make anything else look like this," he adds holding up the wet spoon.

"Precisely."

"I thought maybe I could get one done before church this morning, but the wood burning pen gets hotter than you think."

"I can see that," scrunching up my nose from the smell of the burning wood. Taking the spoon out from underneath the running water, I inspect the charred remains. "I am going to fix a piece of toast. Do you want one?"

"Sure," he says drying his hands.

"Are you going to bury that later or are there more?"

He blows out his cheeks and rubs his neck.

"There may be a few more. What do you think of the idea of asking your folks out for dinner? That way you wouldn't have to worry about fixing anything and we could work right up to the time they come over. I could ask your dad for suggestions on working with the wooden spoons."

"Sounds great. I need to get as much done as possible today."

"I am going to head back out to the garage and clean things up and then get ready. We can ask them when we see them at church."

"You're going to clean up the sink before you go back out to the garage, aren't you?"

"Yes dear," tearing off sheets of paper toweling.

***

Once home from church, I change into something comfortable and clap my hands, Operation craft bazaar, I announce. I plug in the glue gun and set up shop. I begin with assembling the wreaths, then start snipping, and cutting flowers and leaves and gluing them onto the frame. Satisfied with how it looks, I move onto the next one. After having three done, I stand up to stretch.

Chris walks in and gasps, "Wow!"

"It's a mess, I know," I say. There are twice as many flower parts and flowers on the floor as there are on the table and bed.

"You have gotten a lot done," he says looking at the wreaths lying on the bed.

"They just need a bow and then they are done. I am trying to do them like an assembly line," as I talk with my hands. "You put all the flowers on, then add the finishing touches, and then the bow, last."

Chris bends over to pick up a stray flower and tosses it onto the table. "Are you keeping Mommy company?" Chris says as he bends over to scratch behind Gracie's ears.

"She's doing an excellent job."

"Do you want anything from downstairs?"

"Something to drink would be great."

Chris returns with apple slices and peanut butter and a glass of iced tea. "How many wreaths are you planning to make?"

"I have 6 done and plan on doing 10-12. Remind me to ask Mom if she wants to sell any jewelry she's made."

"Will do, but remind me if I don't, okay?" Chris smirks as he walks out.

I can hear the faint tinkling sound from my wind chimes on the front porch. I walk over to open up the window as a gentle breeze stirs. Standing in front of the window, I take in a deep breath as I close my eyes and concentrate on the music from the chimes. My concentration is broken when I hear the words, "the message," in a gloomy tone.

Caught off guard, I turn around bumping the table and knocking the glue gun onto the floor. I quickly reach for it, carelessly touching the tip and burning my finger. I blow over the burned finger which feels like it has its own heartbeat. I carefully peel off the hot glue and in doing so break the blister that has formed. I get the first aid kit out of the hall closet and open up a band-aid.

"What happened?" asks Chris. "I heard something fall."

"I knocked over the glue gun and burnt my finger," I admit. "Chris, I heard a voice say, " 'the message'." He hands me my glass to take a drink. "I am trying to stay afloat myself," comparing myself to the ice floating in the glass.

"Are you talking to the ice cubes?"

"No, just making a statement."

"I pray this all comes to light very soon," Chris says.

"Me too!" as I set my glass down and continue with the wreaths.

"Are we going to discuss that you were talking to ice cubes?"

"Nope!"

"I will go back downstairs then."

As he heads out the door, "I'm sorry Chris."

"I know," he says.

I take a minute to tidy my work area and I lighten my mood by picking up stray pieces of wire and flowers. With just a few wreaths left to make, I push through.

An hour goes by and Chris walks into the room with his hands behind his back. "Shut your eyes and no peeking. Now hold out your hands," he tells me.

I cautiously extend my hands as he deposits something in them.

"Okay, now open them," he commands.

I open my eyes and I can't believe my eyes as I look at two wooden spoons reading "More sprinkles please!"

"I love them!"

"I am proud of them," he gushes.

"Have you made any others?" I ask.

He quickly changes the subject.

"Wow, you have been going like gangbusters in here. Do you have them all done now?"

"You didn't answer my question Chris. What about the spoons?"

"The good news is, I am getting closer. They are starting to look like spoons. The bad news is, I called and asked your Dad to pick up spoons on his way over. We can work until it's time to go out for dinner."

Hearing a yell from downstairs, "That's them now," Chris says walking downstairs.

As I walk into the kitchen, I see Dad is kneeling, getting kisses from Gracie. "Hi, Dad," leaning over and kissing him as he stands up.

"How's my girl?" giving me a hug.

"A busy one," I reply. "Where's Mom?"

"She's outside admiring your flowers."

Just then Mom walks in and sets her purse down. "Beth your flowers are just beautiful. I had to take a closer look," Mom says.

"Do you need a vase for that one?" pointing to her hand, I ask. Reaching under the cabinet, I retrieve a small jelly jar and fill it with water. I set it on the counter beside Mom as she carefully snips the flower and places it in the jar.

"Smell it. It's just wonderful," Mom grins.

Chris then interjects, "Here are the spoons. These are what I have so far," handing them to Dad to inspect. Dad adjusts his glasses and examines them closely.

"Your iron is still too hot. They can be tricky to work with. If you don't watch out, you can end up with a charred kindling," says Dad.

Chris clears his throat as he ushers Dad to the garage, smirking as he walks past. Trying to hold my composure, in a low tone, I hear Chris say, "I'll show you my pile of trials and errors."

Once the men retreat to the garage, Mom turns and looks at me. "Are you feeling any more relaxed?" she asks. "You still look so tired."

I smile at her and say, "I have made some good headway with the bazaar items. The wreaths are all done now, I just need to start on some flower arrangements."

"Show me what you have gotten done."

As we walk into the room, I can tell by the look on her face that she's caught off guard. "It's like a flower shop blew up or something," Mom says.

"I think I have heard that a couple of times now," I answer with a smirk.

"It's a good thing you have a big bed in here!" She looks at all the different wreaths. "I especially like these two," she says, holding them up.

"You've got to be kidding," I laugh. "Those were the last two I did and didn't care anymore. I just wanted them done."

"You are much too hard on yourself. Did you have to buy very many flowers?"

"I only picked up a few the other day. The majority I had tucked in bins under the bed."

She grabs a chair and for the next couple of hours we assemble a variety of flower arrangements and nosegays.

"We will have them all done once the bows are made and placed," I announce.

Hearing voices coming up the stairs, Mom turns and looks at the doorway in anticipation and she places two more finished arrangements on the bed.

Just then the bodies matching the voices enter the room.

"You two are looking quite cheeky," I chuckle.

"I would have to agree," Mom says.

Chris and Dad hand us each a spoon to inspect and wait for our reactions.

"The design is great!" I smile.

"I second that," Mom adds.

"Your Dad is a genius, Beth!" says Chris. "He got the idea to outline the design first and then we dialed back the temperature along with the pressure exerted on the wood."

Beth adds, "I could tie the spoon onto the loaf of banana bread with raffia. I am planning on twelve loaves of bread so I will need twelve spoons. If I can use these two then you only have ten more to make. I don't want to start making the raffia ties until the flowers are done. I want one project completely done before starting another to try and keep organized."

Mom offers, "If you haven't started baking the banana bread, could I do that for you? Your dad can help me, and it would be less on your plate."

"I like the sound of that," I say with a sigh of relief.

"Me too," Chris says.

"I have the bananas in the freezer that I was going to use. I will pull them out and give them to you along with my loaf pans before you go home tonight. That would really put me ahead of the game if you wouldn't mind."

Chris and Dad stand there looking at each other.

"What do you think of the color of the wood, Dad?" Chris says in a high voice, as he puts his hand on his hip.

"It's just so beautiful, Christopher," Dad says matching Chris' high voice. "They bring tears to my eyes!" pulling out his hanky and pretending to wipe his tears.

"You guys think you are hilarious. We both said they're great. Did you not hear us?"

"I think the bazaar is going to do better than last year's and mainly because of the spoons made by yours truly," Chris says pointing to himself.

He catches Dad giving him the snake eye, and quickly corrects himself. "By both of us."

"Go with any design or saying you want. I just need 12 in the end. You have full carte blanche," I reassure them.

"What time is it anyway?" Mom asks looking at her watch. "My watch shows 1:30 p.m."

"Your watch must have stopped Dad tells her, "It's already 4:30 p.m."

"The day has flown by. I started working on this right after church," I say, standing up to stretch.

"We have a mess to clean up in the garage before going to dinner," Chris says.

"There are only a few more bows to add before the arrangements are done. We will tidy up in here and then we can all go out for a nice dinner," I add.

"Roger," Chris says as he stands at attention and salutes, almost knocking himself out in the process before leaving the room.

"Careful, goofy," I warn.

While I begin placing the finished flower arrangements in a large box, Mom finishes the task of placing the bows in the arrangements. "It's been fun getting to do something with you and talk," says Mom.

"Thanks Momma, I have enjoyed it too. Eventually, all the finished projects will be staged in the dining room before loading them into the car for transport. I just don't want the mess downstairs yet. I have a busy work week and I don't want to stress myself out with a mess in every room."

"I understand. The apple didn't fall far from the tree, you know," she says smiling.

"Did you want to make any jewelry to sell this year?" I ask Mom.

"I have a few pieces I have been working on that I could sell."

I unplug the glue gun and walk downstairs as Mom follows me into the kitchen. We meet the guys in the kitchen who have come in to wash up.

***

"I am going to run upstairs and get the glasses we were using," Mom says. Walking back into the craft room, she looks around and sighs. Beth isn't going to want to leave this mess, I just know it. She begins picking up stray flower petals and stems along with pieces of ribbon and wire that have gone astray. While leaning over she hears a whisper near her ear, "Ask about the message."

She snaps upright and looks around. "Who said that?" She does her best to ignore it while she continues picking up the remaining scraps and dumps them in the wastebasket. Wrapping the cord up around the glue gun, she tidies up the stuff on the table. Reaching over she grabs the drinking glasses off the table. When she begins to take a step, she feels a cool breeze on the back of her neck and hears again, "Ask about the message."

Hearing a noise from the other side of the room, she cautiously walks around to the other side of the bed, and says, "Oh, it's you, Gracie. You scared Grammy. I didn't know you were up here." Leaning down to pet her, she notices a piece of paper stuck under her paw. "What do you have, girl?" She carefully peels it off and reads it. One side is blank while the other side has the word "sister" written on it. I wonder what this is for, she asks herself.

As she walks into the hallway to go downstairs, she hears a ringing. Searching to locate where it is coming from, she walks into the guest room. She cautiously walks over to the black antique phone sitting on the desk, as it rings loudly. Gingerly lifting the receiver from its cradle, she listens and then says, "hello."

On the other end, she hears a female voice ask, "Addy?"

"Hello," Mother repeats. Not hearing anything else, she picks up the phone and looks underneath. "It's not even plugged into the wall," she says aloud. "There isn't anyway someone could be calling." She slams down the receiver, causing the phone to ring. On the verge of tears, she quickly walks downstairs.

Walking into the kitchen, she is clearly rattled. "Where are the glasses?" I ask.

"Oh, I forgot them," she says wringing her hands.

"Is something wrong?"

"I was upstairs tidying the craft room for you, and I checked to make sure the glue gun was unplugged. I was going to bring down the glasses when something happened. Could I have a drink of water please?"

As she takes a sip, I see that her hands are noticeably shaking. "Mom, what is it?" I grab her arm and encourage her to sit down.

"I heard a voice. It said, 'ask about the message', not once but twice."

My eyes widen as I realize what she has just said. Chris and Dad walk in and sense something is wrong.

"Everything okay?" Chris asks, looking over at me.

"Sweetheart," Dad says, walking over and touching Mom's arm. "Are you okay?"

"I'm okay," she replies wearily. "Just a little startled," running her fingers through her hair.

Tears begin to form as I look at Mom, who is visibly shaken. My dad looks at me with concern.

"How do I begin?" looking at Chris. I pull out a chair and bury my head in my hands. Chris walks over and pats my back. The dam breaks as tears flow down my cheeks, with my parents totally confused. Chris hands me a tissue to wipe my tears.

"It was Addy," I announce. "The girl that was in the accident that came to the ER and died. I have been seeing her since the accident happened and recently Chris has even seen her."

"Chris had told us that you were dealing with something from work," Dad says.

Looking into my parents' faces, I question, "He never told you I was seeing or hearing things?"

Mom begins patting the table and playing with her tissue, looking down at the table. "He might have mentioned it," looking over at Dad for some input to get her out of the hot seat.

"It doesn't really matter anymore," I tell them.

"But it does matter Beth! Things are going to be cleared up very soon. You mustn't lose sight of that. Remember your meeting with Chaplain Paul yesterday? You are going to the nursing home Tuesday to talk with the girl's employer and family member," Chris says.

"I have a question for you both," Mom quietly asks. "Has the old black phone you have on the desk ever rung before?"

Chris and I look at each other blankly, and then back at her.

"The one in the guest room?" I question.

Embarrassed by her question, Mom now stares back at the three sets of eyes watching her. She sits up straight in her chair and explains. "Before coming downstairs, I heard a ringing. It turns out it was the old phone. I answered it," pausing as she watches our expressions.

"Yeah, then what," we say in unison.

"There was a female voice on the other end that asked for Addy. Then I didn't hear anything else."

"Shut the front door!" Chris says as he stands up, almost knocking over his chair. Dad sits with a confused look on his face as he looks over at Mom. She continues to play with something in her hand.

"I realize this doesn't make any sense because I checked and the cord isn't even attached to the phone," says Mom.

"Wow, this is some trip to crazy town and it's nice to know I'm not the only one on the bus!" I say in disbelief.

"I found this paper stuck under Gracie's paw when I was picking things up off the floor," Mom says.

Chris reaches for it and slowly reads aloud, "Sister." He flips it over to examine the other side. "It's the only word written on it. What do you suppose it means?" he asks.

Dad who has been quiet up to now says, "Maybe it was meant for you to find it."

"I have no idea where it came from. I cleaned up the floor earlier this afternoon and never saw it," I sigh.

"With it stuck to Gracie's foot it makes her the messenger, so to speak," Dad says.

I am caught off guard by Dad's choice of words, with him using the phrase "the messenger". It makes me think back to a previous conversation with Addy when she said, "Gracie knows the message". I swallow hard as I wonder to myself what's next.

Chris glances over at the clock and says, "It's already 5:30 p.m."

"I think I have lost my appetite," I say quietly.

"What if we order takeout? Your dad can go pick up a pizza or whatever else sounds good," Mom suggests.

"Dad and I will go," Chris says. "Dinner is on us tonight."

"I will stay and keep Beth company," Mom says. "Why don't you go upstairs, wash your face and put on some lipstick and then come back down when you're ready."

"Just order whatever you guys feel like. Anything is fine," I tell them walking out of the room to go upstairs.

"Is pizza okay with you, Mother?" Dad asks.

"Fine, fine," she waves. "I will keep her company while you guys go, just don't get lost or sidetracked."

"Yes, ma'am," Chris replies, "I will keep my eye on him."

Dad then makes the gestures that he will keep an eye on Chris as well. Mom shakes her head and shuts the door after them.

I feel just the way I look, exhausted, I think to myself, staring back at the mirror. Trying to pinch some color into my cheeks, I put on some lipstick and brush my hair. Chris is right, things are going to be cleared up very soon. Looking back up into the mirror, I see Addy standing behind me and I feel something touch my shoulder. "I am growing very weary, Addy," I say to the ghostly figure of Addy. She nods then slowly fades away. I take a deep breath and walk downstairs.

Mom has a pitcher of iced tea and glasses set up for us on the patio. "I thought sitting out here would give us some fresh air."

"I'm okay. Gracie, come on girl," I say as I pat against my leg.

"Dogs can sense when something is wrong, or someone is sad. I know our Sadie girl does," says Mom. Hearing voices, Mom stands up. "They must be back."

Chris walks out with paper plates and napkins, stacked on top of the pizza box.

"That smells good," Mom says, opening up the box. Dad hands out the napkins as Mom dishes up the pizza. Once everyone has their plate and is eating, Chris breaks the silence. "It's been a very interesting `day."

Dad wipes his mouth and says, "You may have gotten more accomplished than you think, Beth."

As I look around at their faces, I feel so much love and support. This is when I know everything is going to be okay and soon.

Mom and Dad leave shortly after dinner. Chris offers to run a bath for me and I quickly accept.

Chris turns on the water and adjusts the temperature, while I pin up my hair. Reading the box of bath salts, he questions himself, how much do I add for mildly stressed compared to over the top stressed? Deciding on the latter, he adds more.

Seconds later, he announces in an official voice, "Madam your bath is ready for you," and bows.

"You're a nut," I laugh.

"Yeah, but a good nut," he grins.

EIGHTEEN

Chris says, peeking his head into the doorway of the craft room, "Are you watching the time?"

"Yes. I'm wearing my robe over my uniform, so I don't get anything on it. I am just tweaking the wreaths," replies Beth.

"I'm glad to see you divert your energy from Addy to the craft bazaar. I'm leaving early to pick up donuts for a meeting."

"Well, eat one for me."

"I will and maybe even two."

As I start to walk out of the room, I hear a noise. Walking over to the window, I check to see if it's Chris coming back for something. Walking down the hall, I stop in the doorway of Addy's room and hold my breath as I listen. Looking at the flower on the dresser, several petals have fallen. "Hello Addy," I say while looking at my reflection in the mirror. A white haze then appears as her image comes through.

"Hello," she answers.

"I'm trying to help you, but I've got so much going on."

"Time is precious -- you see that every day. You need to know that when all the petals are gone from the flower, it will be too late for you to deliver the message."

"There are just a couple that have fallen so far," opening up my hand and showing them to her. She nods, and as I hear the clock downstairs chime, I turn away only to see her image fade away.

***

Thankfully, the day was calm at the hospital and several of us could talk in between patients. My phone rings while I am walking to my car. It's Amber Lynn again. Ugh, I really don't want to answer it.

"Hi." I answer guarded.

"I wanted to check with you about the bazaar and tell you I have already added your name to the flyer," says Amber Lynn.

"Flyer?"

"This year, I am having flyers printed that will be placed in the church bulletin and circulated around to area businesses and schools. I think it will help drum up business and let people know what they can expect this year. Since you've been preoccupied, I went ahead and put you down for your usual. So - everybody knows they can expect your cinnamon rolls and apple dumplings. You can thank me later."

"You what?" Holding the phone tightly to my head, I put a finger in my other ear, blocking out the noise from the street. "They're not cinnamon rolls, they're bundles. I'm only doing them this year and not the dumplings. I have decided to make banana bread this year in place of them."

"Well, since you never contacted me to get your changes approved, you need to think again. It's listed on the flyer and people will be counting on them."

At a loss for words, I'm silent.

"Are you still having your issue?" asks Amber Lynn.

My mouth drops open as I feel the heat in my cheeks. "Amber Lynn why haven't I been told about any of the bazaar meetings? I ran into Carolyn and she told me someone asked why I wasn't there. You told everyone that I was seeing dead people and having a nervous breakdown," I say in a shaky voice.

"I simply stated a fact. You yourself told me you were seeing a dead girl. And if you ask anybody, they will agree you're having a nervous breakdown. I was protecting everybody from you."

"Protecting everybody?" I yell. "What are you talking about?"

"You never know when people are going to go crazy. You hear it on the news all the time."

"I admit I have been preoccupied, but that's no reason to deliberately exclude me."

"Well since you weren't at any of the meetings, I will update you on a few things. Only a portion of the crafters' entrance fee will be donated to the Make-A-Wish foundation. The other part of the entrance fee will be put towards the use of the church and advertising. We won't be collecting a percentage of everyone's sales for donation like we have in the past."

"How is that going to help increase the amount of money donated? The bazaar has always been done to help a charity and has been a successful one."

"Get with the times Beth! Change is good and were doing it like Penelope did."

"Who is Penelope?" I ask.

"She is the highly respected chairperson of the Christmas Shop craft bazaar. She tripled her total sales and they even passed around a bucket at the end of the day adding to their total."

"So, this has gone from giving to charity to seeing who can raise the most and outdo the other! How would someone even find out how much each bazaar raised?" After the words are out of my mouth, I can't believe I said them.

Immediately she asks, "What did you just say? Word gets around and I would know!"

I'm not going to play her game, I think to myself. I need to keep thinking about the real reason behind the bazaar and stay grounded. "I need to go, Amber Lynn," and quickly hang up without saying bye.

***

I take a seat in the family room and turn on the TV. "We're going to sit here until Daddy comes home, Gracie." Tenderly, I play with her ears. She sighs deeply, fully content. *Why is Amber Lynn so mean, Gracie?*

The peacefulness is broken when the phone rings. "Hello," I answer.

"Well, hello there. You have been chosen to receive a free set of ...," says an unidentified voice.

I hang up the phone, disgusted. Sales calls! Not today friend. Not two seconds later, the phone rings again. Hesitantly I pick up the receiver, and say, "Hello."

"Don't hang up," I hear on the other end, "it's me," says a familiar voice.

"Not funny, Christopher! You know how I feel about solicitors."

"I know, I'm sorry. I was just trying to be funny, and it backfired," apologizes Chris.

"Big time!"

"What's for dinner?" he asks.

"I don't know. Gracie and I are sitting on the couch talking about it."

"I'm anxious to hear what ideas she comes up with."

"No, I mean I was talking to her about it."

"I know what you mean. Wow, you're really in a bad mood. Did something happen at work?"

"Amber Lynn called me as I was leaving work. She wasn't nice. It soured my mood."

"I will be home soon, and you can tell me about it then."

While fixing dinner, I talk to Chris about my conversation with Amber Lynn. "I confronted her about not telling me about the meetings and she said she was protecting herself and others from me. I told her I didn't agree with her trying to outdo the chairperson from the Christmas Shop and that isn't what the bazaar is about. I knew it was the Christmas Shop's chairperson that Amber Lynn was competing with before she told me. Mom had heard a couple of people talking about it when she got her hair done. She heard they tripled their sales and that is what Amber Lynn had said also."

"Isn't that the one where they have a police officer directing traffic?" Chris asks.

"That's the one," I answer.

"That bazaar is huge."

"When is she going to see that it's not about outdoing the next guy? You want everyone to succeed."

"She has changed, Beth. I know you have considered her a friend in the past, but she is playing dirty. It will all come out some time, mark my words. Are you okay?"

"Yeah, I'm just perturbed. I would bow out of the bazaar all together but this year it's to help the Make-A-Wish foundation. I'm also back to making the apple dumplings in addition to everything else."

"Why?"

"Amber Lynn had flyers printed this year and went off of what I did last year, only she has the cinnamon bundles listed as cinnamon rolls."

"I know you really didn't want to make the dumplings, but it will make the guys at work super happy. Besides helping with the baking next week, what else can I do to help?"

"I could use something to help display the wreaths and flower arrangements."

"I will putter out in the garage and see what I can come up with."

"Well, you know where I will be -- knee deep in flowers."

A little while later, I open the door to the garage to let Chris know I'm going to bed. Chris shows me the display he's working on.

"Take a look at this and tell me what you think. If you can spread out all the wreaths on your display, it will help the customer see what you have. You can use hooks to hang the wreaths from the lattice and it will stand beside the booth, one on each side. With the little shelves here and here," he points to the diagram, "you can put your flower arrangements on them. This will help fill out your display but also free up table space for the bundles, dumplings, bread, and your mom's jewelry."

"Keep in mind we have to be able to get to the kitchen. Last year the door was behind our booth. I don't know, after my last conversation with Amber Lynn, if I will be in the same spot as last year or in the parking lot."

"This should still work. I will be in shortly."

By the time he makes it upstairs, I am already in bed. He leans over and kisses me goodnight as I drift off to sleep.

***

"What an awful dream," I tell Chris. "I was answering the black antique phone and the voice sounded like Amber Lynn's. She was saying, 'You're a terrible messenger!' At some point in the dream, we walk into the room of the nursing home and when Paul pulls back the sheet, Amber Lynn sits up in bed and is laughing at me."

"That sounds terrible!" he sympathizes.

While fixing my coffee, I imagine that I hear the announcer on the radio say, "Folks, if you have something to tell someone don't ask Beth. She is an awful messenger." I reach over and shut it off. "You think this is easy? It's not! Why don't you go talk to Addy's family member?" I holler at the radio.

Chris walks back into the kitchen and hears me yelling at the radio. "Who's winning?" as he looks at me and then the radio.

"I didn't sleep well. I'm hearing things," I grumble.

"Do you want any toast?"

"No, I'm not hungry."

He looks over his shoulder and gives me a look. "When are you planning on eating today?"

"Really Chris!"

"I am merely asking you a question. I think you might be in better shape if you eat something before you go to your meeting. It is only a suggestion. I realize you are going to do what you want to do."

I take the slice of toast he has fixed and take a bite. "I'm going to start getting ready for work."

"You're working today? I thought you had your meeting with Paul."

I stop in my tracks, trying to remember what I said.

"Tell you what, Beth. You go upstairs, and I will wake you in an hour."

"I really shouldn't."

"I'm not taking 'no' for an answer on this one. I mean it. March!"

An hour goes by and Chris comes into the bedroom with a piece of toast and coffee.

"I feel like I have been asleep for hours."

"I'm glad you're not driving today. I'm leaving for work now," he says leaning over to kiss me.

Paul arrives promptly at 12:45 p.m. and I get into his car. Self-conscious of the dark circles under my eyes, I put on my sunglasses.

Paul looks over at me and says, "You didn't even give me a chance to walk up to the door. My dad taught me that was a 'no-no' growing up."

"I'm just anxious to get this over. I'm a wreck inside," I share.

"You too? I didn't sleep much either. My poor wife, Susie, kept saying I was mumbling and calling out Bible verses. She even told me that I have bags under my eyes this morning."

"If yours are bags, mine are suitcases! It's a good thing I'm not flying, because they would charge me extra!" I laugh.

"That was bad," he laughs, shaking his head. "The nursing home administrator called me. Adeline's family member has taken a turn for the worse. She's glad we are coming today."

"Do you know who the family member is?"

"She didn't say, and I didn't ask. We will find out soon enough."

We pull into a visitor spot and as I get out of the car, I begin to try to smooth out the wrinkles in my outfit. I put my purse over my shoulder and begin the slow walk in. Paul looks over at me and smiles.

"I have butterflies in my stomach," he says.

"Mine feel like bats!" I add.

He pauses before we get up to the door. "Let's have a word of prayer before we go in."

I bow my head and concentrate on the words being spoken.

"Dear Father, I ask that you be with Beth and myself as we learn more about Addy and meet her family. Help us feel your loving presence and guide us to be more like you. In Jesus' name, Amen."

***

After signing in at the front desk, we're promptly met by the administrator of the facility, Mrs. Snow. She is a short, round woman with gray hair and rosy cheeks. She ushers us into her office and we take our seats on an overstuffed flowered couch. She then offers us refreshments from a tea cart sitting in the corner. I watch as she fixes herself a cup and chooses a cookie.

"I always think you need something sweet to go with a cup of coffee or tea, don't you?" Mrs. Snow asks.

Looking around at her office, I see that it's nicely decorated with a homey feel, and the delightful scent of sugar cookies.

"I guess we should begin," she says. "Before I start, I need to let you both know that I am having a very hard time talking about her in the past tense, so please bear with me." She pulls out a hanky tucked in her sleeve and pats her nose. "Let me tell you a little about Adeline or Addy. She is one of the sweetest people I have ever met. Life may have dealt her a bad hand, but it didn't leave a chip on her shoulder. Addy is a survivor and an advocate. She's as beautiful on the inside as she is on the outside. They are more like family to me."

Puzzled by her use of the word "they", I don't interrupt and let her continue.

"Addy works here as a care assistant and also stays here," Mrs. Snow continues.

"She lived here too?" I ask.

Mrs. Snow slowly takes a sip and places her cup on the saucer. "Being the administrator, I am able to turn a blind eye and let her stay with her sister."

I gasp, bringing my hand up to my mouth. Her sister? The image of the piece of paper with the word "Sister" written on it flashes in my mind.

"We're a smaller, family-based home and not a large corporate chain, so it's easier," says Mrs. Snow.

"I didn't entertain the idea of her family member being another young person," Paul says.

"Addy and her sister grew up in an orphanage. They were placed there at an early age for unknown reasons. Addy and I, on occasion, talked about life's lessons. I would tell her about my childhood growing up poor on a farm with my sister. She would say things once and awhile about how they were a package deal and because her sister was frail from a congenital heart defect, they were overlooked for adoption."

Mrs. Snow gets up to warm her tea and chooses another cookie. She then extends the offer to both of us. I select a cookie and continue sipping my water. Paul also takes a cookie and accepts the offer for more tea. She sets her cup on her desk and adjusts the fluffy pillow behind her back. Mrs. Snow resumes the story. "The two of them were turned out on their own at the age of eighteen and left to find their own way," she says stirring her tea.

"Her sister ended up getting sick and after frequent stays in the hospital, needed to be placed in a care facility. Due to their lack of funds and insurance, Addy's sister was having trouble getting placed. Many facilities will check your bank statement and insurance policy before accepting someone. I learned about her after receiving a call from a friend who is a social worker. I went to the hospital to meet the sister and that is when I met Addy.

"As she sat beside her sister's bed, she explained why they had so little and just each other. I just couldn't let them be disappointed yet again by society or the system. Addy told me that if I hire her, she would work for free to help pay for her sister's room. That was four years ago. We were able to help them in applying for state assistance and Addy worked to help pay for incidentals. There were also various donations that helped. Our staff members are like one big family. We treat them as such and by doing so, we take excellent care of our residents."

She sits back in her chair and laughs as she looks up at the ceiling. "Addy could light up a room with her smile and energetic personality." She sighs, cradling her cup in her hand. "She was one in a million and is going to be so dearly missed," letting her voice trail off. A tear escapes to her cheek and she brushes it away.

"I have been talking nonstop," Mrs. Snow says with tears in her eyes. "What would you like to know?"

Paul looks over at me and smiles. I take a deep breath before beginning. "I was working in the Emergency Room when she came in. I want you to know that everyone did everything they possibly could," I assure her.

"I'm sure you did," nods Mrs. Snow.

"You said that Addy lived here also. Do other family members live here with their loved ones?" I ask.

"Addy was a special circumstance. At first, she left after her shift or when visiting hours were over. But then we started finding her sleeping on the floor next to her sister's bed. After several weeks of this and my learning she had no place to go and no one to take her in, I moved a cot in there. We chose a cot rather than an actual bed so that the state couldn't say she was occupying the room. Addy was okay with just a cot and understood. The only thing that mattered to either one of them was that they were together. We fudged, I know, but looking into that young girl's eyes you knew you were looking at the face of an angel."

Speaking of fudge, Mrs. Snow offers, "Chaplain Paul, did you try one of these cookies with the fudge center? They are simply delicious."

I continue the conversation, "Mrs. Snow, I need you to know, I feel Addy has been trying to contact me to deliver a message and now since speaking to you, I now know the message is for her sister."

Mrs. Snow looks over her glasses and says, "That's kind of odd, wouldn't you say? Addy is gone. How can she possibly be trying to talk to you?"

"Chaplain Paul had mentioned to me that he also feels he is being contacted," Beth adds.

"I don't understand how she could talk to either one of you."

"Addy has been giving me signs. I saw her in a mirror asking me for help." Feeling my nerves starting to get the better of me, I go to take a drink and in doing so, squeeze the bottle, spilling water on my pants.

Mrs. Snow quickly hands me a tissue. After blotting up what I can, I take a sip.

"What were the signs?" she asks.

"Well, occasionally, I will smell lilacs," I begin to explain.

"Then it is Addy. They were her favorite.

"Addy had a good relationship with everyone here from the staff clear down to the residents. She treated everybody like family. She was just the sweetest. She started helping in the kitchen and then moved up to a care assistant. She wanted to become a nurse. The two of them had a dream of someday getting their own place. Addy knew with her sister's heart problems, there was a slim chance, but it gave them hope and something to look forward to. We have a collection jar at the front desk for guests, families, and staff to throw in their loose change. Then at the end of the month, we choose someone who is in need and give it to them. It could be a resident, a resident's family member, a staff member – sometimes it's been Addy."

"I need to excuse myself," she says pushing herself away from her desk. "All that tea has gone right through me. I will be just a few minutes and then we will go meet Sophie. She's just as sweet as Addy."

As she leaves the room, I turn to face Paul. "We're going to meet Sophie and I don't even know what I'm going to say."

"I don't know how I can help," Paul says.

NINETEEN

When Mrs. Snow comes back to her office, Paul asks, "Does Sophie know what happened to Addy?"

"She knows something isn't right and keeps asking for her," replies Mrs. Snow.

She escorts us down the winding hallways and at last, we stop in front of Sophie's room. A nurse walks up to a med cart and smiles at us.

"Good morning Gabby," Mrs. Snow says. "This is Sophie's nurse."

"Hi," Gabby says, extending her hand to both of us. Her handshake is firm and when she smiles her whole face lights up. A firm handshake says a lot about a person. Just as much as looking a person in the eye when you are speaking to them.

"How is Sophie today?" Mrs. Snow asks Gabby.

Gabby replies, "She is having to wear her oxygen more often. She thinks Addy is mad at her. We have all been trying to take extra time with her to sit and talk."

"You are all truly amazing with your compassion and care," I tell them, swallowing hard.

"Yes, we are!" Mrs. Snow boasts. "We all know we are just an extension of God's grace and love."

Gabby looks over at Mrs. Snow and nods affirmingly.

"Could you excuse me?" I ask. "I need to find the ladies' room."

Mrs. Snow begins to give me directions when Gabby offers to show me.

"Thank you, I know you are busy," I say.

"No bother, this will give me a chance to get something to drink and a fudge cookie that everyone is talking about," says Gabby.

As we walk down the hall, I observe the unique interaction between the staff and residents, many laughing and hugging one another.

A gentleman comes out of his room and stops Gabby, "Could you help me please, Gabby, with a crossword puzzle?"

"This is Henry," Gabby says. "He is a whiz at crosswords."

"Nice to meet you," Henry says.

"Hi," I say smiling.

"It's a real tough one. I'm not sure if you will get it," Henry says.

"Well, let's have a look," Gabby says, as he points to 7 down.

I look over her shoulder as she studies it. Suddenly, a call light alert goes off across the hall. Gabby hands me the crossword puzzle book as she goes to help.

While we wait for Gabby to return, Henry and I continue looking at the puzzle. After several seconds, Henry says, "You are not seeing it with an open heart. Close your eyes."

Surprised by his comment, I go along with it and close my eyes.

"Now open them," he says.

When I open my eyes and look at the puzzle, the answer is in large bold print. As I read it to myself, I look at Henry's face.

"Beth, you knew the message all along. There are angels all around trying to help guide you," he quietly says.

I look at the puzzle again and can't believe what I am seeing, "I'm here waiting for you" is in bold print.

With the emergency resolved, a woman I believe to be a resident follows Gabby out of her room. The woman smiles when she makes eye contact with Henry. He then gives her the thumbs up sign and she nods. When I glance back down at the puzzle, the words in bold are gone, leaving letters written in pencil.

Gabby takes the crossword and reads it over several times. "Henry, you have misspelled a word. Seven down isn't 'massage'. It should be 'message' – 'a way of communication as in a text, phone call, letter or email'."

"Wow, that was a hard one," he says looking up, giving Gabby a wink. He nods at me and goes back into his room.

"I haven't forgotten about you Beth," Gabby says. "I promise no more interruptions."

After walking down several hallways, Gabby directs me to the restrooms which are just past the nurses' station on the left. As I start to open the door to the restroom, I hear her ask someone, "Where are the fudge cookies I am hearing so much about?"

Standing at the sink, I look in the mirror. What just happened? Smoothing out my hair, I adjust my sweater and smooth out my slacks. As I wash my hands, the coolness of the water feels good.

After coming out of the restroom, I continue walking past the information desk, and head outside for some fresh air. As I take a seat on the bench, I watch a squirrel looking for something to eat. Drawing in a breath, I close my eyes and silently pray. I'm scared, nervous, and confused. Jesus, please let me be your voice...

I make eye contact with the girl sitting at the information desk and walk on by. As I go around the corner, Gabby walks out a door carrying a cup of coffee and a plate of cookies.

"Shh," she tells me as she holds up her plate and cup signaling her hands are full. "Don't tell anybody that I found the fudge cookies. If anybody asks, they're regular cookies."

"Got it," putting my lips together and nodding.

"You will want to keep going down this hall until the carpet stops and then hang a left. That'll be Sophie's room."

As I make the turn, I find Paul and Mrs. Snow waiting outside the room for me. "Everything okay, dear?" Mrs. Snow asks.

"Fine," I answer, trying to be convincing.

As we enter Sophie's room, it is not what I expected. I try not to stare at her small frail body. When I look at her, I swear it's Addy. While trying not to be obvious, I study Sophie, looking for similarities. Mrs. Snow is reading my face and before I open my mouth, she answers. "To answer your question, Addy and Sophie are twins." She walks over to Sophie and leans down, stroking her forehead. "Sophie, I have some people I want you to meet. Can you open your eyes?"

Sophie stirs as she tries to raise her head and look around.

"Hi, Momma," she says, her voice weak.

Mrs. Snow holds Sophie's hand while she explains. "The girls asked a couple of years ago if they could call me 'Mom'. I didn't think it would be of any harm. I feel like I am "mom" to a lot of people here." She takes a deep breath while she wipes her eyes and swallows hard.

"I am sure you have helped fill a void for them," Paul says.

"Well, they have certainly helped fill a void for me, too."

"Sophie these are my friends Beth and Paul. We need to tell you something about Addy."

As I look over at her, my eyes tear up. I hadn't even thought about needing to tell her. Gabby comes in to check Sophie and then adjusts her bed, so she can sit up. "You're doing really good, sweetheart," Gabby says. "I know the oxygen tubing is bothering your nose. We will put some more ointment on in a little bit." She leaves, shutting the door.

Struggling, Mrs. Snow once more tries to get out the words. "Sophie, I'm afraid Addy was in a very bad accident," wiping at her eyes and nose.

"Can I see her?" Sophie asks as tears flow down her cheeks.

Mrs. Snow walks over to the window with her back to us, but everyone can tell she is sobbing.

"Sophie, Chaplain Paul, and I were in the emergency room when Addy came in. She was hurt so badly that she couldn't be saved." The words begin to flow out of my mouth as I begin to tell her. "Your sister loved you so much and didn't want to go to heaven without you knowing that. She also wanted you to know that she is there waiting for you and will be there to take your hand and walk with you. And she wanted me to tell you that there is no sickness or pain in Heaven. Everyone is healthy and at peace.

"Do you like ice cream, Sophie?" I ask.

"Yes." she replies.

"What is your favorite flavor? Mine is chocolate." I then point to Paul and ask, "What's yours?"

"Well, how about thirty-one flavors," Chaplain Paul laughs, patting his stomach. "I would have to say," clearing his throat, "butter pecan."

Gabby walks in and stands by Sophie.

"Mrs. Snow," I ask, "What is your favorite flavor of ice cream?"

"Hmm, I would have to say strawberry," replies Mrs. Snow.

"Okay Sophie, it's your turn. What flavor?"

"Come on kiddo, tell them what kind," Gabby says.

Sophie looks around at us and then says shyly, "Mint chocolate chip. Addy likes chocolate chip. We always like similar things."

"Well, I bet there is even ice cream in heaven," Paul says.

As tears roll down Sophie's cheeks, she says, "I'm all alone now."

Hearing her say these words has put a lump in my throat. This poor girl has lost her sister and now is truly alone and feeling it. I turn to look out the window, trying to hide my tears.

Gabby taps her leg, "You've got me. What am I chopped liver? You have me, Mom, and everybody else here."

Sophie's eyes scan from Paul to me and she asks, "Could you come back and see me?"

"That would be very nice," Paul answers.

"I would like that as well," I smile.

We decide to leave when we notice her eyes growing heavy. "I'm going to stay with her until she falls asleep," Gabby says, waving.

Outside in the hallway away from her room, I ask Mrs. Snow:, "Do you feel Sophie can process this?"

"Sophie may be frail and a little behind compared to Addy, but she is smart. While you were in the restroom, Noah, one of our care assistants, came and told me that Sophie told him Addy wasn't coming back and that she saw her in a dream."

Gabby walks out of Sophie's room and Paul and I give her our phone numbers. We both offer to help with whatever we can.

Back in Mrs. Snow's office, Paul asks, "Did either of the girls have burial plans?"

"When you are young, you never think of dying," replies Mrs. Snow.

"I may be able to help, but I need to talk to my husband first," I tell them.

"This has been quite an afternoon for everyone involved. Let's check in with each other at the end of the week," Mrs. Snow suggests.

I walk over and give Mrs. Snow a hug. "You are a very special woman and will have a special place in heaven!"

"That's nice. I am just trying to make sure people see a glimpse of it here before they get there."

We wave goodbye as we walk down the hall, both feeling a huge relief. In the car, I settle into the seat and crack the window. "That was not what I had anticipated at all."

"Mrs. Snow is so nice along with all the staff," Paul adds. "What you said to Sophie was beautiful."

On the drive home, I proceed to tell Paul about Henry and the crossword puzzle.

"Nothing surprises me anymore," Paul says. We agree to check in with each other in a couple of days.

"Sounds good," I tell him as I shut the car door.

***

Sitting in the bathtub, I feel drained even though a weight has been lifted. I hear a noise from downstairs. "I'm in the tub," I yell.

He peeks his head around the corner. "How did it go?"

I recap the highlights for him including Henry and the crossword puzzle.

"You poor thing. You look exhausted," he says. "My poor Boo."

"Aw, you haven't called me that since high school. What are you doing home so early?"

"I came home early to check on you. The word on the street is that I'm a nice guy and a heck of a catch."

"I couldn't agree more."

After a long soak in the tub and feeling like a limp noodle, I put on my robe and stand before the closet.

"Why are you staring at your closet?" Chris asks.

"I am looking for something to wear."

"Why?"

"Because clothes are going to look better than my birthday suit."

"That depends on who you are asking," he says with a devilish grin. "Just get ready for bed. Put your pajamas on and lounge around."

"Chris, it's still early."

"So, relax, the Chinese won't be here for a little while."

"You ordered Chinese? How thoughtful! Okay, jammies it is."

Downstairs, Chris opens the door and starts talking to someone as I scurry into the kitchen. He walks in carrying a flower arrangement. As I look at the flowers, my mouth flies open.

"Who are they from?" I ask in anticipation.

"Open the card," he says handing it to me.

" 'For being a perfect messenger. We love you, Mom and Dad'."

"Aw, how sweet," I say, tearing the paper from around the arrangement and removing the vase from the box. "Smell them," I encourage Chris. "Don't they smell amazing?"

"They do, just not as good as Chinese takeout," he laughs. The doorbell rings, and he trades the driver cash for the food. "Do you feel like reading your fortune cookie?"

"Maybe later, I'm almost afraid to read it." I grab plates and napkins, and after we dish up our food we head to the family room to find something to watch on TV. Settling on a game show, we both try guessing at the answers and laugh when neither of us even comes close.

"Can I ask you something?" I say.

"Sure, you look so serious," responds Chris, "Are you okay?"

"Yeah, I will be. You know the two burial plots that we have."

"Yes," he answers looking puzzled.

"Would you mind if I let Addy and her sister Sophie have them? This way they would both have a place to be buried and would be together."

"That sounds fine, especially since neither of us has the desire to be buried or have our ashes placed there."

"I'm glad. I also want to arrange a graveside service for Addy. I will let Paul know tomorrow." I try to stifle a yawn without success. "I'm ready to call it a day. How about you?"

Turning over in bed, I flip over my pillow and sense a light in the room. I sit up in bed and notice the light getting brighter and brighter. Then suddenly, I see Addy standing at the foot of the bed.

"You met Sophie," Addy says.

Nodding, "Chaplain Paul was with me. The message was for Sophie, wasn't it?"

She nods looking over at something. "I need to go soon. They're calling for me."

"Addy, wait... I have some questions. What about the photos? Who are the girls?"

"The pictures are ones I exchanged with my best friend, Millie in a past life."

"Past life? I'm confused how everything ties together."

"Loved ones will always be linked together for an eternity in their lives whether it's the past, present, or future. Your Aunt Millie and I were best friends. You are a lot like her, Beth, very caring.

"God has helped me to understand that I needed to be the one to go home first so I could be there to take Sophie's hand and she wouldn't be afraid or alone. Sophie doesn't have much time. Would you be there for her? I don't want her to be alone."

"Of course we will," I answer without hesitating.

"Addy, I need to tell you we are going to have a graveside service for you. You will be buried in our family's plot, and oddly enough you will be next to my Aunt Millie."

"That will be nice, but what about Sophie?"

"She will be next to you, when her time comes."

"I will have my two best friends on each side."

With tears in her eyes, Addy says, "Beth, I need you to tell Sophie that she was the best sister anyone could ever ask for and my very best friend."

"She already knows how much you love her, but I will tell her. I will make sure she knows."

"Beth, I want to thank you. I know how hard all of you tried to save me. I watched all of you in the room and when everyone left, you stayed. You covered me with warm blankets and held my hand and prayed for me. That is how I knew; and chose you to be the one."

"How did you come to choose Chaplain Paul?"

"He came into the room to check on you and stayed after everyone else left. He held my hand and prayed for me as well. That's when I knew I wanted you both to help me.

"I really must go now," she says as she looks over again at someone and nods. "Please give her a kiss and hug," she says as her voice cracks as she tries not to cry.

"Don't be afraid Addy," I say wiping the tears from my face with the back of my hand.

She then looks over and tells someone, "I'm ready."

The glowing light around her becomes even brighter. A hand then appears, extending from the sleeve of a white robe. She grasps the hand and turns to me, smiling. Then she is gone.

The room is dark and still. I get up to get a tissue in the bathroom and blow my nose while sitting on the toilet, crying. I go over to the sink and wash my face. That wasn't any dream, that was real. I look over at the clock as I get back in bed, it reads 2:30 a.m. I cuddle up next to Chris who wakes up enough to put his arm around me, before falling back to sleep.

TWENTY

"Someone's eager this morning," Chris says as he watches me anxiously await by the coffee maker.

"If I could get my mouth under it, I would skip the cup all together," I respond.

"I wouldn't advise it. A nurse once told me that burns are terrible," he says shuddering.

As I fill my cup and add creamer, I cautiously take a sip.

"Do you feel better after the extra sleep?" Chris asks.

"What extra sleep? I didn't sleep in," I respond.

"According to the clock, you did."

"Is that really the time? I'm going to be late," I shout as I run upstairs.

"I didn't think you were working today," he hollers up the stairs.

I throw on my uniform and quickly grab my purse. I kiss Chris and take my badge that he is dangling from his hand.

"You have got to slow down or you are going to get in an accident," he adds.

As I carefully back out of the driveway, I think about his warning while I wait for a school bus. Stopping for the bus is a subtle reminder to be mindful of kids and people who aren't watching for neurotic nurses who are late for work.

Speed walking into the hospital, I clock in just in time and watch as the long hand winds around. "Nah," I say, sticking my tongue out at the timeclock. "I have beat you once again." A young paramedic student is standing in the corner looking around. I turn to catch the surprised look on his face. "Hi, I didn't see you standing there. It's been a rough morning and I thought I was going to be late," I ramble. "Are you shadowing in the department today?"

"Yes," he hesitantly responds.

"I'm Beth, and welcome," shaking his hand. As I walk out into the department and introduce him to coworkers, I find myself getting funny looks. "What's wrong?" I ask everyone.

"Are you okay?" Karli asks?

"I'm a little frazzled this morning. It's been a rough start. Why?"

"Well, for starters your top is turned inside out, and you have two different shoes on," Paige bluntly states, then laughs.

I look down in frustration. "That explains why I couldn't put anything in my pockets and felt like I was walking peg-leg."

They both come over and hug me, trying not to laugh or hurt my feelings. "I'll fix my top later and endure the shoes. What area do you want me to work in today?" I ask.

Karli and Paige look at each other puzzled.

"What's wrong now?" I sigh.

"You know today is Wednesday, right?" Paige asks.

"I haven't really thought about what day it is, to be honest, but now I do. Am I not supposed to be here today?"

"You traded with Lexi," Paige says.

Lexi sees me and comes over. "We traded so I could go to my little girl's field trip tomorrow."

"I remember now! I also remember I was going to write a reminder for myself."

"It's not that we wouldn't love to have you," Paige says, as she walks me back to the breakroom, "but you have got too much going on in that pretty little head of yours. I'm going to send you on your merry way, and we will see you tomorrow." She waves and closes the door behind her.

As I stand at my locker, I am embarrassed and frustrated. This is why Chris questioned me about working. I call him on the way home. "I'm coming back home. I don't work today. I forgot that I traded with Lexi for tomorrow. I also have been walking around with my uniform top inside out and two different shoes on."

He immediately starts laughing and I can't help but smile.

"I'm coming home to see if I can restart my day."

"Don't stop anywhere on the way home," he advises before hanging up.

***

I turn my uniform top right side out and drape it over the chair with my pants. I then set out a pair of matching shoes for tomorrow. At least I have my stuff ready for tomorrow, I tell Gracie. Cuddling up with Gracie on the bed, I doze off. I wake up to see Gracie with her head on Chris' pillow and laugh. "Did you have a good nap?" She thumps her tail against the bed.

The clock reads 10:00 a.m. I need to get up and get something accomplished. I find the necessary paperwork regarding the cemetery plots and call the office. As I look at Aunt Millie's faded blue handwriting, I think aloud, I know you understand my wanting to gift them to Addy and Sophie.

Finally, I get connected to someone who can help, after being transferred multiple times. The gentleman offers to put the paperwork in the mail, but after explaining to him Addy's situation and time constraints, he agrees to let me come in and fill out the paperwork. I quickly grab my purse and promise to be there soon.

When I get back home, I give Paul a call. "I wanted to talk to you about helping me arrange a graveside service for Addy. I talked it over with Chris last evening and I have two burial plots that I would like to donate to Addy and Sophie. Chris and I have no use for them since we want to be cremated and our ashes spread. By using these plots, the two of them would be together for eternity."

"I don't know what to say except that it is such a generous and special gift," replies Paul.

"It's Addy who gave the gift, in allowing me to be her messenger. She came to me again this morning. She said she saw me putting warm blankets on her and holding her hand and praying with her. She said that's how she chose me to be her messenger. She also told me how she chose you, Paul."

"What did she say?" he asks.

"That you had come into the room to check on me and stayed after everyone else had left. She said you also held her hand and prayed for her.

That's how she knew she wanted both of us to help her."

"Remarkable. This is something only the two of us know since we were the only ones in the room with her."

"I asked her about the pictures and her knowing my aunt. She said she and my Aunt Millie were best friends. She wanted me to understand that you're linked with your loved ones through eternity. She said God helped her to understand why she was called home first. She needed to be there to take Sophie's hand so Sophie wouldn't be afraid or alone."

"Wow," Paul says.

"I also let her know about the graveside service we will have for her as well as Sophie. I told her she would be buried next to my Aunt Millie. Her response was 'a best friend on each side'."

"There was a bright light around Addy the entire time. She kept looking over, like someone was talking to her. Then the light got even brighter, and a hand extended from a white robe. She took the hand, turned to me, and smiled. I told her not to be afraid as I was crying. Then in an instant she was gone along with the bright light."

"I question how someone could not believe in a higher power after witnessing something like this," Paul says letting out a sigh. "I literally have goosebumps. I have always wondered how the hereafter might be."

"Addy told me that Sophie doesn't' have much time and asked if we would be there for Sophie. I told her absolutely. When I went to the cemetery I asked if we could have the service on Saturday. Would that work for you Paul?"

"Saturday is fine for me. I will call and update Mrs. Snow and talk to you later then," Paul says.

I walk into Addy's room and immediately go over to the vase on the dresser. The stem is now bare. A small pile of flower petals sits on the dresser. I pick them up and place them in my hand as I look into the mirror. There on the mirror is a message left for me. I smile as I read it, and it says, Thank you. I watch as the letters on the mirror fade and disappear. When I open my hand, the flower petals are also gone.

With Addy's service set up, things are starting to draw to a close. Now, I just need to be there for Sophie, like I promised. My thoughts are interrupted when Paul calls. He informs me that Mrs. Snow has a funeral home that she is fond of, and Addy has already been transported there. "I told Mrs. Snow about the burial plots and she thinks what you are doing is wonderful. Susie and I will take care of the flowers for the casket," says Paul.

"It sounds like everything is coming together," I say, feeling relieved. I tell Paul about the message left on the mirror and the flower petals. Before hanging up, I give him the name and phone number of the cemetery along with the contact name.

I fix a cup of tea and curl up in the chair and it's not long before I doze off again. I must be sick. I have been sleeping every time I sit down. I don't feel chilly or achy. Chris calls and checks on me and advises me to continue doing nothing and reminds me how nurses make terrible patients.

Chris comes home later with sandwiches and as we eat, I tell him about seeing Addy. "She thanked me. We both were crying. I told her not to be afraid. She had this bright light all around her. She looked over at someone and told them she was ready. Then a hand appeared from a white robe."

Chris stops chewing and looks over at me. "Then what happened?"

"She grasped the hand, smiled and was gone."

"No wonder you are so worn out today. You always wonder what it will be like. That's something," shaking his head.

"Paul said the same thing when I told him about it. What I can't get over is she said she watched me cover her with warm blankets and hold her hand and pray. She said that's how she knew I was the one to deliver the message. She told me she saw Paul hold it as he prayed for her. That's how she knew she wanted both of us to help her."

"Wow. Too bad you're not an author. It would make a good book."

"You know the saying 'Don't quit your day job'. I'm not even going to try."

***

At work, I take a couple of minutes to update everybody on the arrangements for Addy's service. I also hang up a flyer in the breakroom so everybody will know the time and location. I had a hard time not getting emotional when I told them about meeting Sophie. It wasn't a busy morning, so we had time to talk about Addy and Sophie.

After lunch, I take a minute and call Chris. "How's your day going?"

"Pretty good. I ended up going out for lunch with a couple of the guys here, so I will save the lunch I packed for tomorrow. What about you?" Chris asks.

"Typical Thursday. Remember if you get home early, preheat the oven, and stick the casserole in. The directions are next to the stove."

"Very funny. I know how to use the stove."

"No silly! I know you do. I meant the temperature to set it at and for how long, is by the stove," I laugh.

"Have a good rest of your shift."

"I love you and will see you later."

I turn around to see Karli standing there.

"You guys are so cute."

"Thanks," I smile.

***

Walking in the kitchen, I am delighted to see Chris wearing an apron and the dining room table set. "You're home later than I expected," he comments.

"I stayed to help with a patient that came in. Sometimes it's just easier than trying to turn over care. It wasn't long before they were assigned a bed, so I decided to just stay and see it through."

"That's why you are so well liked. You don't dump', I think is the term."

I can smell the French bread in the oven and see the casserole hot and sitting on the stove. "Everything looks delicious," leaning over to kiss him.

He takes his hot mitt off and fans himself. "Just look at my nails, they're a mess. And my hair, it's all wilted I bet, from the heat," he jokes.

After eating we decide to phone my folks and see if they want to join us for ice cream. "Hello Dad," says Chris. "Your daughter, Beth, is going to treat me to some ice cream since I slaved all afternoon in the kitchen preparing a fabulous dinner. Would you and Mom like to join us? Beth's treat, of course."

"We would love to. What time?" Dad asks.

"Hold on while I ask her. I have her doing the dishes now to make up for me working so hard. Your dad says you need to mop the floors after you're done and that you are working me too hard."

"I bet he does! Tell them we can pick them up in fifteen minutes."

"Now don't you get me in trouble with my daughter," Dad says to Chris, laughing. "I have enough problems trying to keep Mother at bay."

On the way to the ice cream shop, we talked about meeting Sophie and the arrangements for Addy's service.

"The flowers you guys sent me are just beautiful!"

"Tell them what you did yesterday," Chris laughs.

"It's not that funny," I tell Chris."

"She went to work on the wrong day and had her uniform top inside out and was even wearing two different shoes."

"That just goes to show your character," Dad says. "You were showing up to work without calling off like so many people do nowadays."

"I suppose you're right," looking over at Chris and making a face. "You keep it up buster and I am not buying you any ice cream."

Mom lets out a giggle and catches herself by putting her hand over her mouth.

Chris is the first to dive into his ice cream as we sit under the colorful umbrella table.

"Are you feeling any better?" Mom asks me.

"Each day I feel I am getting closer to the end. It's like trying to get to the last chapter of a book - if that makes sense."

"What is Sophie like?"

"I didn't expect her to be Addy's twin. She is very frail and has been since a young age, due to a heart defect. They were in an orphanage until they were eighteen and then turned out on their own. Addy wouldn't allow them to be separated and nobody wanted to take on a child with a heart problem knowing there would be frequent doctor and hospital visits."

Dad gently touches my arm and gestures to remind me my ice cream is melting. I look down and see the melted ice cream has cascaded down into a pool of chocolate sauce. Plunging my spoon into the chocolate puddle, I take a bite and savor the taste. "Thanks, Daddy," taking another bite.

"Addy's service is going to be on Saturday at 2:00 p.m. at the Sacred Garden cemetery. We are giving her the plots that we have so that Addy and her sister can be buried beside each other."

"Oh, Beth," Mom says getting choked up, "that is so sweet."

"Don't cry Mom, you'll melt your ice cream," I laugh. "This is what we feel we are supposed to do," looking over at Chris who is smiling. "Sophie is very frail," I continue. "I'm not sure if she is going to be able to attend or not."

"Well, your father and I will be there to support you and will be there for Addy too."

"We sure will," Dad affirms with a nod.

I take another bite of my pool of ice cream and smile back at my audience watching. "I just want to say to you guys that I know the last several weeks have not been easy for any of you. Chris, I know you have been fielding calls from people reporting to you and asking about me."

He looks down, scraping the remaining ice cream from his dish. "It's okay," he says.

"I understand and appreciate that people were worried. Now that you guys know about everything and the fact that Chris has seen Addy for himself, no one should think that I am going bonkers. There are probably a few out there that could still think it but at this point, I don't care what anybody else thinks. You three are the only ones I care about."

Mom takes her napkin and looks away while I notice Dad digging his hanky out of his pocket and blowing his nose. "Darn allergies," he utters.

Chris leans over and kisses me. "Nobody is going to say you are crazy, cause if they do, I will tell them, to: 'Put 'em up. Put 'em up. I'll fight you with one paw behind my back. I'll fight you standing on one foot. I'll fight you with my eyes closed'." He says all of this using his best cowardly lion's voice from the Wizard of Oz.

We all break out laughing and he stands up and takes a bow.

"Finish your ice cream and we will go," he says.

I take another bite and announce, "I'm finished."

Chris grabs the cup and looks like the kid who has been given a second helping of candy. He carefully takes his spoon and gives it a stir. He then decides it's easier and faster to just drink it. Taking my napkin, I wipe the chocolate from the corner of his mouth.

"Is my little boy ready to go home now?" I ask.

We drop Mom and Dad off after I promise to call them tomorrow on my way home.

"You're goofy at times," I tell Chris.

"Right now, I am full," he says patting his stomach.

TWENTY-ONE

"How did you sleep?" I ask Chris.

"I wouldn't suggest going to bed with a belly full of ice cream. I had such crazy dreams. People were chasing me with ice cream to eat," he replies.

"Aw, you poor thing."

"I don't think I am going to eat anything today."

After making him a cup of tea, I'm surprised to see Chris still sitting on the bed half-dressed and looking green.

"Sip on this, it will help your stomach."

He takes a sip and sets the cup down.

"Are you sure you even want to go in today? You're green!" I exclaim.

I hand him the phone so he can let the office know he won't be in and I promise to check in on him later in the day.

***

As I get out of the car, I hear my name called from behind. "Good morning, ladies," I smile.

"I hope it's a decent day like yesterday," Rachel says.

"Do you think it's possible to have two in a row?" Madison asks.

"It's up to the one upstairs," I answer pointing up to the sky.

"Amen to that," Rachel laughs.

As we go about our day, Madison, Rachel, and Karli talk about the service tomorrow. "We know it's been very difficult for you, Beth," says Madison.

"For some reason, I felt a connection with Addy," I explain. "And now I feel I owe it to Sophie to be there for her until the end." They smile showing compassion that I know is genuine.

Paul calls and asks if I can meet him for lunch in the cafeteria. He has a few things he wants to go over before Addy's service tomorrow. After giving report on my patients, I head down to the cafeteria.

Paul sees me and waves as he waits in line to pay. I quickly make my lunch choices and join him as we choose a table by the window. Once settled, we take a few bites, and ask about each other's day.

"I wanted to tell you that Mrs. Snow called me. Addy and Sophie wore matching heart necklaces that she had given them. She found Addy's and gave it to the funeral home," Paul says.

"I'm sure it will mean a lot to both of them," I respond.

"Are your coworkers aware of your donation to Addy and Sophie?"

"I don't think it's important, do you?" I ask.

"It truly shows your heart. Have you gotten any more signs from Addy?"

"Nope."

"I can't seem to get it out of my mind how Addy had said to you that she would have a best friend on each side. How peculiar it is that she knew your aunt in a past life and now is going to be buried next to her.

"I'm satisfying my sweet tooth today," he says. "I bought one of each. You can have your pick --oatmeal raisin or chocolate chip," as he pushes the plate towards me.

I break off a piece of the oatmeal raisin and begin nibbling.

"Last night, Beth, when I picked up my Bible, I found a blank piece of paper sticking out between the pages. I came up with Psalm 4:7, 'Thou hast put gladness in my heart'."

"How did you know it was that one, if the paper was blank?" I ask.

"When I went out to my car last night after work there was '47' on the window."

"You mean written in the dirt on your back window?"

"Not exactly. It was on the driver's side window and before you say anything my car is not that dirty," he laughs. "It looked like a smear, but I could clearly see the numbers."

As he takes a bite from his cookie, he says, "I still have a lot of work to do. My wife, Susie, ordered the flowers yesterday for the casket. I just need to finish writing the service tonight."

His voice trails off as he watches me.

"What's wrong?" Paul asks.

"I can't believe I forgot about the actual casket," I add.

"It's okay, Beth. Mrs. Snow told me that Addy's work family was taking care of it."

"Did she mention how Sophie was doing or if she would be at the service?" taking another bite of my cookie.

"Mrs. Snow said that Sophie is too weak. Gabby will be working so she will be here for Sophie. She also mentioned that Sophie has requested a flower from the service."

"That brave sweet girl," shaking my head.

"Sometimes I think that of you, Beth," Paul says. "For Addy's service, I know I want to finish the service with the Lord's prayer. I just have to come up with the beginning and middle," he laughs.

"Good luck."

"Don't be surprised if you get a call from me tonight for help with it."

"I'm available should you need to, but I doubt if it will come to that."

***

As promised I call Mom on my way home to let her know about my day. After setting up a time for them to come over to the house, I give Chris a call. Thankfully, he has been lying around most of the day but hasn't eaten anything. The poor thing started getting sick after I left this morning. He thought it was related to the ice cream. "Do you want me to stop and get anything?" I offer.
"Like what?" he asks.

"Like jello, ginger ale, soup? Do any of those sound good to you?"

"Soup might be nice and maybe some jello."

"Okay, I will be home shortly."

"I will be the green-looking man lying on the couch."

Grabbing a shopping cart, I set out to only pick up the essentials for Chris. Hitting the produce aisle first, I grab bananas to help replenish his potassium. I then wander to the soup isle and pick out two kinds, chicken noodle, and chicken and stars. Next, I grab a box of saltines because I can't remember if we have any. I pick out several flavors of premade jello and toss them into the cart. I grab a variety of flavors of sports drinks and survey the cart. *That should do*, and I head to the registers.

As I wait in line, I look over the dreaded "last chance" area full of gum, candy, mints, and magazines strategically placed to lure small children and temp those with little will power. I pick out a magazine that I think Chris will like along with a package of gum and some lifesavers. The candy bars are specially priced. I pick out several different ones. The angel on my shoulder is saying, "It's okay, they're for Chris, they're justified." But the devil is saying, "Who are you kidding? There are at least one or two you like!" Shaking them off, they each scoff, and disappear.

The cashier looks at me and asks: "Are you done shopping?"

"Yes." I reply, feeling embarrassed.

"That's okay. You have been fun to watch. Getting one of these, and one of these, two of these, then two of this kind, and then one more of these."

"There are only six," correcting her. "I'm taking them to my husband who is sick at home. I am trying to pick out things to make him feel better."

"Oh, gee lady, I'm sorry. I hope one of the candy bars is for you."

"Actually, if you must know, there are at least two," I smile.

Handing me my receipt, "Have a lovely day and I hope your husband feels better."

"Like tomorrow," I say under my breath. Before leaving the store, I look back over my shoulder for any familiar faces. They must all have the day off, I sigh.

***

I unpack the groceries and get out a pan to warm up his soup as he walks into the kitchen. "At least you don't look as green as you did this morning," I remark.

"I'm a little better and Gracie has been keeping me company," he says surveying the loot. He grabs his magazine and begins leafing through it and then finds the roll of lifesavers and opens them.

"Which kind of soup do you want, chicken noodle or chicken and stars?" I ask, holding up the cans.

He chooses and then I ask him to decide which sports drink he wants before pouring it over ice and handing it to him.

He fishes out a star on his spoon and says, "They never look like the ones on the label, do they?"

"Eat your soup. I hate to sound heartless, but I need you to be with me tomorrow."

"I will. I'm feeling better already," taking another bite while trying to seem convincing.

While Chris eats, I tell him about having lunch with Paul and his message with the Bible verse he feels was from Addy.

Before bed, I walk into Addy's room and get the vase and the dead flower stem. Chris walks in and asks, "What are you doing?"

"Throwing away the remainder of the flower. Addy is gone and so is the flower," I answer.

"About the flower," he pauses "I replaced it when it started to look dead a while ago."

"Why would you do that?"

"With the flower dying so quickly, I wasn't sure what it would do to your frame of mind. I only changed it once."

"I'm not mad because I know you were only trying to help."

"It will all be over very soon," he says kissing the top of my head.

***

Chris walks into the bedroom carrying a tray and says, "Your folks brought by croissants this morning. They will be here around 1:30 p.m. for us to all ride over together."

"That was sweet of them," I respond.

"How did you sleep? You sure were tossing and turning. You were even talking in your sleep."

"What did I say?"

"You said that you didn't know what you would do without me, and you think you need to do something special for me. I clearly remember you saying, 'I need to buy Chris a new truck'."

"I doubt that very much but nice try," I laugh.

Getting dressed, he asks, "Do you think this looks okay?" as he smooths out his tie.

"It looks great."

"What are you going to wear?"

"Well, I can't very well go in my nightgown, so I better get it in gear."

After rearranging hangers for a while, I settle on an outfit of black dress pants and a coral colored sweater. "Does this look okay?"

"It looks great. I can't see anybody judging someone's outfit at a funeral."

As I stand at the mirror trying to fix my hair, I'm glum.

"Instead of being sad about today, be happy. You honored Addy's request and delivered her message to Sophie. You were the messenger," Chris says.

"All I can say is that I'm trying," I add.

"Is there anything that needs to be done before the service?"

"I feel I need to go and see Sophie."

"Do you want me to go with you?" Chris asks.

"I would love it. I won't be there long."

Paul calls just as we're about to leave. I let him know I'm going to see Sophie before the service and that I feel it will help me get through it better.

***

Standing at the front desk, Chris and I are in the process of signing in when I hear a familiar voice. Looking up, it's Gabby. I introduce her to Chris as she instructs us to follow her to Sophie's room.

"How is she today?" I ask.

"As well as can be expected. We have all assured her she is not going to be alone. We adopted her and Addy into our hearts and families a long time ago!" says Gabby.

I silently say a quick prayer before walking into her room. Gabby walks in ahead of us.

"Look who I found roaming the halls," Gabby tells Sophie.

"Hi Sophie, do you remember me?" She looks over at me and nods while watching Chris. "This is my husband, Chris. I told him about you, and he wanted to come and meet you. How are you feeling today?"

She looks over at Gabby and begins to cry.

"We are all going to miss Addy, but you need to remember she is always with you right here," pointing to Sophie's heart. "She is also right here, in all of us," Gabby says putting her hand over her heart. Chris and I nod in agreement.

"Sophie, you know the necklace you are wearing. Addy has hers on too. Every time you touch your necklace, I want you to know that Addy is thinking about you. She loved you very much. I have had a few of my loved ones die. What helps me to cope is knowing God must have needed them as special angels to take them so soon."

Gabby wipes Sophie's tears as Sophie nods and asks, "Will you bring me a flower?"

"I sure will," I answer squeezing her hand.

Gabby stands up and straightens her covers. "We will talk to you later. Sophie is looking a little tired," Gabby says. She makes a silly face, causing Sophie to smile. "We might even take a nap!"

***

The drive back home is a quiet one, mostly on my part. Chris tries to engage me in conversation, but I find myself just answering his questions with one word. Looking out the window, I silently talk to Addy. Sophie is trying to be strong. You would be proud of her. Turning my head, Chris sees my eyes filled with tears and grabs my hand but doesn't say anything.

When Mom and Dad arrive, Dad asks, "Does my little girl need a bear hug?"

"Always!" I answer.

Mom walks over and kisses me on the cheek. "How are you holding up?" she asks.

"We saw Sophie a little while ago. She wants me to bring her a flower from the service."

"This has got to be so hard for her," Dad says clearing his throat.

"She's showing us that she's stronger than we think," I sigh.

***

The drive to the cemetery seems longer than it should be. I find Mom, Dad, and Chris carrying on a conversation while I stare out the window. Thankfully, nobody is pressing me to talk, and I can be lost in my thoughts.

Paul and Susie walk up as we get out of the car. Paul introduces us to Susie, and I introduce them to my parents.

"I think you will be pleased, Beth. We have had to ask for more chairs to be set up," Paul says.

"Really?" I ask.

"They're setting them up now."

The canopy makes it easier to find. I read the headstones and markers as we make our way toward the gravesite. Locating her marker, I squat down beside it. Kissing my fingers, I touch Aunt Millie's name. "Hi, Aunt Millie. You're going to have company. It's your best friend, Addy."

Mom hears me and smiles.

Susie walks up as I walk up to Addy's casket. She says, "I hope the flowers are okay."

"They're so pretty," I remark as I work to remove a flower. "I'm honoring a request from Sophie." Holding a single white rose, "The lilacs are really strong."

"That's funny-- I didn't ask for any in the arrangement," Susie says. Looking through the arrangement, neither of us can see lilacs. "I don't see any, but I can sure smell them."

"I do too," Paul says. We then turn and look at each other and smile, "It's Addy," I nod.

"I have seats in the front row for you," Paul says, "along with Mrs. Snow."

I am pleased to see so many people attending. Mrs. Snow was right when she said they were a family, seeing Addy's coworkers and residents with their family members. I notice Henry waiting to take a seat. He looks over at me, tips his hat and smiles. I'm even more surprised to see the faces of Autumn, Karli, Madison, Paige, Lexi, and Rachel, from work. They smile and wave as they take their seats several rows back.

Mrs. Snow walks up to the casket and pauses for several minutes, standing there quietly. She comes over to where I am sitting and before taking her seat gives me a hug and tells me that I'm an angel. Paul makes his way over and she points at him and says, "And there's another angel," giving him a hug. Paul then helps her to her seat. Turning around in my seat, I understand what Paul meant about the chairs. Even with the extra chairs, several people are left having to stand.

Paul does an amazing job on the service and although he never knew Addy, he was able to share a piece of her heart with everyone there. He told me he had talked a great deal with Mrs. Snow, Addy's coworkers, and of course, Sophie. I know if Sophie would have been strong enough to attcnd, she would have approved. During the service, I studied the flower I selected for Sophie. So delicate, just like Sophie. At the conclusion of the service, we all stood and recited the Lord's

Prayer. Throughout the service, there was a strong scent of lilacs with several people commenting on it.

When it was over, people stood around and talked. The girls from work came over to say hello. "The flowers are beautiful and smell amazing," one of them said.

"Did you smell the lilacs?" another one asked.

"Lilacs were her favorite," I told them.

"The service was very sweet, Beth," Lexi said.

Karli looks at the others, and hands me an envelope. "We took up a collection at work. Maybe you can use it towards her marker."

"You are always doing fundraisers and bake sales. This was our time to help," Madison says.

"You guys are the best," I said through tears giving them each a hug.

"See you on Monday," Rachel says waving.

Paul and I watch as Mrs. Snow stands at the casket. She takes her hand and softly pats the casket. Fingering one of the flowers, she plucks it from the rest. She smells it and closes her eyes. Watching this, I swallow hard as I try not to cry. She walks over to us fighting to maintain her composure. Looking over at Paul, he too has tear filled eyes. She hugs us both goodbye, then Paul walks her to her car.

Mom and Dad head to the car while I ask Chris for a few minutes with Addy. Silently, I let Addy know, I don't think I will ever forget you.

You have taught me some things about myself as well as others. You don't have to worry; I will be there for Sophie and continue to tell her how much you love her. No longer able to keep the tears from falling, I say aloud, "Goodbye Addy." I turn around and walk into Chris' outstretched arms.

As we pull away, I see Paul and Susie holding hands, standing in front of Addy's casket. Closing my eyes, I take a deep breath and look down at the flower in my hand. "Can we stop by the care center so I can give Sophie her flower?"

As I walk down the hall, Gabby meets me. She looks at the flower in my hand, smiles and says, "Sophie has had a rough afternoon. We gave her something to relax her and she's sleeping now."

Holding up the flower, "Here's the flower I promised her."

"It's beautiful," Gabby says. "I will put it in some water and set it beside her bed. She can see it when she wakes up. I will let her know you came by."

"Could you also let her know that everyone could smell lilacs? The funny thing is, there weren't any in the flower arrangements. We took it as a sign from Addy."

"Those were her favorite!" Gabby laughs. "Take care, Beth."

As I open the car door and get in, I ask, "Who's ready for an early dinner?"

"It sounds wonderful," Mom answers.

"What do you feel up for?" as Chris begins listing names of area restaurants.

"How about a nice juicy steak?" I ask.

"Barney's has the best steaks," Dad says.

"And the best rolls," Chris adds.

During the ride to the restaurant, Mom talks about the bazaar and their plans to start baking this week.

***

The food was delicious and a nice end to the day. Before heading to bed, I stop at Addy's room. I hope the service was okay, Addy, I silently say. I'm glad it's over. Looking at the pictures on the dresser, something is different. Addy is gone from the picture again. As I look at the remaining two pictures, it becomes evident. Addy is now in the picture with Aunt Millie. They're arm and arm and smiling! I flip over the picture to read the back "Addy and Millie, Best friends and together forever!"

Chris walks upstairs and sees me sitting on the bed. "Everything okay?" he asks, taking a seat beside me.

"Look at this," I say, handing him the picture.

"What is this?"

"It was the picture of Addy She's not in it anymore."

"I can see that."

"She's now in the picture with Aunt Millie," I point out.

"They're together again, just like you said."

"It gets better, read the back."

"Addy and Millie, Best friends and together forever!" he reads aloud.

I take a deep breath and turn to Chris. "I just want to say thank you for everything today and for the past several weeks."

"I'm relieved things will be getting back to normal," he sighs.

TWENTY-TWO

As Chris and I sit in the kitchen, I review my agenda for today as well as the next several days. "I have my shopping list for the items needed for the baking marathon. I'm going to pop to the store after I finish my coffee. This week is going to be a busy one, between work and getting ready for the bazaar."

"Leave the breakfast dishes and I will do them. This will help you get your shopping done quicker," he offers.

"I appreciate that. I can't believe the bazaar is this Saturday."

"Can I make a suggestion that next year you skip the bazaar all together and write a check instead of having to go through what you did with Amber Lynn?"

"I'm not going to make any decision concerning next year, right now."

Returning from the grocery store, I jockey the bags in my arms and try to open the door into the house. Setting the bags on the table, I sling my purse onto the chair. Chris walks in from the backyard with Gracie.

"Is there more to carry in?" he asks.

"There's just a few more if you don't mind. I can start emptying the bags then," I reply.

Chris makes several trips to the car. "Here's the last of the bags unless you have more being delivered," he jokes.

"Funny. I picked up a few extra ingredients and I'm glad I did. As I was leaving the store, I got a call from Natalie. She is also doing the bazaar. She told me that there was a sign-up sheet at the church for preorders that Amber Lynn had put up. She sent me the list on my phone so I can count them in my tally. I asked that she write on the bottom of the sign-up sheet that no more preorders will be accepted."

"I don't understand why Amber Lynn wouldn't share that information with everyone."

"Thankfully, we don't think like her. Maybe she is doing it to be mean." Wanting to change the subject from Amber Lynn, "Mom should be starting on the banana bread today. They will stick them in the freezer, and we will pull them out the day before the bazaar to finish them. It's such an immense help to have one less thing to bake, especially since I am back to making the apple dumplings."

While I am busy doing laundry, Chris looks at the picture Natalie sent me. "Why is Amber Lynn calling your cinnamon bundles, 'cinnamon rolls'? The bundles are way better anyway."

"Beats me," I answer.

"What does your work schedule look like this week?" Chris asks.

"Well," I sigh. "I work tomorrow and Tuesday and I'll be baking all day Wednesday and Thursday."

"What then?"

"Friday we will finish setting up for the bazaar. Saturday is the bazaar and I work Sunday."

"You are going to be so tired on Sunday. Can't you ask someone to pick it up for you?"

"I'll get through it. I will feel so much better knowing that the bazaar is over," I say as I grab the laundry basket and walk upstairs.

Chris yells up the stairs, "I am going to call your folks to see how the bread making is going." It rings several times before someone answers. "I thought I would call and see how it's going at your place. Are you two ready to open your own bakery yet?"

"Not a chance," Dad says. "Mother is working me to the bone. I'm so tired. The only break I got was when I sat down to eat lunch."

Walking back into the kitchen, Chris switches the phone to speaker. "I had to beg to sit down during my lunch break," Dad whines.

"Wow, she is tough," sympathizes Chris.

"Don't listen to a thing he is saying," Mom says. "He is such a whiner. It wouldn't be so bad, but he thinks he needs to sample every batch. I keep telling him that if you slice the loaf up and take a piece out of the middle, someone is going to notice."

"Well," Chris says, "that depends on how you cut it. If you use a really sharp knife, it will make cleaner edges. You can then piece them back together with hardly anyone noticing. Trust me, I am a pro!" as he moves closer to the phone.

I walk back in just in time to ear the last part. "That explains a lot around here," I add.

"Well, the last loaves are in, and I think we are going to call it a day soon," Mom says. "I'm exhausted. I've been on my feet all day and my back is aching."

"You need to take a couple of ibuprofen and go sit down. Let Daddy load the dishwasher and clean up the kitchen."

"Whose side are you on, pumpkin?" asks Dad.

"Daddy, she would do the same for you if you were hurting and you know it," I scold.

"Yeah, you're right," he says.

"He just brought me a glass of water and the bottle of ibuprofen," says Mom, sticking up for Dad.

"I am kinda getting fond of wearing this apron," Dad laughs.

"How are you guys doing over there?" Mom asks.

"Well, I got all the shopping done for the baking marathon," I say, "and have been busy organizing things for the bazaar. I have everything from upstairs moved into the dining room and it's getting full. I got an interesting phone call from Natalie who is also selling things in the bazaar. After her church service today, she was walking around with her little girl and noticed that Amber Lynn had put up sign-up sheets for preorders. Amber Lynn didn't even bother to tell anyone. Some people are having to get more supplies in order to be able to fill the orders."

"That girl! Honestly, what's wrong with her?" Mom asks.

"I don't know. I hope someday she learns that you can't treat people like that."

"I told Beth to just write a check next year and not even be involved with the bazaar. Amber Lynn has soured the whole thing for me." Chris says sternly.

"I would have to agree with you Chris," Dad says. "Well sorry to cut this short, but if I am going to get any dinner, I need to start cleaning this kitchen."

"Thankfully, we have our leftovers from last night," Mom reminds Dad.

"It's nice nobody has to cook tonight," I respond.

***

The next morning, as I'm checking the assignment sheet at work, I see that I am to take over for Jesse. Naomi, who is working at the desk today and manning the phones, asks about the craft bazaar after seeing the flyer I posted in the breakroom. "I want to go to the bazaar so I can maybe start my Christmas shopping early," says Naomi.

I respond, "It's a nice bazaar with a variety of items. Good luck with your shopping and be sure to stop and say hi."

I walk over to Jesse and put my hand on his shoulder. "Hello there, sir. I'm following you today. Would you like to go home?"

He looks up and smiles. "Always! I'm sure my little munchkins at home will be glad to see me. I'm off tonight, so I am going to surprise my wife, Haley, by taking the kids to the park and getting them out of the house. I hope Haley can just maybe have some quiet time to herself or take a nap."

"You better watch out, or you might be in the running for Father of the Year," I tell him.

"Haley goes out of her way to keep the kids quiet while I'm sleeping."

"Did you have a busy shift?"

"It wasn't bad. I only have a few patients to turn over to you this morning."

The shift change routine is the same and begins with Jesse introducing me to the patient and any family members that are present. He summarizes why the patient is here, including signs and symptoms. As he talks, I check the patient's name band.

As Jesse reviews the tests ordered, results obtained, and clarifies what is still pending, I get a current set of vital signs. We then review any allergies, fall risks, and medications given. Erasing Jesse's name, I sign my name on the information board and ask the patient about their current pain rating. Jesse then asks them if they have any questions or need anything. With no further questions, we proceed to the next patient.

Jesse wishes me a good shift as he gathers his stuff and leaves. I take my seat and reach for my drink. Looking around the nurses' station, I don't know where I set it. I walk back to the breakroom to see if I left it on the table when I clocked in. After checking my locker and coming up empty, I retrieve money to buy a bottle of water from the vending machine in the lobby.

Taking a long drink, I feel like a camel. The coffee this morning has made me thirsty. Before heading back, I stop at the triage desk. "Good morning, ladies."

"Hi Beth, how are you today?" Madison asks.

"Pretty good, thanks."

"It was a nice service on Saturday," Rachel says.

"Yes, it was," Madison joins in. You and Chaplain Paul were so kind for arranging all that. I just can't get over how you donated the burial plots."

"Where did you guys hear that?" I ask.

"Chaplain Paul told us after some of us were asking where she was going to be buried. He said you were doing the same for her sister, so they could be together. You have such a big heart," Madison says.

"Me? What about all of you here taking up a collection for her marker. Chris and I weren't going to be using them and this way they can talk with my family."

Rachel laughs, "What did you say?"

"They're in our family plot and she is going to be next to my Aunt Millie, so they can talk again."

She then gives me a puzzled look. "I just look at things differently," I laugh. I almost spilled it about Addy and Aunt Millie being friends in a past life. "Well, I came out for this," holding up the bottle of water. "I better get back and check on my patients. Talk to you later."

While sitting in the nurses' station and reviewing my patients' orders, Karli walks up and asks for help. I follow her into her patient's room. "Mrs. Reynolds, this is Beth, and she is going to help me get you comfortable," says Karli. Positioning ourselves on each side of the patient, we slide her up in bed.

"That feels so much better. Thank you girls."

***

The morning flies by and it's not long before I'm waiting for the elevator to take my lunch break. After glancing at all of my options, I decide on soup. Out of the corner of my eye, I see Paul.

He walks up with his tray and leans over, "We must stop meeting like this," he grins.

"Try the soup," I suggest. "I got the beef barley. It looks really good. I'll grab a table if you want to join me."

"That would be great. I'll finish getting my lunch and look for you."

Paul sits down, and after we talk briefly about the morning, the conversation turns to Addy. "You did a wonderful job on Saturday, Paul." Taking a spoonful of soup, I say, "This hits the spot today."

"I didn't tell you earlier, but I may have told a few people about you donating the cemetery plots."

"Someone mentioned it to me this morning," I tell him taking another bite.

"I hope I haven't upset you," he says as he unwraps his straw and sticks it in his drink.

"No, it's alright, I just don't like the attention on me."

"It just shows what kind of person you are and how big a heart you have."

I take a sip of my drink and change the subject, "Have you spoken to Mrs. Snow?"

"Yes, I called her this morning to check on Sophie. Mrs. Snow said she is getting weaker."

"She has lost her will to live now that Addy is gone," I say quietly.

"What does your schedule look like for the rest of the week?"

"I work tomorrow and Sunday. I have the craft bazaar Saturday, so I will be making cinnamon bundles and apple dumplings on my days off."

"Where is the bazaar on Saturday?"

"Grace Point Church. It runs from 8:00 a.m. to 5:00 p.m. You should come check it out if you aren't doing anything."

"Susie loves craft bazaars."

Checking the time, "I better be getting back." We wish each other a good rest of the day and part ways.

While at lunch, my patients were discharged. I offer to watch Karli's patients so she can go to lunch. I increase my patient load by picking up a family of three with flu symptoms and a young boy with an injury who was playing football. Sitting in the nurses' station and looking over my patients' charts, several of the girls ask about the bazaar. I end up taking preorders for the cinnamon bundles and apple dumplings. Boy am I thankful I picked up extra supplies.

***

I call Mom on my way home to see how her jewelry making is going and she in turn invites Chris and me over for a barbeque tonight. "It sounds great. What can we bring?"

"Just yourselves with Gracie of course," she answers.

"I'll come up with something and we'll be over after Chris gets home."

Something chocolate would be nice, looking in the freezer. Spying a Texas sheet cake in the back, "Eureka," I yell out. Carrying it into the house, I do a happy dance as Gracie watches. Chris arrives home to see the cake on the counter.

"Is this dinner?" he asks.

"Funny! My parents invited us over for a cookout tonight and that's dessert."

Gracie enjoys the ride over, sitting in the backseat with her head peeking out the window. "Nothing like the wind at your ears, huh Gracie?" Chris laughs.

As we walk in the door, Mom says, to Gracie, "Sadie is in the backyard waiting for you."

Setting the cake on the counter, Mom looks over, "That looks yummy."

"Texas sheet cake," I say smiling, "for our chocolate fix."

Dad walks into the kitchen and gives me a hug and a kiss. "Did I hear someone say we are having dessert first?"

"No, you did not," I answer.

"You behave yourself," Mother urges. "Chris, help him do the grilling, so we aren't eating charcoal tonight."

"Ouch," Dad says, playfully grabbing his heart. "That hurt!"

Chris looks over at me, "We better get out of here. It's starting to get a little warm in here if you know what I mean." Dad carries the plate of meat outside while Chris carries the spatula and tongs.

Mom smiles, "Those two are like two little kids when they get together."

"We're lucky they get along so well!"

"So, just one more day to work this week?" Mom asks.

"Yup," yawning. "I will be glad when this is over, I can tell you that much. This whole thing has really zapped my energy. I thought with the stress from Addy gone, I would have more energy."

"Well, it takes time. I haven't really seen you slow down any."

"That's for sure!" Chris says carrying in the platter. "Soups on," he announces as we begin fixing our plates.

After we've finished eating, I begin cutting the cake while Dad gets out the vanilla ice cream. Dad and Chris go into the family room to watch TV while Mom and I stay at the table and talk.

"This cake is so moist. I need to make sure I have the recipe," Mom says.

"You make it with buttermilk. It's not bad with the ice cream on the side either," I say. "It finished off the dinner quite nicely. Thank you for inviting us over."

"This way you didn't have to cook, and I could see if you needed to borrow any baking things," Mom says.

"Do you think it matters which I bake first?"

"You could do either one, really. It's not like they won't keep. I hope you aren't going to need an army to do the baking."

"Maybe just a small one. Like the one that just ate cake," I laugh, pointing to Chris and Dad.

Kissing them goodbye, I say, "Thanks again for dinner."

"Thank you for bringing dessert. It was delicious," Mom says.

"Don't you want your leftover cake?" Dad asks.

"No, I'm leaving it here for you. We're going to be bombarded with sweets soon. See you bright and early Wednesday," I say waving goodbye.

On the drive home, Chris turns to me and says, "Well, just one more workday for you, sweetie. I hope you don't fall asleep counting apple dumplings and cinnamon bundles."

"Nope, that's tomorrow night!" I laugh.

TWENTY-THREE

Walking out of work, the day is a blur other than having additional orders for baked goods. On the drive home, I play over in my mind what else needs to be done for tomorrow's baking session. I can't even recall the number we made last year. I will have to ask if Chris remembers. It doesn't really matter anyway, because the remainder left at the end of the day, I have decided to take to Mrs. Snow and her staff. I'm thankful that I have reinforcements again this year. I want to get to bed at a decent time tonight, so I am ready to face the day!

While busy fixing dinner, I get a phone call.

"Hi Beth, it's Peggy, Christopher's Mom."

Trying not to laugh as she reminds me who she is, I respond, "Hi Peggy, how are you guys doing since you got back from your trip?"

"We're doing great. It was so nice getting away and visiting with friends. I wanted to thank you both for watching our place. I hope it wasn't too much of an inconvenience for you with you both working and adjusting your schedules and all to accommodate my demands."

Wincing at her choice of words, "No, Peggy, it was fine. Demands?"

"Apparently, Chris and Andy told their father my list read like ransom demands."

My mouth flies open, as I try and think what to say. "I'm sure the two of them were just kidding."

"I suppose," she says quietly.

"You know your boys love you and Pop very much and would do anything in the world for you."

"I know they do. And I know that you, Faith, and baby Charlie do too. I'm so lucky to have you and Faith for daughters-in-law and Charlie for a sweet grandson."

"Absolutely."

"Speaking of babies," she starts.

Here it comes, I think to myself,

"You need to go and see for yourself how well Faith and Andy are getting along with Charlie."

"We'd love to, it's just things have been a little hectic around here."

"Well, we are anxiously waiting for more grandbabies to love. You know, maybe in the future from you and Christopher? It's your turn."

"Yes, I know. We're just leaving things to the man upstairs at this point."

"I understand, dear."

As I work in the kitchen, I try to stay focused on the conversation.

"I guess people don't realize that when you're older and retired, it sometimes gets lonely," continues Peggy.

"It's been a while since we have gotten together and gone out to dinner. Why don't you check your calendar, and we can make a date to go out, the four of us," I offer.

"That sounds wonderful. We could even extend the invitation to Andy and Faith if you wouldn't mind. I'm sure they would love a chance to have a night out with adults."

"That's sounds perfect. We should be free after the bazaar on Saturday. I'm busy making cinnamon bundles tomorrow and apple dumplings on Thursday. Friday we're busy getting last minute things done and setting up at the church. So, after Saturday is over, we should be free."

"You know what you need?"

"What?" I respond hesitantly.

"Another set of hands helping you bake. What time do you want me, Captain?" she asks enthusiastically.

"Are you sure, Peggy?"

"I would love to spend the day with my daughter-in-law and feel needed."

"My folks will be helping as well."

"That's great. I would love to catch up with them too."

"Well if you are sure, we are starting at 8:00 a.m. tomorrow," I sigh.

"I will see you then and thank you."

I hang up just as Chris walks in.

"Who have you been talking to? I have been trying to call you for the last forty-five minutes."

"Your Mother," I reply dryly.

"That's not the answer I was expecting. Is everything okay? And Pop?"

"They're both fine. She called to thank us for helping to watch the house."

"I'm sure that didn't take forty-five minutes."

"Well let's see. Let me try to summarize the conversation. She knows about the list of demands comment, and I tried to downplay it and to reiterate how much you and Andy both love them."

"Yikes! Pop must have 'spilled the beans'."

"She told me that we need to go and visit Charlie again."

"Which we do," he nods.

"I agree. As soon as the bazaar is over, we will have some free time. We can even offer to babysit so they can have some time alone."

"And? Did she talk about babies and us?"

"Yup. She said she is anxiously waiting for more grand babies and that it's our turn. I did tell her that we are leaving it up to the one upstairs and she said she understood. She also told me how sometimes even though you are retired, you get lonely and want to feel needed. I told her we need to set up a date to go out to dinner and she thought it would be nice to include Andy and Faith."

"That sounds like a fun night!"

"She is also coming over tomorrow to help with the baking."

"Wow," walking over and feeling my forehead. "She must have caught you at a weak moment."

"Now stop! I like your parents. It's just sometimes, I get tired of hearing about babies."

"I understand and thank you for including my mom in the baking. I am sure she is calling her friends telling them what she is going to be doing," he laughs.

"I decided on the way home that you could eat the rest of my leftovers from the other night for your dinner tonight."

"I can't," he says looking glum. "I already ate your leftovers for lunch today. I will just make myself a sandwich or have a bowl of cereal. What are you going to eat?"

"I might just have yogurt or something light," patting my stomach and making a face. "And before you ask, I ate soup for lunch and Paul is my witness."

"Okay," holding up his hand, "I believe you."

"What's in your hand?"

"You got something in the mail."

I open up the envelope to see it is a thank you card from Mrs. Snow, Sophie, and the staff. She wrote that Addy and Sophie would both have been happy with the service. "That's so sweet," propping it up on the counter.

While Chris eats, I begin staging the kitchen. Mom called to make sure nothing else is needed for tomorrow. I let her know that Peggy has offered to help as well. Chris waits until I have hung up to pull out the list from his shirt pocket. He carefully smooths it out before handing it to me. "Here's the rest of the preorders from the guys."

"This is everything now, right? No more preorders? You aren't going to pull anymore out of a hat, from behind your ear, or out of one of your other pockets, are you?" I tease.

"Correct! We are officially closed for preorders. I will stick to my guns. No matter how much they beg or bribe me. I will tell them they have to come to the bazaar."

"What's our total anyway that we need for the orders? I took a few orders myself today at work. I laid the sheet by the tally you started. Don't forget to add your orders from today too."

After several minutes, he says, "Okay drum roll," as he begins hitting the table with his pencil and hand. "It brings the total to 19 dozen cinnamon bundles, 15 dozen baked dumplings, and 8 dozen frozen dumplings. This doesn't even include what you need to have on hand to sell."

"It sounds worse than it really is. One muffin tin will make a dozen bundles and the dumplings actually go pretty fast when you do it like an assembly line."

"That's the spirit!" Chris yells.

After the kitchen is set up with the necessary bowls, utensils, measuring cups, pans, and ingredients, I shut the light out and go upstairs. Slipping on my nightgown, Chris asks, "So how are you feeling since Addy's chapter has closed?"

"There have been a couple times I felt like something might happen, like when I went to the grocery store for the baking stuff and picked up things when you were sick. But it turns out none of my dead relatives were working," I say smiling.

"Maybe it was their day off," Chris teases.

"I feel really sad for Sophie. I know in my heart that had their situation presented itself to us, we would have adopted them and not have let Sophie's heart condition stand in the way."

"Not everybody feels the way that you do."

Sitting in bed, I reach into the drawer of my nightstand for hand lotion. To my surprise, I pull out a packet of forget-me-not flower seeds. "How did these get in there?" showing Chris.

"Instead of sawing logs tonight, you are going to try and sow a row," he laughs.

"You're a regular comedian today!" Gracie is curled up at the end of the bed and sighs heavily. "She even thought it was bad." Rolling over on my side, I try and get comfortable. I wonder if the seeds are a message from Addy.

***

Mom arrives right on time, wearing her apron. Dad will come over later. Chris went into work already in hopes of finishing early. After making a pot of coffee, I see Peggy arriving bearing gifts.

"My goodness," Mom says to Peggy, "Let me help you lighten your load."

"I stopped and picked up some Danish pastries to have while we work," says Peggy.

"How thoughtful!"

"It's the least I can do for my daughter-in-law," Peggy says as she gives my arm a squeeze.

While she puts on her apron, I go over the game plan. The idea is to start with six batches of dough. After they are all baked and iced, we will repeat the entire process all over again. With the kitchen warm, the dough will rise quickly. I don't want to get too ahead of ourselves and overproof the dough.

Over the next several hours, the three of us work well together. Dad pops in at eleven. "It sure smells good in here. You can smell them from the driveway," Dad says.

Dad is quick to start assembling the boxes. Chris' Dad, "Pop," also arrives to help. "This is so sweet," I say, kissing him on the cheek. "You didn't have to come over."

"Peggy wanted me to and I didn't want you to think I didn't want to help," says Pop.

He and Dad begin working on the preorders. Once a box is filled, they print a name on the box and cross them off the master list. With everyone getting hungry, Dad and Pop run out for sandwiches.

While we take a break and eat lunch, Madison from work calls. She wants to see if I could trade days. It would give me the Sunday after the bazaar off. It isn't until I look closer at my schedule that I realize it would also have me work several days in a row. I will be tired, but at least I will have the day after the bazaar off, I think to myself.

It was Peggy who stands up and claps her hands together, declaring the lunch break over. As we laugh in surprise, we get back to work as ordered. Feeling tired from the routine, I pour myself a glass of water and continue to work. Chris comes home to find us all laughing and kidding one another.

"Now this is what I like to see," he says smiling. "Boy does it smell good in here!" Giving me a kiss, "Your hair even smells sweet," he jokes.

After the last batch was boxed, Chris looks around, trying to be nonchalant. "What are you looking for?" I ask.

"I was wondering if you guys saved me one. Have you even tasted them? What if they're awful and you can't sell them?" he asks.

"We will sell them anyway," we all say in unison and laugh.

Reaching into the cabinet, I pull out a plate of bundles, as his eyes light up. I cut a few bundles in half for us all to sample, as Chris reaches for one.

"They're light, with just the right amount of cinnamon and sugar. I give it two thumbs up!" he blurts.

Laughing, we all agree our hard work has paid off. After the last dish has been washed, "This kitchen is now officially closed," I announced.

"What's for dinner?" Chris asks.

"You are a bottomless pit!" I reply.

"Come on. We all have to eat dinner. Let's order pizzas for everyone. We can all eat together, and then everybody can go home and crash," Chris suggests.

"To do this all over again tomorrow except were making apple dumplings," I smirk.

Pop and Dad rode with Chris to pick up the pizzas. Chuckling to myself, I remembered how Dad offered to pay if he could have an advance in his allowance from Mom. "I want to get the table ready for when the guys get back," I tell Mom and Peggy. Getting up from the chair, I quickly sit back down.

"What's wrong?" Mom asks looking at my face.

"I must have gotten up too quickly," I answer.

"Just sit there," Mom says sternly, handing me my glass of water.

After several minutes, I am feeling much better.

"It's my own fault. I haven't drunk much water today," I confess.

"Just sit there," Peggy said. "You have been on your feet all day."

It's not long before the fellows return with dinner, and we eat with many of us feeling too tired to chew. Peggy and Mom help to tidy up the kitchen before leaving so we can start with a clean slate in the morning. As my head hits the pillow, I am thankful to call it a day.

***

"How did you sleep?" Chris asks.

"Awful!" I answer. "I dreamt we were at the bazaar and trying to sell the cinnamon bundles. We would open a box and it would be empty and then we would open another box and it would be empty. People were in line and yelling. Amber Lynn was there, too, with a smug look on her face."

I walk into the dining room and open up a box.

Chris stands frowning as he watches. "What are you doing?" he asks.

"Just checking," I answer.

"Are you satisfied that it was just a dream now?"

After opening two more boxes, "Now I am," I answer.

As I slip the apron over my head and tie the strings, I quickly glance over at the clock. "Our folks will be over soon to start the process all over again. I was so tired yesterday; it slipped my mind to tell you that I have traded and have Sunday off to recuperate. I will have to work several days in a row, but I think it will be worth it."

"I'm not crazy about you having to work that many days in a row." Chris frowns.

"Well, sometimes you just have to take the good with the bad," I tell him.

"I have a surprise for you," he says cheerfully. "I have taken the next two days off to help you."

As my eyes fill with tears, I put my arms around him and kiss him. "You don't know what this means to me. Really? Do you know how wonderful you are?"

"I do, I do," he answers unabashedly. "There's no denying it, so I won't," he shrugs smirking.

The cavalry arrives and a game plan is discussed. Chris and Pop work on peeling and preparing the apples while Peggy and I make the pie crust. Mom and Dad have the task of forming the apple dumplings and putting them in the oven. With fewer steps than the bundles, we were able to make, bake and package them in record time. While taking a break, we survey the kitchen and dining room. The kitchen looks like a bakery blew up, but it smells delightful.

With Dad, Pop, and Chris having all the orders accounted for, boxed, and labeled, we girls set to cleaning the kitchen. Mom and Peggy made meat and cheese sandwiches while I got out the condiments and opened some chips. Most of us didn't feel like eating with the exclusion of Chris. Later, when everyone was leaving, I made sure to thank them and let them know how grateful I was for their help.

After my much deserved bath I crawled into bed and sighed. When Chris rolled over in bed to kiss me goodnight, it was sweeter than usual. "Hmm, I think I tasted a little apple dumpling, if I'm not mistaken," I accuse him, playfully.

"It's your imagination," he said rolling over, aware he was caught.

***

As we walk downstairs, the sweet smell hits us in the face. "There is no way I could work in a bakery," I say. "I'm tired of smelling and looking at them, already." As I get out the pitcher of orange juice and pour a glass, Chris surprisingly agrees.

"So, what's on today's roster, Mrs. Davis?" he asks.

"Mom is going to come over and we will get the banana breads all packaged up. Then I thought we could start loading the truck. They're allowing us to come in at 4:30 p.m. The church isn't responsible for anything loss or stolen, so I won't be taking the food and crafts until tomorrow, but at least our booth will be set up. I will pack my car up later to make a quick getaway in the morning. I also need to get cash from the bank and gather up some office supplies to have on hand."

"As organized as you are, we will get it all done. I have no doubt."

"I want to be at the church early tomorrow to set things up. The doors open to the public at 8:00 a.m."

***

On our way to the church. Chris stops by the bank. As the teller is busy counting out the bills, she becomes distracted when she notices someone has written on one and has to start over.

"Honestly! I don't know why people do that," she scoffs.

"What does it say?" I ask, being curious.

She picks it up and reads it out loud. " 'I'm waiting Sophie'. Weird!" she says, shaking her head, clearly upset.

I will myself to stay calm, while chewing the inside of my cheek. She places it back in the stack begins recounting, and then says, "I can give you another one, if you don't want this one."

"Don't worry about it. I don't mind." I tell her.

She then shoves the stack in an envelope and hands it to me.

Once in the car, I tear open the envelope and fan out the bills to hurry and show Chris.

"What's wrong?" he asks. "Did you get a message from Addy?"

"What makes you say that?" I ask. "I haven't showed you anything yet."

"You just have that look and you were speed walking out to the car."

"Look what is written on this five-dollar bill? The teller was counting it out and noticed it. She became upset and had to start over counting it back to me. I tried to stay calm after she told me what it said.

"Addy wanted you to see it, Beth."

"I need another five-dollar bill. I want to hang on to this one and not use it." I ask for Chris' wallet, and I watch as the writing slowly fades then disappears. "It's gone. Just like when she wrote on the mirror."

"That's because the message was meant for your eyes only."

I look over at him with a puzzled look. "Who are you?"

TWENTY-FOUR

The morning is busy as Chris and Dad make several trips into the church while Mom and I begin placing things. Chris and Dad stay around until we are set up to make sure we don't need anything tweaked. "Everything looks great. Now we just need to sell everything, so we don't have to lug it home," I tell Mom.

"I second that," Mom grins.

As the first couple of hours creep by, I stand up to stretch my legs. Walking to the front of our display, I straighten things that people have moved while looking. "Your jewelry is so pretty, Mom. What a neat combination of the wood and stones."

"Your Dad gave me the idea to use some of his woodworking scraps."

A woman walks up to the booth that I recall from seeing earlier. Mom and I both commented on her vivid blue scarf that she had tied to her brown handbag. She carefully looks at all our items on display. "Could I see some of your other stock?" she asks.

Mom and I look at each other confused. "Other stock?" I repeated back to her. I give Mom a look as I assure the woman that all of our items are out on display.

She then goes on to explain she is looking for a wreath with purple. After leaving the table and then returning for one more look, she finally buys one. As she walks away, I sigh heavily and voice, "It's going to be a long day if we have very many more like her."

Not long after, a woman walks up holding a lengthy list in her hand. "I'm determined to make a dent in my Christmas shopping today," she declares. "I have a preorder of cinnamon rolls and apple dumplings to pick up."

I feel like a broken record explaining there was an error on the preorder sheet. They are cinnamon bundles and not rolls but just as delicious if not more.

As items sell, Mom and I take turns in filling the empty space and moving things around. Chris comes to help during the afternoon and to give us a break.

Another woman hurriedly walks up to the table, appearing upset. Chris gets her name and pulls her order card. As we look over her order, we read it out loud. "That's not right!" she says loudly.

Chris and I look at each other surprised.

"I'm sorry," she pauses. "I don't mean to be testy. I'm just really upset," she sighs. "I stupidly left my wallet at a booth and luckily it was turned in. I had asked someone to hold a necklace for me while I went to get my wallet. When I went back to pay for it, they told me it had been sold. I asked why they didn't hold it for me and she said the chairperson for the bazaar told her she couldn't hold items. The gal that had the booth said she felt bad."

"Oh my, I am so sorry."

"The lady that is the chairperson came up to the booth while I was there and told me 'a sale is a sale'. She was snarky about it. She was tapping her clipboard with her fancy pen. I had a necklace picked out for my mother-in-law's birthday. She's hard to buy for, and to make matters worse, her birthday is tomorrow."

"I will be right back with your order," I tell her, trying to help her calm down. Surprisingly, when I return to the table, Mom, and the woman along with Chris are all smiling. While they were waiting, Chris encouraged the woman to look through the jewelry that Mom had made. Happily, the woman picked out a necklace set for her mother-in-law that she liked even better. As Mom handed the woman her shopping bag, I grabbed a cinnamon bundle from the cake plate and gave it to her.

"What's this?" the woman asked, surprised.

"To help sweeten your day," I told her. "Enjoy it with a cup of tea," I suggested.

"Thank you," she said with tears in her eyes. "I will!"

Peggy and Pop came by to chat and to look at all the crafts. Peggy surprised us when she hinted that maybe next year she would make something to sell at our booth.

The afternoon was much busier than the morning. I was thankful that Chris was there with an extra set of hands, especially running to the back to get the orders from the freezer.

"Chris must have gotten lost," I tell mom and the woman waiting for her order. Now with another order for a frozen goodie, I leave Mom to staff the booth. I'm surprised to find Chris standing around and talking to Peter, who is also there helping his wife, Dana. They have a booth selling fresh baked cookies.

"Hi, Peter, how's it going?" I ask.

"Dana decided this year, that if people could smell her fresh baked cookies, she'd sell more. And I think her strategy is working!" replies Peter.

"That's great!" I say. Pointing to the chocolate on Chris' mouth, "I see Chris is helping too."

"He asked me to taste it, honest!" Chris exclaims.

"I did ask him to taste it," Peter said. "I can't eat anymore let alone smell anything sweet."

"We feel the same way about our stuff."

"Please don't tell Dana," Peter begs.

Putting her hand on Peter's shoulder, "Tell Dana what?" she asks.

His eyes widen as he stammers, "Uh, nothing."

"Your cookies smell amazing," I tell Dana. "We will have to get some unless Chris decides to eat them all back here," I tease.

"You don't have to explain, Peter, I'm not mad," Dana says. "I get the gist of what he was helping you with. I can't stand looking at or smelling them either. Chris, honestly though, how are they?"

"It was the best cookie I have eaten today, and I say that truthfully."

"I hate to break this party up, but I have some more orders. Chris, here are the slips. Please put their names on the shopping bags as you bring them out."

Chris stands at attention and salutes, as I shoot him a look, shaking my head.

Dana follows suit and rattles off instructions for Peter. "I need more boxes for the cookies, and I promise to stop asking you to sample them. I don't want to have to take you to the Emergency Room to have your stomach pumped," she laughs. "See you later, Beth."

The same routine of retrieving orders, wrapping, and bagging purchases repeats itself well into the afternoon. Chris, Mom, and I shared a cinnamon bundle while sipping a cup of tea. "Now we just need to sell everything, pack it up, and try to put this behind us until next year, right Beth?" Chris asks.

"What a nice thought Chris," I nod.

With the remaining orders of cinnamon bundles and apple dumplings picked up, the rest of the afternoon is spent visiting with shoppers. Getting up to stretch my legs, I walk around to see the other booths. Not long after, I walk back to our booth, fingering a new scarf around my neck. "Don't you just love it? I traded it for a flower arrangement."

Mom smiles and picks out a few necklaces. When she walks back to the booth, she is holding a wooden paper towel holder with a chicken painted on the front of it.

"Wow, look what you got. A chicken." I say.

"She marked it down because she didn't think it was going to sell. Bernice's husband, Harold, made it and Bernice painted it. Isn't it cute?" Mom gushes.

"Adorable," I fuss as Chris looks at me with raised eyebrows.

"You are just going to have to come over to my house and admire it. I bought the last one," Mom says proudly.

"Darn," pretending to pout.

"You want me to go ask her if they can make you one?" as she starts to walk off.

"No!" Getting up to stop her. "Like you said, I will just have to admire yours."

***

"Five o'clock couldn't have come soon enough!" I say yawning. As we watch a few stragglers hurry to make their last-minute purchases, I begin to gather up the items that are left. Several crafters are walking around trying to barter their wares. After watching Mom eye my remaining wreath, I unfasten it from its hook and hand it to her. "You can have my last one."

"Really? I know just where I am going to put it," she says beaming.

Boxing up the remaining cinnamon bundles and apple dumplings, I draw a smiley face on the box. "I will take these to Mrs. Snow."

As the donation box makes its way to us, Mom gathers up a few pieces of jewelry and places them in gift boxes. With only one flower arrangement left, I carefully place it in the box. This is something the crafters did yearly and was a thoughtful way for the charity to collect items for their silent auction.

As Dad and Chris get ready to start dissembling the booth, Mom and I finish boxing everything up. After the tablecloths are folded and placed into a box, we begin making several trips to the cars. With our area swept and cleaned, we begin saying our goodbyes before leaving.

As I am telling Gina goodbye, Amber Lynn stops me. "I need your totals," she demands.

I look over at Mom as Amber Lynn repeats herself. I respond to her by saying, "I will have to get back to you. We didn't bother to add it all up."

"Well, that's unfortunate," clearly sounding perturbed. "Everyone has given me their numbers I don't understand why you can't do what everyone else is doing."

Puzzled by her outburst, I look around to see people standing around and watching. I'm embarrassed by the audience and how she is acting. "Amber Lynn, I don't understand what the big deal is. I told you I will get them for you later."

"I'm trying to find out if presale orders helped and you aren't giving me the information I need. You need to sit down and tally them before you leave. Everyone else is doing what I have asked. I expect you to do the same."

As I look around, the people I had said goodbye to a while ago are nervously sitting down and going through their sales to produce a total for her. Upset with how she has spoken to me, Chris starts to intervene. I put my hand on his arm to stop him.

"It's okay, I got this," I tell Chris.

I turn and face her head on. "I don't know how you can ask any of us to do that when most of us have already been here over eight hours. We are tired and want to go home. Several of us have kids and families we need to get home to."

"Oh really, Beth?" she lashes out. "Last I heard you only had a mangy little dog waiting for you, unless you have adopted a child or had a baby recently that nobody knows about." She fluffs her hair and looks around at her audience to see how's she scoring.

"Amber Lynn, until now, I hadn't realized how hateful and insensitive you have become. This whole thing of you being made chairperson and raising the most money has made you an ugly, spiteful person. It doesn't matter what amount I made. I plan to donate it all to the hospital's Children's Ward. We paid you the entrance fee and because you aren't taking a percentage of our sales for donation, the total shouldn't matter."

Amber Lynn takes a step closer and holds her finger up in my face. As she begins to speak, I cut her off.

After a deep breath, I continue, "The totals wouldn't matter unless you wanted to rub them in someone else's face, like maybe the chairperson from the Christmas Shop Boutique." Soon, many begin to voice their disagreement as they file by, and several walk out the door with a few squeezing my arm in support.

Later as I stand in the parking lot, still smoldering, I begin shaking. Dad walks up and asks, "What did I miss? People are talking in the parking lot about a cat fight."

"I will fill you in on the way home," Mom tells him. "I am very proud of you," Mom says as she hugs me goodbye.

"I don't know what came over me."

"A person can only take so much," Chris says. "I'm proud of you, too."

Later, I snuggle in bed with the comforter around my neck, I silently thank the one above for giving me the courage to stand up to Amber Lynn.

Smiling, I'm elated the bazaar is done and I have tomorrow off.

TWENTY-FIVE

While making the bed I'm puzzled by the way the light is coming through the window. Pulling back the shears, I can't believe my eyes. Toilet paper is strewn through the trees and dangling like Spanish moss. I run downstairs and open the front door. "You have got to be kidding me!" I yell.

Chris walks downstairs and asks, "What's got you so upset this morning?"

"Take a look for yourself. Great! Here comes someone walking their dog," I fume.

"Don't worry about it, we're not the first people in the neighborhood to have this happen to them."

"I'm embarrassed!" I quickly throw on some shoes and walk outside to survey the yard. Chris gets the pole from the attic that we use for stringing Christmas lights, to get the harder to reach areas. As neighbors walk by, they tell us they hope the kids are caught.

"I wonder why we were targeted and no one else on the block?" I ask.

"Maybe someone got the wrong house or maybe you aren't looking at the full picture," Chris replies.

"What do you mean by that?"

"You really don't have any idea who could be behind this? This has Amber Lynn's name written all over it."

"Her kids are small and aren't old enough to do something like this."

"I wasn't talking about her kids. I was thinking of Amber Lynn herself. You really set her straight yesterday and in front of a lot of people. Better yet, in front of those who maybe didn't have the courage to stand up to her."

After several more handfuls are stuffed into the trash bags, I go to the garage to place them in the bin. Reaching for another bag, I hear the phone ringing. Running inside, after several minutes of speaking to the caller, I return outside. "You won't believe what I just found out," I say to Chris. "It turns out were not alone."

"How so?" Chris asks directing the pole high up into the tree.

"Natalie called and said instead of recuperating from yesterday, that she, Jack, and the kids are busy cleaning up toilet paper in their yard. I gave her your idea of using the pole. I told her how you thought Amber Lynn could be involved. She told me Jack feels the same way."

"Nothing surprises me anymore after her display yesterday," Chris says grunting as he lifts toilet paper from the branches.

***

An hour later, we're in the kitchen getting ready for lunch, the yard is cleaned up and showing no signs of the cheap 2-ply. "I'm thankful it didn't rain last night. That would have made the clean-up so much worse."

Chris sits playing with the cap on his water. "I'm curious just how many houses were targeted," he says quietly.

Before I can say anything, we both hear the doorbell. Chris answers the door and soon voices flood into the kitchen. Looking around, I see many faces from yesterday's craft bazaar with their spouses. "Is everything okay?" I ask.

"We're sorry for coming over unannounced," as I realize it's Natalie speaking. "I know I just talked to you on the phone. Tyler Dixon called us, and my husband, Jack, felt we all needed to talk."

Jack begins, "As you know, everyone here participated in the craft bazaar and were impacted by what you said to Amber Lynn."

"Sorry," I say, as I look around.

"Impacted in a good way," Natalie goes on. "Amber Lynn has a very overpowering personality, and she uses it to belittle and manipulate people."

Someone then said, "She's a bully," as others agreed.

Jack then continues, "Well it turns out Vanessa and Owen Baxter along with Olivia and Tyler Dixson both have security cameras. I knew we needed to get together to share the photos they captured on video. I hope you don't mind us barging into your home?"

"Not at all," Chris answers, looking over at me with raised eyebrows. "Videos don't lie as to who was involved."

As they set up their laptops on the kitchen table, the rest of us file around them and wait. Gina stands beside me and says, "I wanted to thank you for standing up to her. I've tried in the past but have been too intimidated."

Jack gets our attention, and we start with the Baxter's video first. The footage shows a car pulling up with a driver and two others getting out. Then it shows them tossing toilet paper back and forth to one another trying to get it into the trees. In one scene, close to the house, the person looks right at the camera. "That looks like Amber Lynn," I hear someone say. After watching both videos, it was the group's consensus that Bridgette and April were the other two women involved and shown on the videos.

Mom and Dad appear from within the crowd. They seem very confused by the crowd. "What are you guys doing here? Is everything okay?" I ask.

"We knocked at the door, but no one heard us. We saw all the cars in the driveway and wondered the same thing," Dad says.

"We're watching surveillance videos," Chris announced.

"Momma you look tired," Beth says.

"We have spent all morning cleaning up the yard," Mom sighs.

"Some kids pulled a prank on us last night and threw toilet paper all over," Dad says frowning.

"It was actually three big kids and we have them on video." Kyle says.

I introduce Mom and Dad to the group. Mom and Dad watch the videos as the rest of us look on. Chris goes to the phone and calls the police to make a formal complaint. Thirty minutes later, an officer arrives. Mom and I along with some of the wives offer refreshments to the group.

We watch as Dad and Chris, along with several other men, sample several of the cookies and various crackers and cheeses. It was funny to hear them comparing their favorites. Dad spots Mom watching him and quickly says, "Why I don't think these are stale at all, Christopher."

The officer, after seeing the videos and getting a copy of them, asks the group what we want to see happen to Amber Lynn. As we look around at each other's faces, we are reluctant to answer.

"There wasn't any real damage except the time and inconvenience of cleaning up the mess," I offer.

"I want her to quit bullying people once and for all," Gina boldly said. "But I don't think there is anything really to take to court."

The officer says he will talk to Amber Lynn as well as April and Bridgette. "Maybe just knowing that all of you have met and have the videos might be enough to rattle them in their boots."

"I know it would me!" I tell the group.

"I would give anything to be a fly on the wall when you go to talk to them," Chris said grinning.

"I feel sorry for Bridgette. She is just tagging along to try to fit in," I tell the group with many agreeing.

***

After everyone is gone, I take something for a headache and go upstairs to lay down. Covering up with the throw from the foot of the bed, it's not long before my muscles relax, and I feel myself sinking into the bed. The noise of Chris and Gracie downstairs grows fainter and fainter as I fall asleep.

I roll over when I hear the floor creek.

"I'm awake," I say out loud. "My headache's gone."

Chris sits on the edge of the bed as I yawn and stretch.

"Good, do you feel up to going for a walk with us?"

As we walk around the neighborhood, Gracie is busy sniffing for squirrels. "You're quiet. What gives?" asks Chris.

"You know me too well," I answer.

"Well, we have known each other for a while."

"A few years," I giggle. "When I look back it has been a very interesting last couple of weeks."

"That it has."

On our walk, a neighbor stops to ask us about the police car. Chris fills them in so that they can at least get the story right when they pass the information along. "I guess they're right in inquiring, so they can at least be informed if anything is truly going on," he adds.

***

During a lull at work, I thanked those who preordered and attended. Many were shocked when I told them about my confrontation with Amber Lynn and the toilet paper incident. The day went by fast, which I was thankful for.

Chris comes home from work and is actually in a good mood. "Did you get a nap at work?" I smirk.

"Funny," Chris responds.

"I felt bad when you told me you didn't sleep well and were edgy from the whole Amber Lynn thing."

"Kyle called. He told me to watch the news tonight. There is a new segment called, 'On Your

Side'. He says it's something they are doing since the news is always so glum. It's like when you have paid for a service and aren't satisfied or can't get your money back, they step in and try to help. I guess it's popular in a lot of the bigger cities. Kyle said his neighbor across the street works at the news station. Kyle helped him with an idea for a segment. He thought we might be interested."

Chris and I get comfortable on the couch with Gracie lying between us. As the program begins, the broadcaster says, "This is a special news segment about wrongdoing that could be happening even in your own neighborhood. 'Wrongdoing' is defined as illegal or dishonest behavior. A lot of things could fall into this category. We are going to take a look at a few tonight. Our goal with this program is to educate you on what you need to know and do." The show goes on to show people knocking down signs and mailboxes and breaking into homes that are vacant and for sale.

"It takes all kinds, I guess."

The announcer goes on to say, "What would you do if you knew the person and it was a malicious act? Let's take a closer look."

"Those look like our videos," I yell at the television set.

"Wow, she's famous. You can clearly tell it's Amber Lynn and anyone that knows her will spot it's her!" Chris says.

"I feel bad for her."

"You have got to be kidding me! Well, I don't. Not in the least!"

Our heated discussion is interrupted when Chris leaves to answer the phone. A couple of minutes later he returns. It was Kyle again. "He said his neighbor called him and told him that since the airing, they have been flooded with people calling to identify the people in the videos. They want to do another segment where they confront Amber Lynn. Pretty good, huh?" he laughs devilishly.

"Yeah," I say, frowning.

"What?"

"She is going to have all this negative attention."

"All this negative attention that she has brought upon herself," he says, raising his voice.

"I'm too tired for this tonight," I say walking upstairs. This is unusual for Chris and I to go to bed mad and not talking. I think we have both given way too much time attention to Amber Lynn.

***

I want to talk to Chris before he leaves for work. I don't want this to continue to fester.

"Sweetheart, I got upset when you seemed excited that Amber Lynn was getting into trouble," I explain.

"I'm sorry too," Chris answers, "but she put herself in that spot. I'm glad about the prospect of her having to face the consequences for her actions. I'm standing up for the ones that don't feel they have the courage or a voice. Weren't you ever bullied at school or work?"

"I know a lot of people who have been bullied. I think I'm just overly sensitive right now," Beth responds.

"I called your folks last night to let them know about the news segment. They are going to come over tonight to see it. They were really surprised about it too. You are so much like your mom."

"How so?"

"She's bothered by the idea of Amber Lynn getting into trouble as well."

***

After getting a call from Mrs. Snow about Sophie, I decide to spend my lunch break sitting in the chapel. Taking a seat next to Paul, I find out that he too received a call. "She's missing Addy," he says quietly.

"I know," sighing. "Addy is wanting her to come home. When I went to the bank to get money for the bazaar, the teller gave me a five with 'I am waiting, Sophie', written on it. The teller is the one that brought it to my attention. She could clearly see it. I was able to show it to Chris before it disappeared."

"That's amazing. I was planning on going to see Sophie after work. If you'd like to go see her, too, I could pick you up at your house and that would give you time to change."

"If you wouldn't mind, that would be great. I don't like wearing these scrubs any longer than I have to. Plus, I could grab a sweater and Chris will like the fact that I'm not going alone."

***

When Chris doesn't answer his phone, I leave a voicemail letting him know where I'm at. I don't want him to worry when he can't find me and my car is sitting in the garage. Paul and I make small talk on the way over.

"I'm sorry we didn't make it to the craft bazaar. We wanted to but Susie's parents showed up unexpectedly," Paul explained.

"That's fine, you didn't miss anything," I comment.

"That's not what your cohorts are saying about all your yummy baked goods."

Signing in at the front desk, I recognize several staff members from Addy's service. Several make eye contact and smile. As we walk to Sophie's room, Gabby looks up from her med cart. "I'm sorry we didn't call ahead that we were coming. We wanted to come and sit with her."

"Her color isn't good, and her blood pressure is really low. I don't think it will be much longer," Gabby says.

I nod and take a deep breath before walking into the dimly lit room. Mrs. Snow is sitting beside her and holding her hand. Mrs. Snow says, "Sophie and I have been talking about how you were Addy's friends and are her friends as well."

Paul slides a chair over for me as Mrs. Snow stands up and looks out the window.

"Hi Sophie," caressing her hand. "It's Beth. Chaplain Paul is here too."

Sophie opens her eyes and weakly says, "I'm tired."

"I know you are sweetheart."

She tries to pull down her oxygen mask. "I don't want this."

"Could I hold it by your face?" I ask.

Paul walks to the other side of the bed and sits down in the chair. After a little time has passed, she opens her eyes and looks at Paul.

"Am I going to be with the angels soon?" Sophie asks him.

With tears in his eyes, Paul nods and says, "Yes, Sophie."

Tears fall to my cheeks, but I try not to make a sound.

"I will be with Addy again," Sophie says sweetly.

"Yes you will," Paul affirms. "You will be together again."

"She is there waiting for you," I tell her as I blot my cheeks.

"She's going to take your hand, Sophie, and the two of you will be together, forever," Mrs. Snow says through her tears.

"Sophie, you and Addy will be in our hearts forever," Gabby adds, wiping her eyes. "We love you and Addy so much."

I look away as Paul swallows hard and wipes his tears with his handkerchief. He stands and recites the Lord's Prayer. As our voices unite, I turn to see the room filled with staff members. Sophie takes a few more breaths and then breathes her last.

As the staff console each other and offer their final goodbyes, they leave the room. Mrs. Snow and Gabby comfort each other as they look at Sophie's lifeless body. Paul and I stay for a little while longer and then leave.

I walk out of the building with Paul, taking a deep breath, welcoming the fresh air. Standing in the parking lot, by his car, is Chris. "You weren't answering your phone, I thought…" says Chris. Before he can finish is sentence, I run into his arms crying. Paul nods to Chris.

"Thank you, Paul," I say, trying to compose myself and wiping my eyes.

"Come on you, I'm getting you home," says Chris. As we hold hands in the car, I look out the window with my head pressed back against the seat. I'm thankful for the peacefulness.

It's not long after getting home, I pick up the phone and call work to let them know I won't be in tomorrow. As I explained to Chris, I just need a day to feel sad. Later, as I stare at myself in the bathroom mirror washing my face, I think to myself, *Goodbye sweet Sophie.*

TWENTY-SIX

Waking up, I look around confused. Is it a.m. or p.m.? The blinds are shut, which makes the room even darker. The clock reads "9:30 a.m." Chris must have shut off my alarm. Suddenly feeling sick to my stomach, I rush into the bathroom. I wet a washcloth and put it on my face. The cool water feels good. Brushing my teeth, I try to get rid of the sour taste. It's probably stomach acid from not eating yesterday. Checking my temperature, I wait for the beep while looking cross-eyed trying to read it. I feel like I have a fever even though it reads normal.

Chris left a note for me posted on the fridge that says "I'm glad you called off. Just rest today. I love you, Chris." After I fix a cup of tea to try to settle my stomach, I cuddle up on the couch and begin flipping through the channels. The phone rings and I see that it's Paul.

"I hope I'm not bothering you. I just wanted to check in on you. When I was seeing a patient in the ER, the girls told me you called in."

"I think I'm fighting a bug or something or maybe it's just an accumulation of everything," I reply.

"Do you think you will be feeling better by Saturday? I was going to see about having Sophie's service then."

"I'm sure I will. I'm just lying around today. I set up Sophie's arrangements to be the same as Addy's."

"Well, if Saturday works with you, I will call and confirm everything. Get some rest and I will be in contact with you later."

"Roger that," I laugh.

With Gracie content and curled up at my feet, I take a sip of my tea, which has now turned lukewarm I close my eyes for only a few seconds, but later realize I have been dozing off and on for several hours. Gracie perks her head up as we both hear my phone. After wandering through the downstairs, I finally find where I laid it. The caller turned out to be

Paul who left a message confirming the arrangements had been set for Saturday.

As I reheat my cup of tea in the microwave, I look through the cabinet for something to eat. I spot a box of animal crackers. Chris must have bought these. Holding the box by the string, I remember having these as a kid and pretending the box was my purse. I take a seat at the kitchen table and call Chris while I open the box.

"Wow, I love that sound," he says.

"My voice?" I ask.

"Yeah, and the sound of cellophane," he laughs.

"I just opened a package of animal crackers. My stomach isn't feeling so hot."

"Do you have a fever?"

"No, I checked. I'm normal according to the thermometer."

"Well take it easy and just relax."

"I'm not even dressed!"

"I promise I won't call the fashion police."

I hang up and take another cracker. "I feel like a bum," I tell Gracie as I hand her a cracker. I tell myself that I have to do something productive today. I carry the laundry basket down and smile as the smell of apples and cinnamon lingers on the clothes. I bet we're the only house in the neighborhood with laundry that smells like apples and cinnamon.

The phone rings and caller ID shows it's Mom calling. Chris must have told her I was home. "Did you get off early today?" she asks.

"Actually, I called off. With the bazaar and Sophie dying, I just needed a break. How are you guys?" I ask.

"Were worried about you. Would you please make an appointment to get a checkup?"

"Okay. I probably just need a stronger vitamin or something. So, when did Chris call you?" I laugh. After I hang up from mom, and as promised, I set up an appointment. This will get several monkeys off my back.

Chris calls just before leaving work to see if I need anything from the store. I let him know about making a doctor's appointment and tell him the animal crackers must have done the trick along with the nap.

***

I look on, as Chris stands at the kitchen counter emptying bags filled with an array of soups, salads, and bread from The Soup Kitchen.

"You bought enough to feed a small village," I tease.

"I wanted to make sure you had something for tomorrow," Chris says, kissing me on the cheek.

"Paul called earlier and Sophie's service is going to be held this Saturday at noon."

"Please don't take this wrong, but it will be nice to have this all over," he says folding up the bag.

"I totally get what you are saying."

***

The next day proves to be a repeat with more lying around and dozing. *Nurses make terrible patients.* Scanning through the TV channels, I become frustrated trying to find something to watch. Looking through the cabinet, I search for more animal crackers. To my delight, I find six more boxes with a note that says, "Feel better, Love Chris." Gracie and I happily resume our place on the couch.

Later in the day, Chris comes home to find me asleep on the couch. As I open my eyes, Chris and Gracie are both staring at me. "How are you feeling?" he asks.

Taking a deep breath, I say, "My hair hurts."

He leans over to feel my forehead. "Stick out your tongue and say 'ahh'."

"Do you even know what you are looking for?"

"No, but you see them do it on TV all the time. I wonder if you have some wild safari animal illness?" he asks trying to be serious while looking at my empty cookie box.

"One that is only cured by consuming large quantities of animal crackers," I grin.

***

Chris walks into the kitchen and is surprised to see me standing there. "Good morning, early bird. How long have you been up?" he asks.

I smile at him and answer, "Early enough to have the newspaper read. It's from all the sleep I have been getting and knowing I am off today."

"You look better," kissing my forehead.

"My hair doesn't hurt anymore either," folding up the paper.

The phone rings and startles me as I look over at the clock. "Whose calling this early, I wonder?" I ask.

"Hi Beth, it's Kyle. I hope I'm not calling too early. Is Chris still there by chance?"

"Sure, I'll put him on," handing Chris the phone. "It's Kyle."

"Hey buddy, what's up?" Chris asks.

"I wanted to catch you before you left for work," Kyle says. "I wanted to tell you the second news segment is airing tonight, the one where they confront Amber Lynn."

"Any teasers you want to give out?" Chris asks.

"I wouldn't want to spoil anything, but let's just say it's not pretty." Kyle answers.

"Thanks for the heads up."

I look at Chris, shaking my head. "You guys talk about us girls gossiping. You have no room to talk."

"This is juicy," Chris says smiling, rubbing his hands together. "We never did have your folks over to watch the first segment."

"I cancelled when I went to see Sophie."

"I have an idea. Let's have them over for dinner and we can have them watch both segments. I will give them a call later and set everything up with your dad. We can get takeout and have them pick it up on their way over."

"This has really got your motor going, Chris."

"I am making the prediction that it is going to be very interesting." Chris changes the subject to my upcoming doctor visit. "What do you think the doctor will do?"

"They'll probably just get some blood tests. There's no reason for me to get an x-ray," I answer.

"You have been taking your vitamins, haven't you?"

"Yes, Chris, you sound like my mother."

"No, hear me out. I was just wondering if the vitamins could be causing you to be sick to your stomach off and on."

"I suppose so, but I have even tried taking them at different times. Let's not play doctor and leave it to the professional."

"If that's the case, I better leave for my day job," he snorts.

After Chris leaves and I'm wandering around the house, I decide I need to get out. I pick up the phone and before I can dial, I hear a voice on the other end.

"Hello," I say laughing into the phone.

"This is Mrs. Snow," she says.

"How are you today?"

"Not the best," she says quietly."

I can hear in her voice that she has been crying. "I'm so sorry. This has got to be such a difficult time for you -- first Addy and now Sophie."

"They were like my own, you know. Not having any children of our own.... Oh, it's not that we didn't want them. God just didn't have them in our plan, not the typical way anyway.

"I also wanted to thank you for the baked goods. The staff and I enjoyed them very much. I didn't know if I would get a chance tomorrow to tell you and I just wanted you to know that you have made such a difference. Some people never get the chance to understand why they are truly here. But you and Chaplain Paul certainly do."

"Thank you, that's kind of you to say. You take care and I will see you tomorrow."

Sitting on the bed in Addy's room, I think, this has been so hard on Mrs. Snow. I silently say a prayer for her. As I stand up, I look over at the dresser. Something doesn't look right. When I look at the pictures. I'm confused. There are now three girls in the same picture. How can that be?

Flipping it over it reads Best Friends Forever, Millie, Addy, and Sophie. Thanks Beth! The girls are arm in arm and smiling with Addy in the middle. Hearing the tinkling from the windchimes on the front porch, I think to myself, Addy has a best friend on each side now.

Speaking of best friends, I need to call mine.

"Good morning sweetheart," Daddy says answering the phone.

"How did you know it was me?" I ask.

"Caller ID. I can't go around calling everybody sweetheart now can I," he laughs.

"Not if you want to stay out of the doghouse."

"So, what are you up to today?"

"I have my doctor's appointment later, and I didn't know if Mom wanted to go to the Fairy Garden Shop with me."

"Is that the place with the relaxation stuff?"

"That's the one."

"While you guys are there, I want you to see if anything fancies her and let me know. I can give it to her for her birthday. She hasn't told me about anything she wants and you know how hard she is to buy for. She told me I could buy her a new skillet and I told her, 'No'."

"Why, if that's what she asked for?"

"I don't want our friends to think I'm a schmuck!"

"You know Mom isn't like that, but I guess I can see your point."

"I'll have your mom call you. I think she is drawing on her face."

I laugh aloud as I hang up the phone thinking about his comment.

***

Upon entering the shop, we immediately smell lilacs, causing my heart to skip a beat. I take a good whiff as we look around to locate the source. Mom pats my arm and points over to the incense burning on the table. Mystery solved.

"Hello ladies," the young man says as he walks from behind the counter. "Out for some retail therapy?"

"Could you point us in the direction of your fairy figurines?" Mom asks.

We follow him over to a display case with a variety of fairies. There are some that look quite feminine with their beautiful butterfly wings and others that look like they could kick some serious butt.

"I don't care for those," Mom frowns. "They look mean."

"I would have to agree. What about this one?" I ask.

"She's pretty with her light brown hair and soft dainty features. She has such a sweet face. What's her name?"

He carefully lifts her out of the case and looks at her tag. "Her name is 'Maranda'."

"Oh, I like her. I will have to think about her," Mom says as she turns to look at something else.

"We have more fairies in the other room, sitting next to the window. You can't miss them," he tells her.

Once I know Mom is out of ear shot, I tell the clerk, "I want to buy the fairy. I want to surprise her on her birthday. I will take it out to my car while she continues to look around. Could you please tell her that someone else bought it?"

After several minutes of trying to persuade him that he was not telling a lie and actually someone else did buy it, he agrees to go along with the charade. With the fairy tucked safely in the trunk of my car, I walk back into the store and ask to use the restroom.

Several minutes later, Mom walks up. "I've been looking for you," she says.

"I had to use the bathroom and the clerk was nice enough to let me use theirs. Did you find anything else?" I ask.

"No, so I think I will tell him that I'll take Maranda." She finds the clerk who promptly tells her it's been sold. "That's terrible. She was so sweet," says Mom, clearly disappointed.

"What's the matter?" I ask, trying to be more believable than the clerk.

"The fairy I was going to buy. Someone else came in and bought it!" I didn't plan on Mom taking it so hard.

"Maybe you can find another one some other time. Let's boost your spirits and go to lunch," I suggest.

"Could you order me one?" Mom asks the clerk.

Rats! I didn't think of that, wrinkling up my face. I cautiously stand behind her and mouth the word 'no' making arm gestures. The clerk looks at her and then at me, frazzled. Mom was watching the clerk's eyes and turns around.

"What are you doing?" she asks me.

"Who me? Nothing. I'm just trying to sing along with the music that is playing."

"The CD that is playing is a selection of Native American flute music. Most people use it for relaxation. I don't think it's one you can really sing along to," the clerk says dryly.

Rolling my eyes at him, "I would agree, it's extremely hard." We thank the clerk for his time as I quickly usher Mom out of the store. "I have the cutest diner to take you to and lunch is on me."

***

As we take our seat, I watch Marie stock the pie case. When she's done, she places water and menus on the table and lets us know about the specials. I look around to see if Millie is working.

"Who are you looking for?" Mom asks.

"I was looking for the other waitress named Millie," I answer. "She was the one I told you about that was so sweet to me and gave me a free piece of pie the day I had lunch with Amber Lynn. She was also our waitress when I brought Chris here."

Marie takes our orders and tells me Millie is busy in the back putting the finishing touches on her chicken pot pies for tomorrow's lunch special.

"I didn't know she did some of the cooking too," Beth says.

"What a lot of people don't know is, the three of us own the diner together," says Marie.

"Who's the third?" I ask.

"Her name is Emma. She mostly works in the back cooking."

"I don't think I have met her yet."

The next thing I know she is yelling to Emma to stick her head out and wave and to tell Millie someone wants to talk to her.

"Order up," Emma says as she rings the bell and waves from the opening below the warming lights.

Millie walks over to say hello.

"Hi, Millie," Beth says. "I'm gradually bringing my whole family in. This is my mom, Jennifer."

"Nice to meet you. Business is good for just starting a couple of months ago. Enjoy your meals and we will check with you later," Millie says.

Having thoroughly enjoyed the soup and pie, we order a piece to take home to the guys.

With the bill paid, we walk out carrying our goody bags.

"Your father will be elated," says Mom.

"So, will Chris," I add. "The crust reminds me of Grandma's pies."

"You probably don't remember, but Grandpa would tease Grandma and tell her she really knew how to shake a stove."

"That's cute. I could see him telling her that."

When I drop Mom off, Dad meets us at the car. "How are my girls?" he asks.

"We're very sweet," I respond. "We just had lunch and finished it off with a piece of pie. And we brought you one!"

"That sounds delightful!"

"There's the lady with the goods," I tell him, pointing to Mom. He leans in and gives me a kiss goodbye. As Mom gets out of the car, I quietly tell him I picked up her present and it's in the trunk.

He quickly turns and holds out his arms to Mom. "Sweetheart, that bag looks heavy," Dad says to

Mom peeking inside. I honk the horn and wave as I head to my doctor's appointment.

***

Checking in at the desk, I fill out my paperwork and wait. Bored, I watch the people in the lobby to pass the time. Finally, it's my turn. The nurse walks me back and we stop in front of the scale.

"What all can I remove?" I ask jokingly. The nurse is clearly not amused and didn't even crack a smile. She could be a drill sergeant.

"You've lost weight, according to your chart," she barks.

She goes on to get the rest of my vital signs and history. "Dr. J. will be in shortly," she said sharply before closing the door.

Not long after, Dr. J. walks in with his usual casual demeanor. "Isn't Melanie here anymore?" I ask.

"She's due to come back in another week or two. She had a baby girl," Dr. J. replies.

"Well, you need to give her a big fat raise. She has quite a personality compared to…"

"I know who you are referring to. Nurse Hatchet was what she was called yesterday by one of my elderly patients after drawing his blood.

"So, I hear you have been feeling under the weather for a while and you thought it might be related to the stress at work and home."

"I didn't say anything about stress at home."

"I just figured you'd have stress being married to Chris," he chuckles. "Have a seat over here," he says patting the exam table, "so I can take a look at you."

I go onto explain how even my hair hurt and how I was feeling achy the other day. After being examined and having answered the usual health questions, he asks the question I have been waiting for, about when we are thinking of starting a family.

"It's not that were preventing starting a family, it just hasn't happened yet," I answer.

"Maybe you just need more practice," he teases.

"Let's run some labs and see if you are just low on iron, making you anemic," he continues. "You know that being anemic can make you dizzy, sweaty, and nauseated too. Since you haven't been running a fever, you may have just had a virus related to where you work and the germs you encounter. Do you want a prescription for nausea medicine?"

"I guess write me one and then if it gets worse, I will get it filled."

He tears off the prescription and hands it to me. "It was good seeing you again and I'll be in touch. I'll send Nurse Hatchet back in to collect your labs," he says smiling.

***

Mom and Dad walk in carrying the food and immediately asks about my doctor's appointment. "They're doing some labs to check if I'm anemic," I answer. "Hopefully, I will know something by Monday."

In between bites, Chris gets the TV ready to watch the first segment of the news program. As the program starts, we hear, "This is Lauren Hart, news anchor, with a special segment of 'On Your Side'. Tonight, we bring you, part one of 'What is a Citizen to Do'?" She goes on to explain how several homes were vandalized with toilet paper. "We feel this was an adult's attempt at bullying. Some may say it's just toilet paper, but just how far is too far? The people responsible have been identified and we are going to interview one of them now."

The footage shows them going up to Amber Lynn's house and knocking. "Hi. Are you Amber Lynn Maynard?" asks Lauren. Amber Lynn nods.

"I'm Lauren Hart with 'Eye on Five News'. We are doing a special news segment of, 'On Your Side' and would like to feature you. Do you mind speaking to our audience and being on camera?" Amber Lynn shrugs her shoulders, runs her fingers through her hair, and steps outside.

"First," continues Lauren, "We have a video clip we would like to show you and get your comment on."

As Amber Lynn watches the video, she looks around, confused, until she slowly realizes that she is watching herself. The anchor then continues. "We understand you were chairperson for a holiday bazaar last Saturday and you had angry words with several of the participants. The video shows that you defaced several homes with toilet paper. Is that what you would say happened?"

"No," says Amber Lynn, shaking her head. "I mean, maybe I got upset."

"Do you understand that the people involved have gone to the police and are trying to have charges brought against you?"

"Over a little bit of toilet paper?" Amber Lynn laughs. "It was only 1-ply, people!"

"How do you like that," Chris says. "We didn't even get 2-ply!"

"The 'Eye on Five' news channel and viewers do not believe this to be a laughing matter. Don't you feel this was a poor attempt of bullying?" asks Lauren.

"No, I…," stammers Amber Lynn.

"Were you ever bullied in school? Or were you the bully?"

Amber Lynn says, "I'm not a bully on any level. This whole thing is a misunderstanding."

"Well," the anchor says, "the news footage would suggest otherwise. With the police now being involved, this is a whole new matter.

Mom and Dad can't believe their eyes as they watch. "I'm almost afraid to watch the second one," Mom says.

"She has it coming," Dad says. "Bullies don't change, they just get older."

"There's a lot to what you are saying, Dad," Chris says.

"What would you say if all parties involved came to an agreement on the damage you caused and what you could do to make things right again? Would you go along with it?" Lauren asks.

"Maybe," Amber Lynn says with her arms folded.

"Since what you did was deliberate, we would like for you to see what it is like being on the other side. The people you targeted had to spend a comparable amount of time cleaning up your mess. You will pick up trash around town for four hours a day for the next three days and we will have a camera crew documenting you."

"Why does there have to be a camera crew?" Amber Lynn asks frowning.

"Ms. Maynard, we are trying to detour any similar activity," Lauren answers. "Your first shift starts tomorrow at 8:00 a.m. and a driver will pick you up and bring you home."

"I get a driver?"

The second video segment begins, and my stomach is in knots. We hear Lauren Hart announce part two of 'What is a Citizen to Do'?"

The next several clips go on to show Amber Lynn, April, and Bridgette wearing yellow jumpsuits and picking up trash along main street. At one point, Amber Lynn is trying to wipe the stains off her jumpsuit and then runs her hands through her hair. She must have forgotten that she was wearing her dirty gloves because she had stuff in her hair. She began crying and screaming when she realized she was on camera as she tried to pull it from her hair.

"So, to anybody else out there who thinks they need to be a bully, remember we're watching you. This is Lauren Hart reporting for 'Eye on Five' news with a segment of 'On Your Side'."

Chris looks over to see my mouth wide open, shaking my head. After watching it over and over for at least another five times, I take a deep breath. "I applaud her for going through with it," I announce.

"She knew she was in a tight spot, so what else could she do?" Chris says.

"That poor girl," Mom says. "I will pray for her tonight that she has learned her lesson."

"Do you think you two will stay friends, Beth?" Dad asks.

"I think it's best that we cut ties. I don't need a friend like that," I say.

"I couldn't agree with you more," Chris smiles.

TWENTY-SEVEN

Mesmerized by the realistic flames in the fireplace, my thoughts feel like pages turning in a book. As I take a sip from my cup, I pray for guidance and composure. This is it, I tell myself as Chris walks in and turns on the light.

"Nice pillow perm," I tease.

"Thanks! I worked on it all night," he answers back. "What time did you get up?"

"Early! I couldn't quiet my mind, so I got up."

"Are you going to be okay today?"

"I have to be for Addy and Sophie."

Chris sets the plate of scrambled eggs in front of me and watches as I push the eggs around my plate for several minutes. "I should warn you, I have them all numbered. Pushing them around the plate isn't going to convince me you've eaten anything."

Giving in, I take a bite. The phone rings and Chris hands me the phone. "It's probably for you anyway. I'm going to go upstairs and finish getting ready."

As I put the receiver up to my ear, I hear the voice on the other end say, "She's coming to the phone." I check the caller ID screen which reads caller unknown. A male voice then says, "Good morning, Beth."

"Yes," I answer curiously.

"This is Dr. J. We got some of your lab results back and I wanted to go over them with you. You are a little anemic so maybe that is why you have been feeling so tired. We will put you on some prenatal vitamins which should boost your iron count and help with tiredness. Take them at night because sometimes they can upset your stomach. You will also want to start taking folic acid every day."

"Okay."

He then goes on to say, "And if you think you are tired now, wait for several months and you will really know what tired is."

"Excuse me?"

"Motherhood can do that," he declares. "Congratulations!"

My mouth drops, as I lose my grip on the phone, sending it bouncing to the floor.

"Oh, dear lord, I think she fainted! Beth? Hello? Beth, can you hear me?" Dr. J. yells.

I hurry and pick up the phone. "I'm here. I'm okay. I didn't faint, I just dropped the phone."

"Good! Call the office on Monday and we will set up an appointment for an ultrasound to see how far along you are."

"Okay," I answer in disbelief.

"Tell that husband of yours it's about time he got you pregnant. Take care now."

"Bye Dr. J."

I walk upstairs and sit down on the bed.

"Who was on the phone? Do you think anyone will notice that I wore the same shirt and jacket for Addy's service?" asks Chris.

I shake my head but don't answer.

"Who was that on the phone?" asks Chris again.

I look up at him dazed. "What?" I answer him.

"Beth what's wrong? Who was on the phone?" Chris asks for the third time.

"It was Dr. J.," I finally answer.

"What is he doing in the office on a Saturday. Don't doctors usually play golf on the weekends?"

"I guess he wanted to call to tell me he knows what's wrong with me. I'm anemic."

"Okay, so why are you anemic and how do people get it?"

"Well, women can sometimes be anemic when they're pregnant."

"But that doesn't explain why you're anemic." I shrug my shoulders and look at him, making a face. Chris looks at me and hollers, "Wait, are you telling me we're pregnant?" He grabs me and swings me around, "Woohoo!" He sets me down and the room is still spinning. "When will we find out how far along you are and if it's a boy or girl or both?" he continues questioning.

"Wait a minute buster, one thing at a time," trying to recover from the spinning motion. "I need to schedule an appointment next week for an ultrasound, so we can look at our schedules to see when you can go with me if you want to. As for finding out the sex, I'm not sure I want to know. I want to think about it."

"Well, how do I look, as a newly expectant father?"

"You wear it well," I smile, straightening his tie.

"Since you're now going to be a mother, I must really ask if you finished eating your eggs. You know you need to eat something before we go and that's an order."

"I will try and take a couple more bites and drink a glass of juice. My stomach felt a little queasy before the phone call and after that twirling and news, it's doing flip flops."

"I'm ready so I will go downstairs and warm up the eggs and fix you a nice cup of tea."

While we wait until it's time to leave, Chris reads off baby names from his laptop while I daydream and sip on my tea. "We're going to be the only two feeling elated at the service, I bet," Chris says.

"We need to keep the news on the low down," I explain to Chris. "I don't want to tell everybody right away. I don't know how far along I am, and things can go wrong. I don't want to jinx anything."

"I understand. When are you going to tell your parents?"

"I need time to process it myself, first."

"Well, I will wait until after you tell your folks, just in case they bump into each other at the store or something. I don't want anyone getting their feelings hurt because they heard the news secondhand and not directly from us."

"That makes sense," I tell him as I get up to rinse out my cup.

"I think I have an idea how we can tell our folks," he says. "You could make it part of your mother's birthday present. You could have a sign made up that says, 'Grandma I will be here in so many months'."

"That's a really cute idea. What time is it now?" I ask.

"It's after ten o'clock. Were your folks going to Sophie's service?" Chris asks.

"I don't think so. If they were, Mom would have mentioned something yesterday."

"How about if I call them to see if they want to go to the service and we can pick them up?"

"Christopher Davis! I know what you are trying to do. I get it. You want to tell somebody. I am dying to tell someone too, just not yet. I'm not going to call them and make them feel obligated that they need to go. Like it or not, it's just the two of us for this service.

"I'll tell you what. I will let you tell someone, but I get to pick who."

"Deal," he says. "Who?"

"You can tell Gracie," I laugh.

"That's not fair. You said someone, not a dog!"

"Did you hear what Daddy just said about you?"

"Okay, Gracie, you are going to be a big sister. You can share your... What can she share with a baby?"

"Her heart of course!"

"Good one!" he says, giving me the thumbs up sign.

Chris continues to browse at the baby names while I glance at my phone for baby furniture and décor ideas. "Did you know there is even a site that tries to match your baby's name to their personality. That's dumb, how can you tell the personality before it's born?"

"Keep looking, for something useful," I teasingly scold him.

"There are a couple of names I am going to insist that we don't name our child or future pet."

"I have a feeling I already know one of them, Amber Lynn."

"Bingo," he says touching his nose. "Give that lady a prize!"

"This is cool," pointing my phone at him. "This site tells you the baby's developmental steps, week by week. See?"

Chris lets out a loud sigh. "I don't see how we are going to keep from telling anyone."

"We need to at least wait until the ultrasound is done. Besides, we will have some pictures to show off then. Maybe we could put a picture in a frame and tell our folks that way."

"If I know Mom, she will want to put it on her fridge."

"Then we will make their picture into a magnet."

"What about a puzzle? You know how my mom and dad like games. What if we did a puzzle with a picture of us and a sign with our due date and then cut it up so they had to put the pieces together?"

"They are all great ideas, but we still need to wait until after the ultrasound. We can plan and scheme then. We need to get going."

***

At the cemetery, Susie walks over and asks, "How are you feeling? Paul mentioned you were going to the doctor."

"Can you share any news?" Paul asks.

Chris and I look at each other puzzled. "I found out I'm anemic and have to start taking iron pills," I reply.

Paul and Susie look at each other and smile. "How far along are you, Beth?" Paul asks.

"How did you know I was expecting?"

"You have the same symptoms and glow that Susie had. I have predicted all of our kids, clear down to the gender," he boasts proudly.

"Four times," Susie says holding up her fingers.

"We are delighted for you both," Paul adds. "You're doubly blessed," he says with a twinkle in his eye.

"We aren't telling anybody just yet, other than you two now. If you could keep it quiet until we are ready to share the news, we would appreciate it," I ask.

"Absolutely," Paul and Susie say at the same time, grinning at one another.

As I walk up to the casket, Chris stands beside me for support. Silently, I tell Sophie and Addy that I hope our child is special like them. "You're together now, forever." Smelling the scent of lilacs, I smile at Chris as we find a seat. I see Mrs. Snow and lean down to give her a hug.

"Beth dear, you look so pretty today. You have a glow," Mrs. Snow says.

"I do?"

"Addy and Sophie would be delighted with the news. Wouldn't twins be wonderful?"

Surprised, by her comment, I quietly tell her, "We just found out ourselves."

"Well, you needn't worry. It will be our secret until you want it shared," patting my hand, "I hope you'll stay in touch. I would love to be an honorary aunt!"

"You would make a wonderful one, I have no doubt," giving her hand a squeeze. "I have a feeling there are going to be a lot of honorary aunts."

As I look around, there are several familiar faces from Addy's service and who helped care for Sophie. The service is a wonderful tribute to Sophie with Paul doing another amazing job. As we walk to our cars, Paul reminds us, "It's a beautiful thing when we can say goodbye to one life, knowing in the future, we will be welcoming a new one."

"Would you and Susie like to join us for lunch? I know just the place," taking Chris' hand and kissing it. "We have some celebrating to do."

"Yes, we do, and let us eat pie!" Chris laughs.

***

Some months later, I'm clocking out, excited with the thought of going home and taking off my shoes. I pause to look down at my feet. Gone are the days of my being able to see my feet. It would be just like the girls to avoid telling me if my shoes didn't match. I can't blame everything on pregnancy brain.

Once in the car, I take a minute to catch my breath. With the majority of the afternoon spent with Mr. Kelly and his family, it's left me tired and feeling a little drained. Mr. Kelly was an elderly gentleman who unfortunately passed away after having worked in his garden for the better part of the day. His wife went out to take him a cold drink and found him slumped in the porch swing. Mrs. Kelly reiterated to her family that he spent his last day doing what he loved. One of his favorite things to do was to sit in his porch swing that he had made and admire his garden.

Feeling a sharp pain in my ribs, "Ouch! You two need to behave," I say out loud, rubbing my enlarged belly. "My feet are swollen, I'm short of breath, and one of you keeps giving me an elbow to the ribs."

Gradually, I smell something. As I sniff at the air, the smell becomes stronger and I realize it's cherry tobacco. But where is it coming from? I look in the rearview mirror and then over at the car parked next to me. I don't see anyone sitting in their car or standing outside smoking.

Suddenly, I have an overwhelming feeling that something isn't right. When I turn back around, I'm not alone. Someone is sitting in the passenger seat. "Sweet momma!" I yell grabbing the steering wheel. It's Mr. Kelly! It's the gentleman from earlier this afternoon who died. "Mr. Kelly?" I ask in disbelief.

I watch, engrossed, as he takes a puff off his pipe. He slowly tilts his head back, blowing out the smoke. He sits quietly as he takes a deep breath. I hold my breath, as I wait for him to speak.

After several minutes, he turns to me and smiles. "I heard you're the messenger."

~The End~

Made in USA - Kendallville, IN
11243_9798218153601
05 01 2023 1349